Sole Brethren
Left To Their Own Devices

Sole Brethren
Left To Their Own Devices

B.A. Summer

This is a work of fiction. Names, characters, places and incidents either are the product of the author's imagination or are used fictitiously. Any resemblance to actual persons, living or dead, events or locales is entirely coincidental.

Copyright © 2024 B. A. Summer

All rights reserved. No part of this book may be reproduced or used in any manner without written permission of the copyright owner except for the use of quotations in a book review. For more information, address: info@ElfadoIsland.com

First paperback edition July 2024

Typesetting: Shakspeare Editorial
Cover design by Louisa Fitch from an illustration by Alenarbuz

978-1-7396102-4-1 (paperback)
978-1-7396102-3-4 (e-book)

Elfado Island
www.ElfadoIsland.

Dedicated to Helen M – many thanks being a superfan and jollying me along to finish writing this novel.

Contents

Chapter One 1
Chapter Two 15
Chapter Three 21
Chapter Four 33
Chapter Five 49
Chapter Six 59
Chapter Seven 73
Chapter Eight 83
Chapter Nine 95
Chapter Ten 109
Chapter Eleven 123
Chapter Twelve 135
Chapter Thirteen 147
Chapter Fourteen 165
Chapter Fifteen 183
Chapter Sixteen 193
Chapter Seventeen 205
Chapter Eighteen 221
Author's Note 234
Also By B.A. Summer 236
Author Details 237

Chapter One

'Blanche, you are a mistress of the quick step!' Cordelia cried gleefully, holding her pet dog's front paws and dancing around the room as Elodie played the piano accordion and sang a ditty she had written comparing Blanche to Helen of Troy. Rather than having a face that launched a thousand ships however, the dog had a face that launched a thousand pleas to stroke her long floppy curly-haired ears. As a spangold – golden retriever and English springer spaniel hybrid – her curls were prodigious.

'She's the lovechild of Jackson Pollock and the Hindu Festival of Colour,' Rex tittered, brush in hand, as he noticed Blanche's feathered tail had knocked over a jar of water into a tray of paints and was spraying pigment everywhere, including the sheet of paper upon which he was daubing.

'Wagadougou your splatter paint technique displays dogged determination.' Cordelia kissed Blanche's forehead and the dog grinned because she was not only the world's waggiest canine, but also the smiliest.

'Thanks to Blanche it now has the look of a remote galaxy. What is it meant to be?' Elodie asked, gazing at the artwork.

'Can't you tell? Full English Breakfast,' Rex replied.

'Oh yes, now I see. The baked beans have a look of distant planets.'

This was round three of Left Leaning Society, an activity which entailed Cordelia, Rex, and Elodie drawing or painting, eyes closed, an image using their right hand, despite all three being left-hand dominant. Then the others had to guess what it represented, which was tricky owing to them stretching the term abstract to its limit.

'If that was by a big-name pop-artist it would sell for millions and be titled something meaningless, like *The Divergent Tensions Between Random Structures and Spatial Yearning*,' Cordelia commented.

'I was at an auction in Miami where a small fur ball balanced on an upturned polystyrene cup sold for $20 million. The artist titled it *Eye of the Beholden* and claimed it was composed of the eyelashes of his thousands of lovers and held together by the tears they shed after he dumped them,' Elodie said, with a trill on the accordion keyboard.

'Imagine if the cleaner had chucked it away thinking it was a bit of old rubbish,' Cordelia sniggered.

'I wonder how many collectors pretend to admire what the dealer is flogging cos they are unable to resist for fear of missing out on the latest art trend,' Rex said, as he signed his name beneath the breakfast still life and pinned it on a board by Cordelia's dragon boat, and Elodie's Statue of Liberty which the others thought was a wind turbine.

'FOMO is a powerful motivator. Hype begats hype and it snowballs. Talent is not always obligatory,' Cordelia opined and then told the others of an occasion during her student days when she and her best friend Wilbur watched a naked performance artist being wheeled through the room in a shopping trolley as he coated himself in squashed blackcurrants and chanted, 'No Fish For The Weekend'. 'Almost everyone nodded solemnly as though they were witnessing something profound, but me and Willy-The-Bur were forced to sneak away and laugh hysterically.'

Elodie chuckled. 'How would they react to our nursery-school level efforts? I know, let's convince wealthy collectors that our un-masterpieces are valuable then they'll be desperate to buy them. We'll start a mysterious art collective and attempt to become the next big thing. But no one will know we are behind it.'

'Genius idea She-She, I'll make some notes.' Cordelia grabbed her pad then waved an empty glass at a magnum of champagne on the table and enquired hopefully, 'Is there any left in that one?'

She-She was Cordelia's nickname for Elodie l'Archambeau, super-chic scion of La Maison Bonheur, the best-selling champagne brand, who travelled everywhere with a crate of fizz in her wake, and vintage flutes in an antique binoculars case.

'No, but I might know where we can get some more,' she replied, taking a bottle from the wine fridge and expertly opening it. 'Is it time for a kir royale myrtille?'

'Botticelli!' Rex cried, using his and Cordelia's nonsense answer to a rhetorical question. 'Seeing as it's the same shade as the weave of my trousers.' Rex did not do casual and never left home looking anything less than the finest-dressed man in the city, in sharply tailored suit, handmade shirt and tie, and cufflinks. 'Don't you own a pair of jeans?' the manager at his first job as a computer programmer had asked. 'I have too much respect for my fellow citizens not to look my best,' he'd replied breezily. Not a good start considering everyone else in the building was wearing denim.

Elodie handed them each a glass and they cheersed by touching together the tip of their left index finger with those of the other two. They were at her new London residence, a 1930s Streamline Moderne building that resembled a cruise liner. Cordelia had christened it the Gâteau Bateau because, as a French citizen, Elodie enthusiastically embraced the doctrine of pâtisserie.

Several months previously Cordelia and Rex had unofficially adopted Elodie. From first meeting her they were the closest of friends and it was apparent their deep bond was familial. Beautiful of body and spirit, she was an unexpected combination of academic – specialising in shoe history and symbolism – and reconstructive surgeon – who worked every few months for Rebâtir, the humanitarian medical charity she had founded to rebuild the bodies of civilians injured by war. Cordelia had met her by chance at a Los Angeles auction as they bid, unsuccessfully, for the same pair of shoes once worn by Bette Davis in the film *All About Eve*.

'We were robbed of our reward!' Elodie had said afterwards in the lobby of the auction house. 'How we both wanted them. But I had a plan. We would take one each and then meet annually to reunite the pair and drink cocktails.'

And that was it, instant friendship. They felt familiar to each other, as though they'd already met and their similarities – age, height (tall) and date of birth – made them speculate that they'd been twins in a former life. They had other things in common: both collected historically significant footwear; both had scars in their left eyebrow inflicted on them as teenagers – Elodie's by being accidentally whacked by the racquet of her tennis doubles partner, and Cordelia's from the stiletto heel of a white plastic shoe on a woman in a hen party who'd fallen down the escalator at Leicester Square Tube station and landed on top of her. Rex, who was Cordelia's twin in this life, also had an instantaneous bond with Elodie. He said he hoped she and Cordelia *had been* twins in a prior existence because he heartily approved of twinage and could not bear to imagine his sister being without the companionship of the person who loved her the most. At first, they had wondered if Elodie was real or whether they had conjured her up because she clicked so perfectly with them. Now they were united, the three spent blissful times together – all laughter and mischief – and nothing in life would ever be better.

Art and creativity were fundamental to Cordelia and Rex. Together they owned the eponymous House of Tanner, the luxury bespoke women's shoe brand, where each model was inspired by a songbird. Cordelia was a celebrated designer and her guiding principle, "I have a duty to spread beauty", was spectacularly rendered by her glorious creations and a personal style that was beyond fashion. She was the dictionary definition of a quaintrelle, a woman who finds splendour everywhere and lives to cultivate pleasure. Rex, younger by ten minutes, with his brilliant mathematical mind was the logistics side of the partnership. While not creative in his day-to-day work, he expressed himself through his wardrobe.

Cordelia frowned as they discussed Elodie's jokey suggestion for the art collective. 'Conceptual art is so easy to forge and that's stealing someone else's intellectual property. Unless an artist's DNA is incorporated into the artwork how can a buyer be confident of owning the real thing? We don't want anyone copying our doodles and selling them for their own profit.' She took a sip of kir. 'Art fraud is rife, especially now that celeb collectors are showing off their buying power and inflating the market, which makes it extra-lucrative for the fakers.'

She had personal experience of counterfeiting because House of Tanner designs had two unique elements concealed in its shoes. Inside one heel a tiny speaker transmitted the bird's song; inside the other was a smartphone battery charger and USB socket. Despite both being trademarked, the USB had been copied by a Chinese company that produced footwear under the name House of T'Anna.

'That's our challenge then, to create impossible to fake art,' Elodie declared.

They spent the rest of the day plotting and giggling about their scheme and agreed the name of the underground abstract art collective was Left to Their Own Devices and that works would be motivated by campaigning issues.

'We can do this,' Rex exclaimed. 'I have ideas on how to make them forgery proof, but I'll need to work it out when I'm not tipsy.

Let's have a think how to build hype. Should we reconvene next week, ready to start?'

'We're akin to medieval scientists attempting to convert base metals into gold. Except in our case, it will be the magic of marketing and not alchemy that does it,' Cordelia replied.

Over the following weeks they met on Saturdays at Gâteau Bateau and, fuelled by Bonheur and cake, had a hoot creating their naive art. Themes were chosen by throwing darts at a list of options, or they held up cards on which suggestions were written and let Blanche choose by sniffing the one she preferred.

One of their first pieces was created by diluting paint to symbolise a melted glacier, which they squirted from water pistols in a work called *High But Not Dry* to emphasise the destructive effects of climate change. For another, they used coloured pencils to draw dollar, euro, and other currency symbols and titled it *It's Who You Know*, referring to political cronyism and corruption. Their favourite method was Twoga, a combination of Twister and yoga poses, where hands and feet dipped in watercolours were imprinted on canvas through bodily contortions. To ensure anonymity they wore gloves and socks so there were no finger or footprints to connect them with the project. Blanche joined in on one by trotting across the canvas laid on the floor and, being such a happy creature, spreading the paint by sitting and wagging her tail. That piece was titled, *The Dog Days,* to protest unscrupulous puppy farmers who breed canines with hugely exaggerated, often unhealthy, physical features.

'How will we persuade people to buy them?' Elodie pondered as she leaned another canvas against the wall.

'Scarcity marketing. That's what we do at HoT by not taking just anyone as a client. It makes the brand even more desirable. And if we deluge soshe with endless talk regarding LefDev then there will be a clamour, even though we don't actually want everyone to have one,'

Cordelia said, picking up a cloth to wipe the paint off Blanche's fur. 'We limit our output and the works are never sold, instead we lend them for a specified period and then someone else borrows it. Each time we charge a considerable fee, one with numerous zeros before the decimal point. Availability is restricted to the world's richest people. I bet they'd go for it out of the belief that if something is expensive it must be good.'

Rex applauded. 'Genius. And if we publicly reveal who the borrowers are then other richies will want one too. Ching ching.'

'Some people will desire a LefDev not for the love of art, but because they crave acknowledgment of their wealth and will use it to brag to their rich-list rivals,' Elodie said. As a collector of art she revered, she was au fait with the various purchasing motivations. 'We'll donate the money we raise to the charities we support.'

'If they have so much dosh then we will soak them and make the borrowing of a piece conditional on also donating a proportion of their fortune to the causes and campaigns our art focuses on.' Cordelia was on a roll. 'Competitive giving. A one-upmanship ego trip. We'll start an arms race of philanthropy.'

Rex had a faraway expression and was tapping his fingers on the table. 'We can do this. I shall marshal the power of my 'puter.'

'What, snackety-snack?'

Elodie looked confused. Cordelia and Rex often spoke cryptically, forgetting that she did not understand.

'She means hacking,' Rex clarified.

'Are you telling me that underneath that sophisticated exterior a naughty renegade resides?' Elodie laughed.

'Mea culpa. I know it's hard to believe.'

'He's a bit of demon in that respect,' Cordelia explained, then changed the subject. 'Blanche needs a stroll. Fancy joining me? We need to discuss how to prevent phoney LefDevs entering the market once we launch.'

'Well, aren't we prolific.' Rex was admiring their pile of canvases. 'We have enough here to cover Tate Modern's Turbine Hall.'

'We're the art equivalent of those sushi places where dishes keep arriving on a conveyor belt,' Cordelia added. 'What are we going to do with them?'

'I have a plan.' Elodie always had a plan – epic, imaginative, and brilliantly executed. 'I've been contemplating my art collection, which I barely see now I'm so rarely in France. How about I move it to London and open a gallery so the public can share its magnificence? Then we'll have somewhere to display Left To Their Own Devices.'

This prompted great excitement and they debated their ideal place: 'A space that makes you want to live there among the art' – Cordelia; 'Somewhere to host parties' – Rex; 'It must have a bar and a café for afternoon tea' – Elodie.

'We need to consult someone acquainted with the workings of a gallery. I have the very person, Phyllida, my former mother-in-law. Haven't seen her for an age. Calling right now.' Cordelia picked up her phone and searched for the number.

Phyllida answered, delight in her voice, 'Cordelia, how splendid to hear from you. Julius was saying the other day how it's been forever since we were all together.'

'Oh, I miss you Phyl. As usual, work gets in the way. I know that's a pathetic excuse but I'm on with something that hopefully means I'll get to see you more often. Do you want to meet for tea?'

'Absolutely. I'm free most days and dying to know what you have up your sleeve.'

'I think we deserve a trip to Longton. I'll tell all when we're in the Scarlet Den.'

'What a treat. But if I try and buy anything that cannot be eaten hide my bank card and refuse to give it back. I'm always tempted by everything I see there.'

Phyl will be brill. She'll give the gallery cred, so no one can accuse it of being a vanity project, Cordelia thought as she left House of Tanner. *Wonder if Vulpy is at work yet.* She entered The Weasel, the pub next door she co-owned with her ex-husband Oscar, who she'd nicknamed Vulpy, a shortened version of Vulpini, on account of him being so foxy. Despite no longer being married, Cordelia and Oscar were still in business and still in love. They'd only ended the marriage because their impossible to co-ordinate circadian rhythms meant they hardly saw each other. She always woke early, while he slept until late morning and worked into the night. They deserved the perfect marriage, but they had the perfect divorce instead. Cordelia lived on House of Tanner's roof in a platform boot-shaped penthouse, Oscar's residence was a folly based on the Temple of Apollo in The Weasel's garden. They shared the care of Blanche, who had been a wedding gift from Rex.

'Good morning my mistress of the dawn.' Oscar was seated in the saloon eating his lunchtime breakfast.

'Good midday my lover. I'm off to see your Mum. Me, Rexicles, and She-She are plotting and we need her expertise.' Cordelia kissed him.

'Wish I could join you but today it's What's The Buzz. I've entered R.E.S.P.E.C.T. The Bees and Ice Iceni Baby in this year's show.' He was referring to the annual apiarists' get-together and honey from his two hives, ruled benevolently by the queens he named Aretha and Boudicca. 'I've something to tell so let's give her a video call.'

'In that case, I'll have a quick caffeine.' Cordelia popped behind the bar to pour a double shot of espresso.

He dialled Phyllida's number.

'Hello Mum, guess who I bumped into.'

'Look at you two. What salve for the eyes,' she said happily.

Cordelia waved. 'You may not remember me, I'm that woman who ran off with your son a few years ago. I should be at Sevenoaks by 3pm. Look out for someone who resembles fruit punch.' She was not kidding. That day she was in a canary-yellow metallic leather jacket, highlighted by lime snakeskin insets, high-waisted trousers in lime pinstriped gabardine, and tangerine-coloured suede Chelsea boots.

'Mum, are you busy on Friday? It'll be an overnighter. I can't be any more specific but you'll be very glad you came.'

'Oh I do enjoy a mystery. Yes please! Give me a wardrobe guideline and I'll be there. Oh, sorry darling, someone's at the door. Can I ring you back?'

'Of course.'

Oscar ended the call and turned to Cordelia. 'I bid in a charity auction and won two tickets for an exclusive visit to Frampton Abbey Flower Show on the full moon to see the night-blooming plants. Mum will be mad about it. We won't only see gardenia, four o' clock alba, and a queen of the night, we'll smell them too. It will be intoxicating!'

'What an impeccable son you are,' Cordelia sighed and stroked his hand. 'If we'd ever wanted children I'd have placed a special order for a child bearing your qualities to be delivered as an adult so I didn't have to do any of that bringing it up malarkey.'

'You're good with other people's though. Shame you don't have a ten-year-old niece or nephew, then you could be like Aunty Mame and teach them how to mix a Martini.'

Aunty Mame was one of Cordelia's top films. As teenagers she and Rex had watched it repeatedly, beguiled by the glamorous costumes and sets, and whooping at the titular character's irreverent attitude and sassy dialogue.

'Essential life lessons. Where do I borrow a ten year old?'

'There must be a dating app type matching service somewhere, but you might need to commit some effort to building a relationship.'

'In that case, no. I'm too busy being selfish and pleasing myself. Anyway, mustache, I'll tell you later what me and the others are up to, after I have secured the services of the inestimable Phyllida Rivington.'

Phyllida was waiting for Cordelia outside Sevenoaks station. They had a long warm hug. 'Julius sends his love and asks if you and Rex will be guinea pigs for a new game he's devised for Planet Wildlife. Having access to Rex's analytical brain and your creative acumen is so helpful.' Julius, Phyllida's husband, published board games and he often enrolled Cordelia and Rex for beta testing.

'Count us in,' Cordelia replied, opening the car door.

They were heading to Longton, a crumbling, nineteenth-century, Gothic Revival pile in the Kent countryside, built for industrialist Sir Hubert Tollington and relinquished by his family to the government in lieu of death duties. Throughout World War I it had been a base for allied soldiers, who had mistreated the historic treasure. It had been in need of restoration when a private school moved there in 1922, but by the time that closed in the 1990s Longton was ramshackle, with only the ghosts of prior occupants appreciating its anachronistic battlements, fan vaulted ceilings, and oriel windows. Its current incarnation was as *Once Seen Never Forgotten*, an enterprise run by Nicole Cantfield, furniture designer par excellence. She'd renovated the place, cleaned it of decades of neglect, and filled its rooms with architectural reclaim, antiques, and her own work. It was now like a

National Trust site where the interiors were available to buy. At the centre of the house, Nicole had converted a flamboyant crimson and gilded reception room into the most luxurious ice-cream parlour in the land, she called the Scarlet Den. Its combination of Knickerbocker Glories, ormolu as far as the eye could see, and that Phyllida lived only a couple of miles away, determined it as the location for the overdue reunion.

Early in Phyllida's career, working for a fine art auction house in authentication and attribution, she had checked three Tintoretto paintings owned by bullish entrepreneur Clayton Dandridge and discovered that they were fakes. Her youthful eyes, scrutinising a canvas through a magnifying glass, had spotted miniature letters that read, "GOTCHA, STUPID!" on the bare ankle of the central figure. Her heart had thumped as she'd checked the other two works. It took hours, but she'd found the same message on both. She also found on each the words tempus fugit and the almost imperceptible image of a digital clock. Phyllida had inspected the paint layers under an electron microscope and seen that clocks and slogans were in situ to other strokes and not added afterwards, which meant all three paintings were forgeries. When informed that his priceless Old Masters were worthless copies, the owner had blown his top and refused to accept the evidence. The auction house had declined to sell the remainder of Dandridge's property, which Phyllida considered to be justice, him being a latter-day robber baron who, as well as being devious in business, had procured quality newspapers, converted them to tabloids and vulgarised public discourse.

'This is the type of edible room I dreamt of as a child,' Cordelia said in admiration of the ice-cream salon. Its raspberry ripple-coloured taffeta wallpaper, dado rail encrusted with hundreds and thousands sprinkles, and cornices of multicoloured glass fruit were the epitome of fairy tale chic.

'It's delicious. Willy Wonka would approve. What are you ordering?' Phyllida asked, looking at the menu.

'As a sculpture graduate I am unable to resist The Three Graces,' Cordelia replied, choosing the nectarine, starfruit, and papaya ice-cream version of Canova's marble masterpiece. 'What are you in the mood for?'

'Being a fan of Doctor Who it has to be the Dalek-shaped dondurma. I've never tasted dondurma. It says here it's a type of Turkish ice cream and has a chewy texture. This Dalek comes in coffee flavour, the eyestalk is a chocolate log, and the casing is dotted with spearmint choccie buttons.'

'Mmm. Will you give me a da-lick?'

Phyllida chuckled. 'Oh darling, I've missed your daft puns.'

'So, do you want me to reveal the plot? I'm here to ask you to oversee the establishment of a new London gallery for my friend's art, to arrange transportation from Paris and Reims, and to hang it. She has an extensive collection of works by female artists, possibly the largest in the world.' Cordelia omitted the part concerning Left To Their Own Devices. That was to remain a secret.

'What a delightful proposal. How could I say no? However, I have a caveat. I must be able to fit it around what my boss decrees.' As an ardent gardener, tasked with two acres of land to vivify, her boss was Mother Nature.

'I'm so pleased, you're a dear. And of course horticulture comes first. This will only be temporary and once we're open, you'll be back to primp your petunias and win first prize in Glorious Gardens of Kent.'

Now that Phyllida was signed up the next step was to secure a location for the gallery. Early each morning Cordelia, with Blanche, strolled the streets of Fitzrovia and Bloomsbury in conversation with the muses to find somewhere that was both characterful and big enough for Elodie's paintings and the Left To Their Own Devices super-sized canvases. Then one day she found it, almost on her doorstep. She rushed up House of Tanner's imperial marble staircase into Rex's office and flopped on his sofa.

'You'll never guess which deconsecrated church opposite has a For Sale sign newly nailed above the door. It'll be just right for us. I'll make a viewing appointment.'

When Elodie, working overseas for Rebâtir, saw the roomy interior in the video Cordelia sent she called them. 'It's perfect and I like the church association. Art is a religion and it's meant to be revered in community alongside other people, not be lonely in empty rooms.'

'Wait 'til you see the exterior. Bands of black and white glazed tiles like a Belted Galloway, my favourite breed of cow,' Rex told her excitedly.

'*Ma colombe*, I adore that you have a favourite cow. That seals the deal. Should we call our gallery Worship?'

A fortnight later, Elodie was back in London and they were celebrating the imminent purchase of what had formerly been St Cecilia's. 'Cecilia is the patron saint of singers,' she said.

'Does that include karaoke-performing surgeons?' Cordelia asked, alluding to one of Elodie's musical pastimes.

'*Bien sûr!* I always call on her for celestial assistance to hit the right notes. She deserves a portrait to hang in the entrance. I wonder if any dealers have paintings of her? It's the Berlin Art Mart soon. Should we go shopping?'

Chapter Two

Cordelia poked her head round Rex's door. 'That writer will be here soon to interview me. Can we use your sofa?' She was preparing for the visit of a journalist profiling her for the Observer magazine.

'Of course, I'll go to the caff and eat a sequel to my earlier breakfast.'

Her phone rang. It was Sebastian, her personal assistant. 'Mary Ball is here. She's waiting in the lobby.'

'Thank you Basti, be right there.' Then to Rex, 'Will you come and say hello?'

They clattered downstairs, relishing the sound their shoes made on the steps because it reminded them of childhood tapdancing lessons.

'Mary, welcome to House of Tanner. How do you do? I'm Cordelia Tanner and this is my brother Rex, who is also my business partner. Without him the place would not exist.'

'Hello Cordelia, good to meet you. And hello Rex, it'll be useful to have a chat. Are you free today?' Mary asked, shaking their hands. They set a time to meet. Rex left them alone so Cordelia could give her the full-on House of Tanner experience.

As they climbed the staircase, with its polished handrail and balustrades, Mary said, 'The architecture is stunning. What was it prior to you moving in?'

'The main office of an insurance firm that eventually relocated. It sat empty for years. A millinery producer was initially based here when feathers on hats were the rage, so its original name was Plumage House. Such a coincidence seeing as my creations are inspired by birds.'

House of Tanner HQ was a sight to behold, a nineteenth-century

Italian Renaissance Revival palace with high arched windows, columns, and a colonnade on the ground floor. In its majestic lobby museum worthy sculptures by Edmonia Lewis, Anne Whitney, and Luisa Roldán greeted visitors.

'Do you fancy a cuppa and then I'll explain what we do?'

Cordelia liked talking about House of Tanner, and why not, it was an extraordinary success story, born of her's and Rex's combination of vision and implementation. During their first postgraduate employment – hers as an assistant for a fashionable shoe brand; his in a software engineering firm – they'd often sat in the pub after work, carping on about their jobs and fantasising about starting their own enterprises. 'You'd hate the bro culture of computing. I hate the bro culture of computing. So I'm in the wrong profession,' Rex had complained.

'I'm learning loads but I want my creativity to be liberated,' Cordelia had sighed.

'We'll do it one of these days,' Rex sighed in return. 'Should we have another drinkie?'

'Thought you'd never ask. Pint of mild please.'

After a few months of dreaming Cordelia had said, 'I enjoy my work and my colleagues are ace, nonetheless I want to design what I want to design. Instead of constantly banging on and then doing nothing, I need to be proactive and acquire funding for my own atelier.'

Rex heard Cordelia's frustration and switched on his listening intently empathy face. 'If I had the dosh I'd fund you. Computing is probably more lucrative, so in case we fail to find a crock of gold at the end of the rainbow we should create something computery that makes us money and then when we're loaded, we'll start in shoe-biz.'

Cordelia sang "There's no business like shoe business", then paused for a few seconds before blurting, 'Got it! We'll combine shoes and software. You build some software for footwear manufacturers, and I'll advise on the shoe-y bits. Mass-market producers in SE Asia churn out mountains, including trainers by the million. Production systems need to be seamless. It's a complicated chain that breaks if any of the links are not co-ordinated.'

Rex was all a-quiver at Cordelia's suggestion because logistics was one of his strengths. He had never yet met a spreadsheet that did not stir him in a way that only other mathematicians could understand. In contrast, if Cordelia pictured a spreadsheet she felt her soul being sucked out through her nostrils.

And that had been the start. Rex developed software with variations for several types of manufacturing. Demand was significant and companies worldwide licensed it on an annual basis, which is how the Tanners went from being juniors in their professions, earning entry-level wages, to building an empire that showcased Cordelia's astounding talent.

Mary was gripped. She was keen on rags to riches stories, especially if they involved families.

'Do you remember your first House of Tanners?' she asked.

Cordelia's expression became wistful. 'Yes. I have a replica pair in the archive. We'll go and see them.'

She led Mary to a vast room where everything ever produced by House of Tanner was displayed.

'I call it The Roost and, as you can see, I have taken the avian analogy to the limit.'

Each model was exhibited on velvet in nest-like hexagonal boxes fastened to the wall, which resembled a giant honeycomb. She walked past the physical manifestations of her ingenuity and picked up a pair of high-heeled platform sandals in iridescent aquamarine, emerald, yellow, scarlet, and electric-blue suede.

'Here they are. The colours are based on the feathers of a Wilson's Bird of Paradise. It has a violet curlicue tail, symbolised here by ribbons that wrap around the ankles.'

Mary made appreciative noises as Cordelia continued. 'They were a one-off for a pal and she has the originals. If it wasn't for her, I doubt House of Tanner would have become so successful.'

She told the tale of her best friend at school, who had later studied at the Royal College of Dramatic Arts and went on to star in Hollywood films. 'Her name is Trudy Dench and seeing as that's almost identical to Dame Judi, she legally changed it to Sabina Bailey.'

'The same one who won the Academy Award for *Where The Earth Meets The Sky*? I loved that film!'

'Me too. Sabina's success is how global recognition for House of Tanner began. She commissioned me to make her a pair of shoes to wear for the Oscars. I made her the Wilson's but she decided they were too gorgeous to be hidden under her frock so she asked if I'd mind an alternative.'

That alternative was her going barefoot on the red carpet, followed by a male model acting as a pageboy, holding aloft a glass case in which the shoes sat on a purple fur cushion. Attention had been on Sabina as a nominee and then as winner, and the shoes appeared in all the reportage. Naturally, she repeatedly mentioned Cordelia's name when asked about her ensemble.

'Those were yours? What an incredible story.'

'I couldn't believe it. Orders were out of control. However, being a start-up we couldn't handle it because even then everything was bespoke. Fortunately, most customers understood the delay. Some of our clients have been with us since the beginning.'

'I'm not surprised. Where did you study shoe design?'

'Cordwainers, a Master of Arts. My Bachelor's was in sculpture at the Courtauld Institute. I'm fortunate to have been educated at such incomparable artistic foundations.'

'Wish I had more pages for this feature Cordelia, there's so much to say.'

'And we haven't even seen what the production team is working on. Do you want to have a nosy now?'

Mary followed Cordelia along the marble-lined corridor into a large room where clickers, closers, and finishers were meticulously working on the footwear fantasies that brought imagination and wonderment to the world.

'As you can see, everything is hand done. These ultra-skilled professionals are maintaining the exceptional craft of cordwaining.'

'It's like engineering.'

'Good description. My brother is a genius mathematician, so he considers cordwaining to be an applied science as well as an art.'

'You two have entirely compatible abilities then.'

'Glad you noticed – will you tell him? I couldn't do any of this without Rex. I tend to get the public recognition cos I do the glam bit, but he's the operating system making sure the machine works as it should.'

Mary glanced at her watch. 'Is it that time? Rex is expecting me in ten minutes.'

'I'll walk you back to his office. So lovely of you to come by. If you need anything clarifying or want to ask more questions, please call. Now, we'll pop in to see my PA, Sebastian so you can arrange for a photographer to make us all look fabulous on film, or should I say, delicious in digital.'

Chapter Three

Heads turned whenever Cordelia entered a room, doubly so if Elodie was beside her, and that day at Berlin Art Mart was no exception. Her hair was in an up-do and she was dressed in a vivid magenta satin skirt suit with statement lapels, the left one adorned with a corsage of sweet peas. Cordelia often wore fresh blooms in her hair or pinned to her outfits and she chose varieties least likely to cause hay-fever symptoms in anyone nearby – as a precaution, she carried antihistamines in her handbag to hand out if necessary. On her feet she was wearing shoes she had created exclusively for herself. They resembled strelitzia, also known as bird of paradise, the flower's dramatic beak as the upper and its orange and purple petal crest proudly rising above the vamp. Elodie, her honey-blonde wavy hair worn loose, was chic in a ruby ankle-length silk charmeuse dress, cut on the bias so it clung in all the right places. She was in a pair of her signature Cuban-heeled cowbike boots, a hybrid of cowboy and biker, handmade by Monsieur Durand, an octogenarian cordonnier in Paris.

They were a dazzling pair who warranted fanfares but, despite their remarkable impact, neither was aloof, both being warm and engaging. Cordelia combined the charisma and authority of a natural leader with playfulness, and she was the type of vivacious character with whom most people wanted to spend time. She always upgraded the ordinary to the extraordinary and the smile in her voice and frequent laughter was an invitation for anyone listening to take joy in life. Elodie, meanwhile, was captivating, utterly charming, and universally adored. She had no idea of the effect she had, which made it even more delightful. A light radiated from her and enveloped everyone in her orbit, and she had a rare gift of making people believe they were the world's most sexy, valiant, and fascinating individual.

Cordelia browsed the show catalogue. 'Ooh, Isabella Cicciano is here. Let's go and say hello.' Isabella was the great-granddaughter of the deceased Minerva Cicciano, devotee of the arts who, in 1930 transformed her private island in the Bay of Naples into a colony for female artists and renamed it Libertas. The intention was to showcase and sell their work in a society where their creativity was largely undervalued. Libertas was also a holiday destination for art afficionados and, as a penniless recently graduated student, Cordelia had visited, courtesy of a bursary. Now, as an internationally successful entrepreneur, she donated generously to the Libertas Foundation so young women on a low income could benefit as she had from what the island offered.

'Cordelia, wonderful to see you. Are you here for work or pleasure?'

'Both,' Cordelia replied, kissing Isabella's cheeks. 'May I introduce Doctor Elodie l'Archambeau. When she told me of her peerless art collection I urged her to visit the island. And it turns out she had already experienced the Libertas lifestyle.'

Coincidentally, Cordelia and Elodie had, without knowing or meeting the other, celebrated their twenty-third birthday on the island.

'*Enchantée*,' Elodie said beaming one of her blinding smiles. 'I loved my stay on Libertas and was so motivated I bought two works. They were the start of my collection. I have your great-grandmother to thank for opening my eyes.'

'That is so good to hear. I am proud to continue her legacy.'

'Coeurdelia,' as Elodie, being all heart, referred to Cordelia, 'Let's return to the island and explore all the places where we unwittingly breathed the same air and then buy some art for Worship.'

'Please do, and you'll see Cordelia's name plaque above the door of the lodge she stayed in. It is the least we can do to acknowledge her generous endowment.'

Cordelia squeezed Isabella's arm, then, noticing a petite dark-haired woman wearing a pencil skirt, tailored jacket, and ultra-high heels, all in black, and flanked by four giant men, said, 'Who's that with the beefcake?'

Isabella murmured, 'Valentina. No surname. She is a prominent dealer, owns an art school in Rome, and also specialises in locating stolen works. That means she has enemies, particularly in organised crime gangs. The bodyguards escort her everywhere, although some say four is rather excessive and that she does it to draw attention to herself.'

'Who's the Lady Boss?' Rex queried as he sauntered on to the Libertas stand.

'Rudolph Valentina. People move out of her way sharpish. Can't imagine why, given her four pet bullmen of the apocalypse,' Cordelia replied.

'Anyone want to bet me a fiver the Hulk is built like a cement wall under that bulletproof vest?' He motioned to the tallest guard, who was holding Valentina's limited edition Hermès Birkin bag.

'She might know the whereabouts of a St Cecilia painting. Isabella, if you are acquainted will you please introduce us?' Elodie asked.

'Of course.'

'Quite scary isn't she,' Rex whispered to Cordelia, as Elodie chatted to Valentina.

'Her pointy ears make me think of La Ciguapa, that folklore character who lures men into the woods to their death,' Cordelia whispered back.

Five minutes later, Valentina had agreed to negotiate a deal with the proprietor of As God Is My Witness, a purveyor of religious paintings whose only client was the Vatican.

'I've invited Valentina to visit Worship when we're open,' Elodie told Cordelia and Rex. 'I mentioned House of Tanner and she's keen to know more.'

Buying from House of Tanner was not as simple as walking in for a fitting. To be deemed worthy of wearing such magnificent footwear potential customers were vetted to ensure they made a positive contribution to society and were not nasty pieces of work. This significant hurdle made wearing House of Tanner even more prestigious. And it meant Cordelia genuinely liked most of her clients.

'As long as she parks the minders somewhere other than HoT. If they sit in Bonatti's Ant can feed them raw liver,' Cordelia said sardonically, referring to their local greasy spoon café.

'Offal tartare. I'd actually eat that. I'm starving,' Rex said. 'Where should we dine?'

'Mutter and Wagner, the city's oldest restaurant, is not far. It's Bonheur's largest German client. Very traditional, Biedermeier style, and usually fully booked. If you like the sound of it, I'll call and ask if they have room for us,' Elodie replied.

'How big's their *Pinkel mit grünkohl?*'

Cordelia sniggered. 'You've been waiting all your life to say that haven't you.'

Over dinner they nattered about the art fair and Elodie's masterstroke in meeting and enticing Sandrine Rivera to visit Worship. Sandrine, founder and CEO of the influential 'Art Is Life and Life Is Art' media conglomerate, was notoriously picky about attending new gallery openings, but she'd immediately said yes to the Worship event.

'She was lovely and seemed keen to hear of my collection,' Elodie said cheerfully. 'What if she includes it in one of her magazines – that would be incredible!'

'Do you reckon rear pews were invented for naughty congregants who need a quick exit after mass has finished?' Cordelia was sitting next to Rex and Elodie in the disused St Cecelia's waiting for Celestine Priestly to arrive and discuss her concepts for its conversion to Worship. Celestine was an Oscar-winning production designer, who also happened to be the Tanners' legal guardian. She'd assumed the role when they were three, following the disappearance of their orchidologist parents during an expedition in Madagascar. Celestine had never wanted children of her own, but she loved her wards, called them her precious jewels and had treated them like adults. She'd given them independence and emboldened their curiosity and sense of adventure. She'd stressed the importance of generosity, empathy, and sharing their good fortune but had always reminded them not to be saints on earth, but to wait until they reached heaven.

'So sorry to be late my precious jewels. Traffic was a horror and the bus was crawling, so I got off and walked from the park,' Celestine announced as she rushed into the church. 'Well, here we are. This is exciting, I hope you'll like my ideas.'

'Everything you conceive is amazamente so we'll be bowing in homage.' Cordelia removed an imaginary hat with a flourish and performed a shallow bow.

'If we take a wander I'll describe what I have in mind.' They followed her and stopped in the aisle in the middle of the nave.

'You asked for Elodie's collection to be in a space that feels homely, so we need to create a room within a room and reduce the cavernous nature of this area by installing wooden walls on which to hang the paintings. The high ceiling will be lowered by a canopy of flowers, leaving gaps in the sides so people can still see the stained-glass windows. They are masterpieces so we don't want to lose them.'

The others nodded eagerly so Celestine continued. 'We'll paint the walls navy blue, because that shade is elegant, calming, and reduces stress, so it will contribute to the relaxing atmosphere you're seeking.'

She presented a drawing that illustrated her plans, including the armchairs requested by Cordelia who had said, 'Squashy seats so people can relax, have a drink, or a snooze, and feel as though they are at home communing with the paintings.'

There were more oohs and aahs and animated comments. Rex asked what would become of the aisle mosaics.

'They are so special, but as they do not cover the whole floor the room will look unfinished in the absence of pews. I recommend hiding them beneath cork flooring across the entire nave. This will help to insulate and warm the place up. Cork is also sustainable, and patterns can be printed on it. How does a parquet flooring effect and then scattering kilim rugs sound?'

'Oh Celestine, I can picture it all and adore your proposals. You have taken our dreams and will turn them into reality,' Elodie said enthusiastically.

'So pleased, thank you. Now for the chancel, and my thinking for the abstract art. We'll keep the altar rails as a distinct boundary between the traditional and the modern.'

'I like the fact that visitors will have to walk past my art on their way to look at the LefDevs,' Elodie commented approvingly.

Celestine smiled. 'Here's another thing for you Elodie. At the risk of being struck down for my sacrilegious intention, the altar will become the bar where water will be changed to sparkling wine.'

Elodie threw back her head and laughed, then she hugged Celestine. 'Everything is perfection. I could not love it more.'

'That's a relief. There are no structural changes to be made, so basically, we are building a set and it can be done swiftly. Rex, we'll need your logistics acumen.'

'What joy. One of my favourite subjects. Let's go and have a cuppa in The Weasel and I can talk endlessly about spreadsheets.'

An hour later they had settled on the plans to bring forth the new gallery. Celestine had a list of carpenters and electricians with whom she regularly worked; the pews and other ecclesiastical furniture that did not fit the new format would be sold to antiques traders; and Phyllida was standing by to accompany Elodie to her homes in Paris and Reims to pack and ship her collection.

'Don't forget the most important factor in this plan – the party.' Cordelia said. 'I'll ask Vulpy if he will produce something splendid.'

Elodie and Archbishop Claudio Albertelli, the Vatican's ambassador to Great Britain, were standing in front of Elizabetta Sirani's portrait of St Cecelia. It had been intended for the papal palace but when the Pope was informed of Elodie's humanitarian work and learned of her interest in purchasing the painting he decided she must have it.

'It is outstanding,' the archbishop commented. 'His Holiness is in Britain for a state visit in January and has asked to see this beautiful work.'

It was 22 November, Cecelia's saint's day, and the launch party for Worship was buzzing with an array of art critics, museum directors, and style commentators conversing underneath Celestine's suspended floral canopy formed of snake's head fritillary, their dark purple and pink lantern-shaped flowers peeking at the guests below. Wait staff circulated holding trays of Bee Double Bs, a cocktail devised by Oscar based on a French 75 and made of Bonheur, Brighton Gin and a hint of The Weasel honey.

In one corner, a group of actors arranged themselves in a tableau vivant of *Elizabeth I Receiving the Ambassadors*, a painting attributed to Levina Teerlinc. On the other side of the room, the skimpy outfits worn by characters in *The Chariot of the Queen and Her Fairies* made the archbishop blush. Natalie Rousseau, the acclaimed coloratura soprano, sang exquisite motets from *Amor Sacro* alongside the Chamber Orchestra of the Baroque. She was Elodie's childhood friend and together they used to regularly sneak out of boarding school to watch the Django Reinhardt gypsy-jazz tribute band in the local bar. At weekends they'd busked by the Sacré-Cœur Basilica, where tourists stood enraptured as Elodie played her accordion and Natalie sang popular French songs.

Elodie, chatting in Spanish with Mateo Castillas, the director of the Museo del Prado, said, 'What a perfect museum you run. Whenever I am in Madrid I always rush there to see the Velázquez portrait of Francisco Pacheco. The way he painted that white ruffled collar is extraordinary.' Mateo preened, and she continued, 'How I wish museums would conduct blind auditions of art so they were unaware who created it and then acquire work on merit. That is a way for more of our cultural institutions to include art by women.' She pointed to the painting of an auburn-haired woman looking side-on to the viewer. 'This is a self-portrait by Victorine Meurent. Forgive me if you are already aware that she is celebrated for being the model for Manet's *Olympia* and the central figure in *Le Déjeuner sur l'Herbe*. She was an accomplished artist in her own right, exhibited at the Paris Salon on many occasions and yet is virtually unknown.'

Cordelia was in the transept, which had been converted into the Left To Their Own Devices precinct. She was standing beside Sandrine Rivera and Vance Dorkin, co-host of TV's *It's Breakfast*. He had a love-hate relationship with Cordelia because she had once politely declined when he'd asked her out on a date. His grudge had never lapsed and he was usually snarky, but Cordelia knew how to handle him and was always courteous, despite him being a rude, narcissistic twerp.

As he inspected a work titled *Absolutely Nothing*, a reference to the song lyric, "War, what is it good for?", she heard him mutter 'amateur hour'. *First time I've agreed with a thing he's said. And he's bound to hate the collective's liberal sentiments,* she thought, inwardly tittering at his mocking facial expression. She sensed he was on the verge of a tirade, which stopped as Sandrine said, 'This is some of the most significant work I've ever seen. It's a bold and necessary voice for a new era. We are witnessing a defining moment and I am tingling with excitement. Vance, I hope you are feeling fortunate, because movements like this rarely appear. It's as momentous as the emergence of Fauvism in Paris in 1905. That shocked the bourgeoisie, and this will shake the establishment from its comfort zone.'

Revolution is only a canvas away. I must dig out my liberty cap. Cordelia wondered if Sandrine was joking. She wasn't.

'I was just saying what a big fan I am of conceptual art that tells a story and makes a comment on society,' Vance pontificated.

Well, well, dumbo Dorkin must have the hots for her if he's lying so blatantly, Cordelia reckoned, watching him leer at Sandrine. Then noticing Rex standing nearby she saw him touch his left eyebrow and left ear, which was their secret code and, in this context, meant, 'I saw and heard what she said and want to stick both thumbs up.' He tried unsuccessfully to stifle a snigger and disguised it by coughing. 'Oh dear, excuse me, I need a drink,' he spluttered, heading to the bar.

Vance shouted after him, 'Get me one too will you pal,' not asking if the others wanted anything. Then he turned to Cordelia, 'Do you want to record a chat for tomorrow's show?'

She said yes and his piece to camera began, 'As you know I'm one of the best-connected people there is and so, it is no surprise that I'm being given an exclusive introduction to the world's newest and most important voice in art. Left To Their Own Devices is a secret cabal but I know who they are, and I actually gave them recommendations for themes.'

He didn't even blink as he uttered those porkies, thought Cordelia as she addressed his comment on why she, a shoe designer, was involved, and why such a zeitgeisty artist collective chose to exhibit at a gallery full of traditional and under-appreciated art.

'Worship is the authorised broker for Left To Their Own Devices in recognition of the female artists highlighted in the gallery who were the rule breakers and disruptors of their era in a discipline from which, due to their sex, they were largely excluded. Even so, they never ceased in their efforts to break through the canvas ceiling. The collective also lauds the humanitarian work of Doctor Elodie l'Archambeau, co-founder of Worship with me and my brother Rex. It's free entry so I hope your viewers will drop by if they are in the area.'

'What do you know about art anyway, you're a cobbler,' Vance said dismissively.

'Well, apart from a degree in sculpture, studying art history, and being the subject of a retrospective at the Victoria & Albert called *The Art of The Shoe*, not much I suppose. But that's the thing – a person does not need to know or understand art because the crucial element is how it makes one feel.' Cordelia was struggling to stop her face communicating her incredulous inner voice, *Each time I believe he's reached the pinnacle of dimwittedness he locates a further peak to scale.*

Vance never recalled that whenever he met Cordelia and posed one of his silly questions she came out on top. As he had no retort, the interview came to an end. Elodie approached and asked, 'May I borrow Coeurdelia ? *Monsieur le Président* is keen to say hello.'

Cordelia gave her a relieved to be rescued look and thanked Vance for coming, then walked over to the French president who was not there in an official role but as the husband of Natalie Rousseau. He shook Cordelia's hand. 'Mademoiselle Tanner, *enchanté*. What a superb gallery. And I am intrigued to hear you own personal items that belonged to King Louis XIV.' He was alluding to one of the highlights of her shoe collection. 'May I be bold and ask to see them during my stay to London?'

'*Mais bien sûr Monsieur le Président. C'est mon privilège. Quelle est votre pointure? Les chaussures du Roi Soleil devraient vous convenir.*'

The President had to listen carefully because, although Cordelia's French was quite good, her accent made it sound a little bit Welsh. There was a slight delay, then he laughed as he registered her question concerning the size of his feet in case the Sun King's shoes fit.

'Don't give him ideas Cordelia. He will be dreaming of absolute power,' Natalie said, giggling and kissing her husband's cheek.

'I will return the favour by inviting you to join me on a tour of the Palace of Versailles. It has some very special shoes. Would you like to see them?' The President motioned towards to a portrait of Marie Antoinette.

Not for the first time Cordelia sent gratitude to a cosmos that was gifting her with such incredible opportunities. She was so excited she cried out loud, 'You betcha bottom Euro Mr Prezzi-al-dente,' when she'd meant to say it in her head. The President did not understand her slang but could tell she was keen, so he smiled and said, '*Merveilleux.*'

All the guests had gone and the TannerBeaus were sitting in the altar bar.

'I think we need to open this,' Elodie said happily, holding up a bottle of Bonheur Prestige Cuvée made in the year of their birth. Whenever a child was born into the Bonheur family it was tradition for hundreds of bottles of that year's vintage to be laid down for them to drink throughout their lives. She opened it and poured out the wine. They sipped and concurred it was divine.

'I wish you'd heard Sandrine's comments and Porkin' Dorkin's complete capitulation from his original opinion of our art being playtime at the nursery,' Cordelia said, rushing her words to enlighten Elodie. 'If she endorses LefDev we're on our way.'

They clinked glasses and cheersed that their wheeze to infiltrate the art market had impressed such a significant figure as Sandrine Rivera.

'We're ready for the moment the billionaires start clamouring, but I'll be sad to see *Full English Breakfast* go,' Rex said.

'So will I. The way you made the grilled mushrooms resemble muddy puddles was exceptional,' Cordelia replied, leaning back in her seat and sighing in contentment. Her favourite occasions were when it was just the three of them.

'Do we have to lose it? I have such good memories of that afternoon. Could you do a brunch instead? Eggs Benedict and a Red Snapper cocktail?' Elodie suggested, then jumped as her phone vibrated. She read the text, *S'il te plaît, appelle-moi* plus the motorbike emoji code.

'It's Manon. We're needed. Operation Rapid Response to the rescue.'

Chapter Four

'I will never not be completely excited to climb these stairs. Aren't we lucky,' Cordelia said as they boarded Elodie's private plane. 'Can I have a go at driving?'

'You can cruise her over the alps Captain, I'll do the easy part of taking off and landing.'

Elodie occasionally used her jet for recreation, although it was primarily for Rebâtir and was large enough to fly medical crews and equipment to deliver the charity's humanitarian work. On long journeys her pilot Collette was in charge, but for shorter journeys Elodie flew solo.

That day they were heading to Marseilles for their latest collaboration with Globo Pol, the international police organisation. They assisted on crimes that proved impossible to solve using traditional methods by using an extrasensory ability a teenage Cordelia had discovered she possessed. She'd held a pair of vintage shoes and glimpsed some personal details of the woman who'd owned them. It had been an exhilarating experience, so she'd tried another pair with similar results. Thereafter, she'd practised every day with various inanimate objects to develop her skill.

'I don't get it, what happens?' Rex had asked.

'It's bonkers cos if I hold someone's personal possessions or things they've touched I can see in my head information about them, and what they've been doing. I can even overhear conversations.'

'Can other people do it too?'

'Well, I did some research on psychic intuition and it's a bit like psychometry, which some peeps have the knack of. Mine seems to be a combination of techniques, including remote viewing, and is unlike the skills others have, so I call it psychomatricks. I'm still discovering the breadth of my ability.'

'Ooh, does that mean you're a voyeur and no one suspects? Please don't try it on me, you'll find out all my secrets.'

'Babe, you're my twin so I already know them. Anyway, I'm only going to do it to historical characters so you're safe. I don't really want deets about living people, although, if there was a good reason, I could have a nosy, but never with anyone I'd known.'

Rex longed to have the knack too but, despite checking regularly, had no aptitude, not even on the occasions he experimented by holding Cordelia's hand to share her vibes. She thought he was unable to let loose due to his logical, disciplined mind. He was disappointed because she made it sound so thrilling.

With Elodie it was a different matter and Cordelia realised that, by doing it in tandem, the effects were doubled and intense waves of energy pulsed in their bodies, making them feel as if they were blasting through space.

'Wowsings – that was powerful! We should offer ourselves to the National Grid as renewable electricity,' Cordelia joked following their first attempt.

The Globo Pol link came after Cordelia psychometrised a man who was attempting to sell a pair of sandals that he claimed had been owned by Mary Magdalene, but were obviously shams. She had learned something else, excitedly saying to Elodie, 'You'll never guess what, he's handling stolen property, including the Degas painting that went missing from the Lenter Museum.'

'*Incroyable*! Can you see where it is stored?'

'Yes, a garage in Istanbul and the insurers will be keen to know.'

'One of my school friends is Manon Jacquet, secretary general of Globo Pol. We can tell her.'

Manon had been impressed when Cordelia's clues led local police to recover the goods and she saw the potential for partnership on other hard-to-crack cases. Cordelia and Elodie, open to all adventures, had heartily approved of the invitation to create the covert Operation Rapid Response. To date, they'd had astonishing success.

'Welcome back. I am so pleased to see you both. How are my star sleuths?' Manon said warmly as they arrived at Globo Pol. She accompanied them to a conference room where they had a coffee and a chat before setting to work. As usual, Manon gave them no clues to the assignment, so as not to influence the answers and handed over an unmarked envelope which contained photographs of a location suspected of having a criminal association, and a man who might be connected.

'Ready to feel the force?' Cordelia asked Elodie, taking the envelope. They held it with their left hands where, as lefties, the power resided, linked little fingers on their right to create a circuit, then meditated. Almost immediately a potent surge forced them back in their chairs and they had psychomatricks lift-off. Providing they were physically in contact, fingers entwined or fingertips touching, what they saw and heard in their mind's eye was identical, as if their brains were connected. This time they registered images of a debonair grey-haired man standing by a black SUV parked outside an anonymous warehouse.

'There's not a lot to go on is there? Although some numbers appeared in my head,' Cordelia said.

'I have numbers too.' Elodie scribbled them on a sheet of paper.

They coincided.

'We're so attuned. Wouldn't it be funny if they were lottery numbers. Did you see anything else?'

'Yes, a rather good-looking man in his early sixties.'

'Did he look like this?' Cordelia swiftly sketched his likeness.

'You're so clever, that's him exactly.'

Manon later confirmed the digits were GPS coordinates for a building situated in Swiss Free Port, one of the world's main facilities for the storage of valuables, including priceless artworks. 'How does a trip to Zurich sound?'

Globo Pol had intelligence that the individual in the photograph was using the warehouse to stow pilfered antiquities, so Cordelia and Elodie's mission was to visit and investigate. Globo Pol had been tipped off by a reputable dealer in New York, who'd been offered a 2,000-year-old Mesopotamian stone sculpted head that he suspected had been looted from the state museum in Baghdad during the Gulf War. He arranged to buy the piece, with the intention of handing it to the police for return to Iraq and had surreptitiously snapped a photograph of the seller, an Austrian named Gerfried Theiler.

'Swiss Free Port is one of the world's largest wine cellars. Bonheur stores thousands of bottles there so that's our excuse to access the site,' Elodie declared.

'Who needs a key when we have Bonheur?' Cordelia said.

This place won't win any architecture prizes, Cordelia reflected from the pillion of Nike, Elodie's high-performance motorcycle, which was driving slowly along the bleak thoroughfares and identikit buildings of Swiss Free Port. Suddenly, Elodie pulled over to the roadside and parked. 'See the warehouse next to that orange shipping container? I have a feeling about it.'

'Right. Let's go for a dekko.'

They removed their crash helmets and approached the single-storey structure. Cordelia placed her hands on its roll-down door. 'You keep an eye out and I'll see if I can read this.'

She concentrated for a few seconds until Elodie murmured, 'Someone's coming.' A black SUV drew up and the driver alighted. They recognised him as the man in the photo.

'Hello there. Are you lost?' he said amiably in German-accented English.

'Yes,' Cordelia replied. 'We're looking for the main office.'

'Sorry, I do not know where that is. This is such a big site, so it may be easier if you go to the security gate and ask for directions. Where is your vehicle?'

She pointed to Nike.

'Impressive. I've always wanted to ride a beast like that.'

'Well, let's go now,' Elodie said, swinging the keys round her finger. 'Do you want to drive or should I?'

Theiler acted like most people did on first meeting Elodie, overcome by an immense crush and transformed from adult into teenager. He smiled bashfully. 'You drive please.'

'Nice move, it'll give me a chance to inspect the door and see what I learn,' Cordelia murmured.

'I'll be fifteen minutes, *cherie*. Is that enough time?'

'Ample, but don't hurry. I'll do his car too. He didn't lock it.'

When Cordelia was alone she leant on the door, palms flat, fingers splayed, and closed her eyes. Anyone passing by might question why a woman in damson-coloured motorcycle leathers had chosen that uncomfortable-looking spot for a nap. Twenty minutes later she heard the growl of Nike's engine.

Elodie parked the bike and Theiler walked towards the warehouse. 'Your friend tells me you are both keen on the British Museum's Assyrian collection, especially the winged lions of Nimrud. I trade in ancient Middle Eastern art. I'd like to show you some special pieces if you're interested.'

'Yes please,' she replied, then said quietly to Elodie, 'You're a genius. If you distract him again I'll do more psy-comming.'

The storage unit was organised in rows of heavy-duty metal shelves, stacked with wooden crates. Theiler opened the nearest one and took out a small item, well protected by bubble wrap.

'Here's another winged lion, a little younger than his Nimrud cousins. This dates to circa 500 BCE and was unearthed in what is now central Iran. A high-status person used it for drinking wine at religious feasts.' He handed Cordelia an ornate golden vessel balanced on a lion's back. Suddenly his phone rang and he apologised, 'Excuse me, I must answer this.'

'I'll listen in to what he's saying,' Elodie whispered.

'And I'll do a quick once-over while you do.'

A few minutes passed and Cordelia heard her say, 'We must be going now. Thank you for showing us that incredible object. Do you have a card? I know someone who is interested in antiquities.'

Oh that's clever, we can psy-comm it.

They waved goodbye to Theiler and climbed aboard Nike.

Cordelia said, 'Total scoundrel. We need to find a café for a debrief. I have things to tell.'

Over raspberry and whipped cream *erdbeerroulade*, Cordelia explained that Gerfried Theiler was a middleman who sold antiquities looted from war zones, in partnership with an English man, name unknown.

'The golden lion dates back to the first Persian empire and was nicked to order. Theiler is aware he's plundering a nation's heritage so that makes it even worse.' She poured out more tea.

Elodie picked up her cup and took a sip before replying, 'Some cultures believe ancestral spirits live in ancient artefacts. I can't bear to think of them being separated from their deceased relatives by thieves who have no respect for the soul of that notion. And Theiler was so affable too. And handsome.'

'Of all the missions we've worked on this makes me feel quite emoshiony and I really want to solve it so we can stop at least one malefactor stealing a country's relics. If we psy-comm the card together there's a chance we'll find out the identity of the mysterious Mr Steal.'

'Foiled,' Rex said to Cordelia and Elodie as they found themselves at yet another dead end. They were having lunch at A-Maze, a pop-up restaurant in Reedly Park, situated inside a living labyrinth of foliage. Diners were only guaranteed food if they stumbled across one of the small dining rooms. Depending on the chosen route, they might end up eating dessert first and appetisers last. The three of them had inhaled Eton Mess before locating the cheese course, so their meal was all back to front.

'This Ticklemore is divine, and the name alone makes me to want to eat it. Such fresh flavour. It works so well with the cider's acidity,' Elodie said delightedly. 'I'm in danger of my French citizenship being revoked by admitting that I yearn for British cheese.'

'You should open a cheese shop and call it From-age to Eternity. I'll be your best customer.' Cordelia giggled then cut herself a chunk and said to Rex, 'So what does your immense intellect make of the info we have so far?'

They were trying to work out the connection between what Cordelia had psychometrised at the warehouse, the words Elodie had overheard Theiler say on the phone, and the information they'd ascertained together from the business card.

'I'll do a Venn diagram. It may not give us the answers but it is a thing of beauty,' Rex said. He drew interlocking circles on a pad and then wrote: Royal Red Horse; International Clarion back page, 4-4; Top right, middle row. He tapped a forefinger on his lips as he looked at what he had written. 'Your psy-comming implies there is to be a shipment of goods leaving Rotterdam for England. Are these random phrases clues to something connected?'

'Newspapers usually have sports on the back page. Is Royal Red the name of a racehorse and 4-4 the date of a big race?' Elodie suggested.

'The Clarion has sports inside and puzzles on the back. I often attempt its crossword,' Rex replied. Then he yelled, 'That's it! Sudoku. Top right, middle row – it refers to one of the boxes in the grid. It might be a message for someone to complete the Clarion's sudoku on 4 April and to focus on specific numbers.'

'Rexicles proving once again he has a supercomputer in his bonce. I'll check on what Rotterdam and Royal Red Horse brings forth from the web.' She soon had the answer. 'It's a boozer on Witte de Withstraat that has a quiz on 4 April. We must enter.'

Rotterdam's Royal Red Horse was one of a chain of English theme pubs conceived by someone who had never actually been in one. It ticked all the cliché boxes but was wrong in numerous ways, including the clumsy title that conflated the three most common pub names. The walls were covered with pictures of long-dead British monarchs and also included Drag King Wenceslas, the very-much-alive male impersonator who ran Monkey Business Ministries and was an acquaintance of Cordelia's. Whoever had included her in the royal hall of fame either had a camp sense of humour or was clueless. The chips in their fish and chips were actually fries (fries!), and mushy peas were of the black eye variety – a crime against pub grub. Cheese and onion crisps came in pink packaging, when everyone in the UK knew that shade was reserved for prawn cocktail; and all the customers were seated, which thwarted the British sport of bulldozing hordes of vertical drinkers to reach the bar. Outside, a plastic statue of the petite blonde-haired landlady of a soap opera hostelry who was notorious for barring people with the bad-tempered catchphrase, 'Get outta my pub', had a sign hanging from her neck that read, 'Get into my pub please.'

'What are we going to drink? I'm Diane von Thirstenberg and nothing grabs me,' Rex sighed, pointing to whatever was pretending to be ale, and the apple-flavoured sugar water masquerading as cider. 'If life was not so short, I'd have Prosecco, but it is, and I won't.' He shuddered at the thought.

'*Ma colombe*, I have a surprise. Last week I spoke to the pub manager and sent him a magnum of Bonheur, which is now chilling for us. Oh, perfect timing, here it is.'

'Darling, if you didn't already so gloriously exist in our lives, I'd invent you,' Rex replied, kissing Elodie's cheek. 'This is an omen. We're going to win.'

He did not admit to being a serial pub quiz winner because he wanted Elodie to assume her Bonheur bounty was the reason for their triumph. She opened the bottle and poured each of them a glass. Rex pulled from his bag that day's International Clarion and the sudoku challenge he had already solved.

'Do the middle row numbers correspond to the running order of the questions, I wonder. What a marvellously old-school method of transmitting cryptic notifications if that's the case,' he pondered, then went on to explain how some female spies during World War I worked coded communiqués into their knitting, using stitches in a predetermined pattern to conceal a secret message in an innocent-looking hat or scarf.

'Look at those blokes over there.' Cordelia motioned with her head towards three burly wide-necked men drinking lager by the door. 'Steroids for breakfast. They look as though hauling a heavy pallet or two would be no effort. Do you think they're our shipment bitches?'

Just then the host welcomed the players and started the general knowledge round.

- What is the name of Morticia Addams' daughter?
- What is an alternative name for a small-boat harbour?
- George Orwell's *Animal Farm* is a satire on which political system?
- Which English island sounds similar to the name of Liverpool's river?
- In Greek mythology who was the goddess of agriculture?
- What hour was Wilson Pickett singing about?
- Are international athletics track races run clockwise or anti-clockwise?
- What type of craft competes in the America's Cup?
- True or false – bamboo can grow up to a metre in a day.
- A dromedary camel has how many humps?

When the first round finished the host bade players swap their sheets with a neighbouring team for marking. An attractive woman in her early thirties, sitting beside an equally pleasant looking man, passed theirs to Cordelia and said, 'They were quite easy. Maybe that's a ploy and the rest are going to be killers.'

'You check the answers and I'll swiftly psy-comm the paper as you do, in case they are the culprits,' Cordelia murmured to Rex, placing her left hand on the sheet and concentrating for a few seconds. 'It's them', she scribbled on her notepad.

He nodded and handed the quiz sheet back to the woman. 'Nine out of ten. How did we do?'

'Full marks. Unfortunately, we can't stay. Good luck.' She stood up, pocketed the sheet and left with her companion, as Elodie took a discreet photograph.

'Now, let's see what message the answers tell us,' Rex said quietly, staring at the questions that corresponded to numbers in the vertical and horizontal middle rows of the top right Sudoku grid. 'Got it. The shipment will be in a yacht departing on Wednesday at midnight heading for the marina on Mersea Island. I've been there. It's off the coast of Essex, famous for oysters, and is connected to the mainland by a causeway that floods at high tide.'

'Top work Tyranno. What a line-up we are with your logic and our magic. Wish we knew the name of Mr Steal though.'

'Perhaps he resembles a baddy in a film,' Elodie mused.

'Going by the rules of the Left Leaning Society, this is him,' Rex said, grabbing the pad and making pencil marks on the page using his right hand. 'Your turn,' passing it to Elodie who quickly drew a few lines.

Cordelia inspected their work and chuckled, 'According to this, Mr Steal resembles the Michelin Man with a face like a pepperoni pizza. We should send it to Globo Pol to help them create a photofit.'

Several weeks later Manon called with an update on the intel they had supplied. Globo Pol agents tracked the yacht to Mersea Island, watched as the cargo was loaded onto a lorry, and followed it to Pyramid Park in Surrey, a visitor attraction inspired by ancient Egypt and Babylon. Pyramid Park was cheap, cheerful, and popular for family days out, with rides on log flumes down the Euphrates (a diverted culvert), chariot-shaped bumper cars, and a ghost train past a burial chamber where mummies jumped up to scare the passengers.

'Rex and I used to go there as children,' Cordelia exclaimed. 'People always got lost because the directional signs were hieroglyphs, and no one understood them.'

Mr Steal was Pyramid Park proprietor Theo Arbuthnot, who had studied history at university but had chosen a career as a wheeler dealer by starting a business sardonically named Off The Back of a Lorry. His favourite film was *Raiders of the Lost Ark* and from his comfortable home in Leatherhead he fantasised about being Indiana Jones.

To ensure the shipment really did contain stolen antiquities Cordelia arranged for her friend Dorothy McInnes, emeritus Professor of Archaeology, to examine it.

It was obvious to Dorothy that they were the real thing. 'Whoever pinched them probably considers this to be a victimless crime. Hardly! It's the equivalent of filching the family heirlooms and that makes me so cross. Each time a relic is taken, cultural identity, history, and memories go too. If I ever meet the culprit they'll get a fist sandwich on the nose. It only needs a little tap to make a memorable impression.'

During police grilling Arbuthnot claimed the artefacts were reproductions to sell in his gift shop but when informed they had been authenticated by one of the country's premier experts and that Theiler had confessed and provided proof of Arbuthnot's role as instigator of the thefts, he admitted his involvement. In a manner that put the smug into smuggling, he boasted that the convoluted delivery method of sudoku, pub quiz, and yacht had been unnecessary. The goods could easily have been flown to Heathrow airport using fraudulent paperwork, but he revelled in the skulduggery, and it amused him to make his employees toil.

'Someone should buy the film rights to my story. I'd have the starring role of course. No one wears a fedora as well as me. Except Indiana Jones on a good day.'

Despite Arbuthnot and Theiler being guilty, the absence of extradition treaties meant they could not be prosecuted in the countries where their offences had been perpetrated. But at least the pillaged antiquities were repatriated. In place of a jail term the court of public opinion was brutal, bestowing on both men reputational life sentences as grave-robbing pariahs.

After Manon reported back to say the case was now closed, Cordelia popped into Rex's office to say, 'To date we've had a 100% success rate, but we couldn't have done this one without you babe.'

Rex was pleased. 'We're Charlie's Angels with better footwear. Will you ensure all your future missions need my mental agility to stymie the villains please. I'm keen on my new position as *éminence grise* of logical thinking.'

'On it. We should have new cards printed – Shoe Moguls With a Sideline in Justice.'

'We have quite distinctive names so we'll need pseudonyms. I know, let's call ourselves after cakes. I'll be Monty Blanc. L.O.D. will be Charlotte Russe.'

'How do you do, I'm Victoria Sponge,' Cordelia said, shaking Rex's hand. 'Except that sounds a bit suspish cos only square pants Bob in that cartoon is called Sponge so instead I shall be Victoria S'Ponge, pronounced essponge, to sound French.'

When they told Elodie their undercover names she giggled and invited them to Gâteau Bateau the following Saturday. 'I have a plan.'

'Welcome to *La Salle de Déguisement*,' Elodie said as she pushed open the door to a dressing room lined by shelves displaying a selection of wigs and spectacles.

'Manon has advice for us on disguises. She said we should have an unremarkable appearance on our missions to make it difficult for anyone to identify us in a picture. Invisibility is the aim, so inconspicuous black or grey clothing. No colour.'

Cordelia and Rex glanced at each other's eye-catching outfits. He was in a plum and pink windowpane check suit, with a cornflower-blue shirt and lilac-spotted tie. Cordelia was poured into a figure-hugging crimson sequinned full-length gown slashed to the thigh because it was one of her Screen Goddess Veneration days and she was channelling Jayne Russell in the opening sequence of *Gentleman Prefer Blondes*.

'No colour? Not even turquoise?' she wailed, gazing at the row of dark suits hanging on a rack in the corner. Colour was fundamental and she had a rare condition called tetrachromacy caused by an extra receptor in her retinas that permitted her to see millions of shades other people did not register.

'And discreet footwear, Oxfords ideally, which means no cowbike boots for me,' Elodie continued.

Manon had also described best practice for hush-hush activity. No perfume, neutral makeup and nail polish, and contact lenses to switch eye colour. Alter normal posture and avoid dramatic facial expressions or gesticulations. Change the habitual manner of walking by bandaging the knees or inserting a small stone in the shoe to cause a limp. Always pay cash rather than use a bank card and never take a receipt. Create a paper trail for an alternative persona, including library card, art gallery or gym membership, and carry them in a wallet. Use Nike only when necessary and with false licence plates.

'She also advised us to tell as few lies as possible so we don't forget the story we invented, and to keep our first name because we will always respond to it, whereas we might forget we are Victoria, Monty, and Charlotte and that would raise suspicions if we did not answer.'

Cordelia, attempting to squeeze a short straight auburn wig onto

Rex's head said, 'It will be a novelty to disappear temporarily into Planet Beige but only if I can revert to my multi-colourism.'

'Richard of York Gave Battle in Vain,' Rex replied. Elodie looked confused so he clarified, 'It's a mnemonic we learn as children to remember the colours of the rainbow.'

'I'm rubbish at memorising numbers so the digits of my phone almost correspond to letters of the alphabet for Phwoordelia.' Cordelia said that word every time she saw her reflection, partly because she was the bearer of the most stunning face, but mostly because it made her laugh and felt good in her mouth.

'In that case if we get burner phones mine will be LeChampagne. How about you *ma colombe?*'

'I've never had a problem with numbers but if you two have aides-memoires then I'll have one too. I'm going for Pythagoras.'

Chapter Five

Cordelia stuck a hand out of the dressing room window in her platform boot house to test the temperature. *Good, I won't need a coat.* It was Sunday morning and she was preparing to depart for her regular visit to Celestine for a few hours gossiping and reading the newspapers. It was their special activity and without it the week felt incomplete.

'Come on Waggy darling,' she said, picking up Blanche's lead as the dog ran excitedly in circles.

Her phone buzzed. It was a text from Elodie. *Don't forget the watering.*

Ta for the reminder. On my way, she replied.

She gazed in the mirror to apply her lipstick, agreeing that she really suited that shade, then left home and popped into The Weasel garden. Tucked away in a secluded area was a hothouse for warm weather orchids, built as a tribute to her parents. In addition to Spotted Cat of the Mountain, Ruffled Dancing Lady, and other vibrantly coloured plants, Orchidelirium was a laboratory to test if chacruhana, a native of the Peruvian rainforest, would grow in the UK. Elodie had been introduced to the hallucinogenic properties of chacruhana during a visit to the Amazon and had brought a stash of seeds and leaves back to London. 'Forest dwellers expand their minds by chewing them, then they have amazing powers, such as being able to translate birdsong,' she explained.

'I want to be able to do that and I'm ready for a bit of mind expansion,' Cordelia replied expectantly.

Elodie had shared a handful of leaves to wash down with Bonheur. It took a few minutes for the effects to commence and with a whoosh they felt they were inside a child's kaleidoscope, surrounded by multicoloured lights forming symmetrical shapes, alternately strobing and shimmering. Then they were hurtling along a mirrored tunnel, tumbling at top speed under an intense G-force before a colossal jolt and sonic boom shattered a solid wall in their minds. Everything was silent as both tried to ascertain whether they were still tripping. Later, it was apparent that chacruhana had reset their consciousness, rewired their brains, and enhanced their capacity to see, hear, smell, touch, and taste. Even more astonishingly, it had given them the ability to communicate telepathically if they were together. Nothing in their lives so far had come close and they wondered if having super-senses might make them eligible to star in a superhero franchise.

'I think we've experienced neuroplasticity. It's a scientific fact that the brain can change in response to life experiences, but I've never heard of the senses being altered so dramatically,' Elodie had said in amazement. 'To maintain the changes I advise regular microdoses. We'll need a reliable supply so let's germinate the seeds and try to grow chacruhana in London.'

'Brilliant scheme doctor. How big were the bushes you saw?'

'A low height and quite compact.'

'That's handy. Did you notice if they have flowers?'

'Yes, exquisite blooms, a bit similar to passionflower.'

'Such beauties. They'll need pollinating. Vulpy's bees might be interested. If the pollen's hallucy they'll have the biggest buzz of their lives, and the honey will be trippy too.'

'There you are my precious jewel.' Celestine kissed Cordelia and stroked Blanche's ears. 'Ooh, what's that?'

'A Stardust Firebird direct from Orchidelirium. Happy birthday for tomorrow.' She handed Celestine a plant with intensely orange flowers confidently standing to attention.

'Glorious, thank you. It shall sit on the table in my bedroom so I see it each time I awaken.'

Cordelia inhaled the scent of coffee as she went into the kitchen and waited for Celestine to say the same phrase she used every Sunday, 'Well will you look at that! A plate of pastries.' Cordelia always replied, 'What pastries?' then ip dip sky blued them and pondered, 'Which delicious confection should I have? That one? Oh go on then, force me.'

Celestine placed a cafetière on the table. 'Pass your cup darling.'

'Sugar and caffeine, exactly what we need to work on those.' Cordelia gestured towards the pile of newspapers then picked up a chouquette and took a bite. 'How were your hols?'

Celestine had returned from a few days in Jerez with Amadeo and Perry, two handsome young men who acted as walkers and escorted her to parties and cultural events.

'A delight. We visited the School of Equestrian Art where Amadeo's sister is one of the instructors. And of course, we drank lots of sherry.' She tore off a piece of pain au chocolat. 'Any gossip since I've been away?' Celestine had a studio at House of Tanner and liked to keep up to date.

'Agnieska is preggles. Our first office baby. Says she'll be back after maternity leave so everyone is relieved. We can't do without her. I hope she brings it to work. Other people have their dogs so why not an infant?'

'And what of King Precious Jewel?'

'He had a date last night. A rare occasion.'

'No one is worthy of our dear boy.'

Rex had once tried a dating app and his disgusted comment on the users' scruffy appearances and dull profiles made Cordelia smile.

'Why waste effort on a boring minger who cares nothing of how they present themselves when I'd rather be with my dazzling sisters?'

'He was on Jermyn Street and saw a well-dressed man on the other side. Both clocked the other and nodded in approval. Then he was browsing books in Hatchard's and bumped into the same fella. His name is Benedict Sterling and, can you believe it, he's a top tailor and owns a firm on Savile Row.'

'How ideal. They will have endless conversations about plackets and notch lapels and spend the evening discussing cloth.'

'Or spend all evening admiring their outfits in front of a mirror. Oh hang on, that would be me.'

Cordelia turned to a tabloid headline, "Bush Trim Refusal Sparks Death Threats". Five inside pages were devoted to a feud between neighbours in Biggleswade and a man named Derek Cropper who refused to prune his leylandii hedge, despite it blocking the pavement and forcing people to walk on the road. He threatened to kill anyone who complained, claiming that as an Englishman his home was his castle and horticultural rights were enshrined in what he referred to as 'Magners Carter'. An accompanying photograph portrayed a group of residents holding a copy of Magna Carta and wearing distinct, he's talking rubbish, facial expressions.

She showed it to Celestine. 'Good job there aren't any hedges in this mews otherwise your new neighbours would insist on cultivating the biggest. Talking of which, are they any more forthcoming?'

'No, the snooty so-and-sos, they barely speak. She's running to be a councillor representing one of those fringe parties in the elections. Her platform is "people who hold my opinions are cancelled" even though they're not because she's often spouting them on local radio.'

'What of him?'

Celestine grimaced, 'Still a merchant banker but the way he acts it's spelled with a w.'

Cordelia felt sorrowful that the house which had formerly belonged to her parents was now the property of such a horrible couple. The Tanners had bought it as a fixer-upper wreck, prior to Primrose Hill's transformation into a gentrified urban village. Their close friend Celestine, who lived next door, had managed the refurbishment and, because the Tanners were botanists and had only modest resources, she'd created an imaginative interior using reclaim from builders' skips. Minimalism was the word – polished floorboards, walls painted yellow for happiness, and colourful flower murals. Neither Cordelia nor Rex had memories of living there, although the décor must have made an impact because Rex had embraced the pared-down aesthetic, whereas Cordelia had gone maximalist with her rebellious, more-is-more attitude.

'You should invite Elodie for a visit and ask her to knock on their door by mistake. She'd chat and be lovely and as no one can resist her they'd become your besties and stop blocking your electric car with their humongous Chelsea tractor.'

'How is my *bijou précieux*? Is she in London?'

'No, at her place near Reims. Someone is writing a book on Bonheur and the house belonged to Apolline, the woman who founded the biz, so Elodie's showing them round.'

Cordelia stood up to clear the table. 'I'll make some fresh coffee then have a wander.' On each visit she cherished a few minutes walking through the house in which she and Rex had lived until they'd left for university. It was not grand, Celestine had been a freelancer and only worked when a film was in production, but it was cosy. Following their commercial success the precious jewels had proposed they buy their guardian a bigger house. She'd graciously declined, saying how content she was in Primrose Hill with its butcher, baker, and 'There used to be a candlestick maker but it's now a retailer of designer baby clothes.'

Surprised to see it, Cordelia picked up a framed sketch she'd done of the futurist Fiat Tagliero petrol station in Asmara and recalled the modernist architecture tour of Eritrea's capital Celestine had taken her and Rex on.

'Cel, where did you find this piccie I did in Asmara?' she shouted.

'I was sorting out some things on the top shelf in your wardrobe. Even as a fifteen-year-old you were adept at drawing.'

Cordelia snapped a photo and sent it to Rex. *Remember this?* Normally, he replied swiftly to texts but not this time. *He's distracted by other things, the minx.*

She went back to the kitchen and slid onto a chair. 'That last pain aux raisins is staring at you begging to be eaten.'

'Then I must oblige.' Celestine picked it up. 'Plenty of mentions of your furtive art collective this week. This is the fourth paper I've seen it in. Whoever they are, they've really pulled the wool. It's complete nonsense. What do you reckon?'

Cordelia giggled. 'Spot on as usual. Most abstract art is a bit rubbish really isn't it. They've been clever in hyping to the max though, and Art Is Life and Life Is Art has blanketed all its outlets.'

Left To Their Own Devices had a formidable ally in Sandrine Rivera and to characterise her endorsement as fervent was an understatement. Fulsome, lavish, and effusive barely described it. Her media organisation reported on the mysterious art sensation and anointed the collective as the brand du jour. Large crowds clamoured to visit Worship, eager to see what the fuss was about. The phone constantly rang with celebrities' personal assistants calling to request private views, their voices adopting a hysterical tone when informed it was not possible due to the gallery being an institution where all visitors had equal access. Concierges of luxury hotels, normally able to wangle favours in exchange for sending high-worth individuals to attractions were peeved to learn there was no preferential treatment. Chauffeur-driven cars blocked the narrow side street and the passengers had the unfamiliar experience of needing to queue. People were offered money to give up their place but not one accepted the bribe.

'Elodie is excited because the focus on Worship means the artists in her collection are finally being lauded.'

'What an advantageous side effect. Now the daubs are all the rage, won't the market be inundated with forgeries? Anyone could do them, eyes closed.' Celestine was not a fan.

Cordelia paused. She needed to word her answer carefully so as not to make it apparent she was part of the collective.

'Worship's website lists the people who have borrowing rights, so there's no point in anyone else claiming one unless their name is there. Each canvas has a concealed tracking device so its whereabouts can be checked. It also emphasises that Worship is the only authorised dealer and that the art is never traded on the open market, so works sold via other sources must be bogus.'

Rex's acumen at computer coding and hacking, combined with Cordelia's ingenuity at marketing, had created a frenzy. Soon after the Left To Their Own Devices launch, Rex started trending #Wherehaveyoubeen on social media in reply to posts from people who admitted to never having heard of it. The thread contained comments such as: 'I've been waiting for Godot'; 'I've been up all night to get lucky'; and Cordelia's favourite, 'I've been to Paradise but I've never been to me', which was prominent in the pantheon of cheesy song lyrics.

Elodie had the notion of hiring operators to fly drones over packed beaches on a sunny bank holiday Monday to release tiny artworks of trees – linden, teak, tamarind, oak, and dogwood (the initials of the collective) – printed on rice paper, to flutter down like confetti on the throng. Videos showed day trippers pouncing, gulls brawling as they swooped to peck at them, and in Clacton-on-Sea some day-trippers doing the brawling.

Philatelists kept their eyes peeled for the postage stamp commemorative issue everyone was talking about which, disappointingly for them, was a rumour started by Rex. Children avidly collected Left To Their Own Devices stickers and swapped them at school. Even the best-selling populist tabloid newspaper joined in the excitement by printing a unique issue emblazoned with a wrap-around cover of the work, *Old MacDonald Used To Have A Farm*, featuring white rhinos, blue whales, and red pandas, a commentary on the extinction of species. It was the best-selling edition in the publication's 180-year history.

One of the most helpful consequences of the hype was when Pauline Westwich, the prejudiced founder of Moral Universe, a movement that disapproved of everything that did not fit the members' narrow-minded view of the world, was solicited for her opinion and said, 'These so-called artists must be communists. Real art is that lovely painting of the couple dancing on the beach where the butler holds an umbrella to shelter them.' Provoking the ire of Moral Universe was a sport the open-minded avidly supported and Left To Their Own Devices shot to the top of the league of brands to revere.

'Aren't you dying to tell me who's behind it?' Celestine asked teasingly. 'No, don't worry, you've probably promised to say nothing, so I won't pry.'

Cordelia was tempted to reveal all. *I don't like keeping this from her. She'd think it was a hoot and be well impressed at how we've managed to blockbusterise it.*

Celestine gathered the scattered newspapers and shuffled them together. 'Which one did you wish you had not wasted time reading?'

'Sunday In A Life, featuring that actor Philip Cromerty, no doubt made up by his publicity agent.' Cordelia riffled the pile for the colour supplement and recited samples of the column. 'Up at dawn for a cold-water swim, fresh fruit for breakfast, a couple of hours responding to fans' social media messages, go to church, take mum for lunch, then to an exhibition at the National Gallery, in late afternoon play five-a-side football with school mates, grilled fish and steamed vegetables for supper, read some Alfred Tennyson poetry, then early to bed.'

Celestine snorted. 'Definitely a work of fiction. I did the sets for a film he starred in. He'll have spent all day in bed watching porn and having takeaway delivered.' She changed the subject. 'What are you doing later?'

'Meeting Vulpy for a Sunday roast, then off to the flicks at that new cinema in Clerkenwell. They have a dogs and owners' screening. That reminds me, I must text and ask him to bring Waggy's Scooby snacks.'

Blanche, who was snoozing on the rug, raised her head, grinned, and made a hurrah-like noise. Cordelia laughed and kneeled to kiss her pet. 'A happy dog, that's my mission.'

Chapter Six

'*Che meraviglia*', Valentina said admiringly of the luxurious room lined with midnight-blue velvet, bearing images of purple Belladonna flowers. She was perched on a curule seat, its curved u-shaped legs painted in old gold, in the middle of an archway of fresh flowers. This was the Boudoir of Pulchritude, a salon at House of Tanner, where clients came to be measured for bespoke shoes. Every contour and idiosyncrasy were recorded so the shoes fitted them alone.

Valentina was in London to visit Worship and doubled up with a fitting for her first pair of House of Tanners. She had chosen the Long-Tailed Widowbird model which, as she always wore black, was apposite. Cordelia waived the standard background check on a potential client because she wanted an excuse to psychometrise her, hoping that even the quickest hands-on would reveal something of interest. However, the plot was frustrated by Valentina being a clean freak who did not shake hands, nor permit anyone to touch her feet unless they were wearing disposable gloves. The latex barrier foiled Cordelia, so the woman in front of her remained a mystery. *How annoying*, she thought, noting the measurements, then said, 'After this we'll go to The Weasel for an aperitivo, then dinner in the Pleasure Gardens. Our host is Oscar Rivington, my ex-husband. Don't worry, we are close friends so your guards will not need to pull us apart!'

As Valentina gathered herself, Cordelia sent a text to Oscar, *Be there in three. You won't be able to miss us. Our guest is reminiscent of a black leather ball in the middle of a rugby scrum of beef mountains.*

Oscar was standing beside Blanche outside the pub waiting to greet them and wearing a big smile of welcome. Ordinarily Blanche would have bounded up to Cordelia with customary enthusiasm but this time she stood still, her tail motionless, and a frown on her habitually grinning face. One of Valentina's bodyguards screamed, *'Via il cane da qua dentro,'* which echoed down Plumage Place.

'Signora Tanner, I am allergic to dogs,' Valentina explained.

'Don't worry, we will be in the garden and Blanche can stay in the pub,' Cordelia assured her. 'Now, may I introduce Oscar Rivington.'

She had warned him that Valentina did not shake hands, so he raised his as though taking an oath and said, *'Benvenuta alla Weasel. La prego di seguirmi per un aperitivo davvero speciale,'* asking her to follow him for a special aperitif made of his new line of bitters sourced from London-grown botanicals.

'Your Italian is excellent Signor Rivington,' Valentina commented.

'Thank you. I learnt a couple of phrases and practised for ages. They felt so good to say. What a musical language. Should I ban English in the pub and we'll use *la bella lingua* instead?'

Drinks were served by the statue of Volupta, the Roman goddess of sensual pleasures, and Oscar gave Valentina his full attention as she spoke at length of her importance in the art sector. Then he took her on a tour of the gardens, which were on a scale that few privately owned properties in central London could boast. Bees foraged for pollen on the wildflowers he had planted specifically, and their honey was used to brew mead in the pub's microbrewery.

Oscar had created a modern-day pleasure garden in homage to its eighteenth-century counterparts, *the* fashionable leisure destinations of the era offering activities including hot air balloon rides, recitals by leading composers, opera, fireworks, gambling, and shenanigans in the bushes which contributed to their louche reputation.

Oscar, a born showman who believed the world needed more jollity, was a purveyor of unforgettable occasions. His gardens included water features (such as a fountain capable of being repurposed to dispense wine), grottoes, tree-lined walkways lit by flaming torches, and hidden glades for playing hide and seek or romancing in (where the air was perfumed by honeysuckle and jasmine).

A Moorish and Indo-Gothic style rotunda, ornamented by an onion dome, minarets, and horseshoe arches, was the primary interior space for mingling. It contained rooms dedicated to dancing, dining, gambling, and a Hall of Mirrors for promenading. For those who wanted to lose themselves temporarily, there was a chamber where computer-generated kaleidoscopic images and a laser light show altered their perceptions without the need for drugs. In a games room the most popular activities were the adult versions of childhood party amusements and the favourite was Pass the Parcel. Each time the music stopped and a layer of wrapping was removed, a truth or dare card dropped out, but at The Weasel the options were all dare and no truth.

Dinner was a cramped affair, due to Valentina insisting the guards accompany her and they were so bulky they used more space than anyone else at the table. They also ate twice as much as anyone else, although it was more like ten times than Valentina, who just picked at her food. Worst of all, their plentiful testosterone smelled unpleasant.

'What a relief they've gone. Such hard work,' Cordelia said to Oscar afterwards. 'She's icy but I noticed how she melted with you. As usual you were a total delight.'

'She was doing the "li'l lady" thing that manipulative women often employ to send a signal to men so it arouses their inner caveman. Not me! I can tell she's a tough 'un. And she has no sense of humour.' To Oscar that was unpardonable.

Next day, Cordelia video called Elodie, who was in Mozambique for Rebâtir. 'You should have seen Blanche's body language as Valkyrie scowled at her. I don't reckon it's an allergy to dogs, she just dislikes them. Being such a cold person she is unable to understand their unconditional love.'

'Oh, beloved Blanche. Did she cheer up?'

'Yes, when me and Vulpy were alone she took turns on our lap for ear fondles. And guess what, Valkyrie was trying it on and playing the "protect me please you big manly man" game. Oscar's the least likely person in the world to fall for that.'

'What was her opinion of Worship?'

'Very complimentary regarding your collection and maybe a bit envious of LefDev. She said, rather witheringly, "What a coup for an unknown gallery to represent a headline art brand".'

'If, as she claims, her clients are in the top wealth bracket then she might want to impress them with a personal introduction.'

'Bet she'd try, and ask for a discount then charge the client full price. It'd be uncomfortable to refuse so we'd need Rexicles to do the deal. He's a demon at negotiating and they have never met, he only saw her at a distance in the Berlin Art Mart.'

'And if she pretends to be a helpless woman trying to appeal to his manliness then he'll snigger.'

'She wouldn't appreciate that. Takes herself far too seriously. Oh, and another thing, she calls me Signora Tanner despite me asking her twice to use my first name, which is odd seeing as she's mononymous. Also, no shaking hands, and I had to wear gloves for the shoe fitting. I couldn't get a single result when I psy-commed her. Must be the latex. She's a sphinx. I don't want to be pals but I am quite intrigued.'

'Then we should accept her invitation to visit the art school for a chance to learn more.'

'Valentina will see you now. This way.' The butler led Cordelia and Elodie along a five-arch loggia that connected two wings of one of Rome's largest private houses, the sixteenth-century Villa Veritas, which served as the hub of Valentina's empire. They entered an opulent room that made Cordelia's eyes happy – patterned marble floor for miles, columns, gold-painted textured plaster, garlands, lion masks, amorini, cornucopia, and arabesques decorated every surface. Her jaw dropped to see frescos representing *The Creation of Heaven and Earth*. She nudged Elodie and whispered, 'I've heard of this place. It was owned by someone who knew Michelangelo and they let him practice on the ceiling prior to working on the real thing in the Sistine chapel.'

Valentina waved from where she stood by a grand fireplace, speaking into her phone. She kept them waiting for five minutes as she finished her fictitious call and then received her guests. 'Welcome. Permit me to show you my business.'

Cordelia and Elodie were genuinely impressed – it was impossible not to be. In one wing the art school operated. It specialised in painting and drawing and enrolled only ten students at a time to study landscape, still-life, portraiture, and more, covering such major movements as Renaissance, Impressionism, and Pop Art.

'Let us listen in to the morning seminar,' said Valentina, leading the way to an understated wood-panelled chamber. A beam of sunlight shone through a window framed by peacock-blue brocade curtains, illuminating the lecturer who was showing slides of works by Delacroix, Goya, and others to illustrate how Romanticism emphasised freedom of form, expressiveness, and the natural world.

The other wing contained Valentina's apartment and gallery, where she bought and sold art for high-net-worth individuals. 'That will be shipped to Doha tomorrow,' she said, pointing to a work by Cézanne and exuding more than a hint of self-satisfaction. 'And the Klimt has been purchased by a Chinese entrepreneur in Shanghai.'

Wants us to be in no doubt of her exalted position in the art world, Cordelia said to herself. At that moment her stomach growled to signal lunchtime. *She barely eats so grub won't be a priority, unlike for us. I'm ravenous,* Cordelia messaged telepathically to Elodie, just as Valentina said, 'May I offer you coffee?'

They went out to the terraced garden and sat at a table under an orange tree, on which the butler had placed cups of single espresso. Cordelia was in the first stages of caffeine withdrawal and, thanks to her chacruhana enabled supertaster status, knew it was decaffeinated. *No biscotti either. Hope she gets pleasure from art cos she certainly doesn't from food and drink.*

As they sipped the coffee Valentina told them about Rightful Owner, a service she provided for locating stolen art. 'It is difficult to sell a well-known work for what it is worth. On the black market it typically fetches 10% of its value. I am well-connected and renowned for reuniting missing works of art with their owner because I persuade the thief to claim the insurance reward instead. Yes, the criminal *is* compensated for their illegal actions, but at least the art does not disappear into a private collection never to be seen again.'

Good job she's not aware we too are in the returning biz with Globo Pol, otherwise she'll assume we're encroaching on her territory and send the guards to warn us off, Cordelia telepathed. *We need to keep Blanche close then they will not come anywhere near us.*

'Doctor l'Archambeau, when I visited Worship I noticed your miniature by Glenora Richards. I know where there is a companion piece if you are interested?' their host proposed.

Elodie was interested indeed, and Valentina promised to be in touch.

'I can't get any impression of who she is under her chilly carapace. What if I'm losing my skill? And did you think she was rather brisk?'

Cordelia said as they strolled down the street looking for a place to eat lunch. She was frustrated by the failure of her innate ability to judge a person's character, which meant she was unaware of Valentina being from a family enriched by various unscrupulous schemes. It was safe to say no income tax had ever been paid, and even safer to say the money had endured a vigorous wash. With rivals a constant threat, Valentina had learnt to be inscrutable and never let anyone become close to her.

'Let's have a gander at her website.' Cordelia scrolled her phone and they giggled at the gushing testimonials and photos of Valentina alongside the grateful-looking rightful owners of art she had returned. One video, blaring Verdi's *Triumphal March* as the soundtrack, showed her on the back of a flatbed truck slowly being driven around a small Tyrolean town. A brass band led the way along roads packed by cheering locals welcoming home their museum's burgled artwork.

'Hugely self-aggrandising isn't it. She's the type to stipulate in her rider that she is to be glorified by the townsfolk. You can tell she rejoices in it.'

'At least they won't have to kiss her feet in homage, considering she is not one to be touched. Oh look, there's the place I mentioned.' Elodie pointed to a restaurant that claimed to stock the world's best vintages. It was called Falernian, in honour of the legendary wine of the Roman empire.

'If only we could psy-comm museum artefacts from that era we'd have a little visit back in time to taste Falernian.' Cordelia paused. 'Need to give this more deliberation cos if we woman-handle the exhibits, security will woman-handle us.' Cordelia was referring to one more astonishing aspect of pyschomatricks, where, thanks to the assistance of chacruhana, they could enter scenarios, interact with others, and participate in whatever activity was taking place. That meant they had a chance of sampling Falernian, albeit in their imagination.

'Lorenzo Borosini is the director of *Museo di Storia Romana*. We had a brief love affair. I'll call him, he might say yes to us examining some artefacts,' Elodie replied as they entered the restaurant. She rarely discussed her personal life, but it was one of grand romance and generosity of spirit. Settling down held no appeal and lovestruck men were wandering the earth, pining to see her again. Elodie, being so considerate and mindful of their hearts, always let them go gently, leaving them with cherished memories.

'Ooh, will you ask him? And if he has any unsolved mysteries connected to the collection we'll be able to help.'

They greeted the maître d' and requested a table. When they were seated Elodie scanned the wine list. 'Château Latour, Château Lafite Rothschild, Château Cheval Blanc. Rare French vintages. *Oh là là* – Bonheur Brut Rosé Millesime 1945. I'm excited. So few bottles still exist, and I've never tasted it. Today is the day!'

The waiter presented the bottle and Elodie asked to open it. She expertly removed the muselet and cork, then poured the wine. She frowned as she moved the glass towards her nose and said quietly, 'This is not Bonheur.'

'Noooo, gutted! How do you know?'

'I've been drinking Bonheur since childhood and never mistake it. Our yeast bestows a distinctive fermentation profile that I can recognise anywhere. And this wine has too much dosage. It should be ultra dry, that's our house style. If you imagine champagne being a musical composition, then a young wine is vivace and mezzo forte, whereas an aged wine is pianissimo and legato. If this was an authentic vintage it would be the ultimate harmony, the drink equivalent of a heaven chord.'

'The label looks old, but we can psy-comm it.'

They held the bottle with their left hand, joined right little fingers, and it took no effort to confirm it was a two-year-old wine by an average producer in Epernay.

'I'll order an alternate vintage in case this was mysteriously mislabelled. They have one from the year of our birth and we know how that will taste.'

The waiter brought the second bottle. However, just like the first it was not what the menu stated.

'I'm so disappointed.' Elodie was downcast.

Cordelia squeezed her arm in empathy. 'Oh honey, we need to work out what's going on. What if we tell the manager you're Bonheurian and impressed with the wine list then ask if we can look in the cellar. I'll psy-comm while you keep her talking.'

As Cordelia predicted, Francesca the manager was pleased to meet Elodie and to show off the unique collection. 'We are so proud of our limited availability Maison Bonheur wines,' she said, showing them the shelves upon which bottles bearing the familiar cream and burgundy branding stood proud.

'May I look more closely?' Elodie asked, then said to Cordelia, handing her a bottle of Bonheur 1970, '*Chérie*, have you seen this?'

Cordelia quickly psychometrised the label as Elodie passed her a 1959 vintage. *Both fakes*, Cordelia telepathed. *I can see a man with a hairy upper lip speaking French on his phone. If you ask Francesca who supplied it, we can visit him and discover if he's the swindler.*

They concealed the truth of the bogus Bonheur and left with contact details for the Luxembourg-based wholesaler Louis Duvel.

'I'm going to call him and say we're collectors then suggest we meet,' Cordelia said.

Unusually, the plan did not excite Elodie. 'I'm upset. If he is selling imitation Bonheur then he's stealing the future from some of the world's poorest people.'

She was alluding to the Bonheur Trust. Apolline Bonheur had bequeathed the business through the female line and stipulated that the beneficiaries must have a career that was valuable to society. As the only girl child born into the family for generations, Elodie's profession as a surgeon meant she was eligible to receive the corporation's significant profits. Conscious that her vast wealth had not been earned, she used it to great effect for her charitable foundation, which funded Rebâtir and other humanitarian projects, including paying for the education of hundreds of medical students in developing countries. Counterfeit Bonheur meant less money for the foundation.

'I totally empathise with not wanting to meet him. If it was me, I'd tug his stupid 'tache and say, "you're a thieving piece of filth", then grab a cut-throat razor and shave it off. But if we go together and find out if he's up to no good then his scam can be smote. Smote, now there's a word I don't use enough.'

'What does it mean?' Elodie was fluent in English and having had a British nanny from birth to her early teenage years, spoke it with only a hint of a French accent but she always checked archaic words.

'It's the past tense of smite and refers to striking someone or something, typically using a sword or rod. Quite a lot of smiting goes on in the King James' Bible.'

'Well in that case Monsieur Duvel will be in line for some divine retribution so you and I need to visit *La Salle de Déguisement* to prepare for a trip to Luxembourg City.' Elodie cheered up at the thought.

'*Bonjour, Hôtel Sigefroid s'il vous plait,*' Elodie said to the taxi driver at Luxembourg airport. She was with Cordelia, heading to meet Louis Duvel. He had chosen the venue to present its exemplary drinks list, most of which he supplied. Both women had altered their appearance. Elodie, hair in a chignon and wearing spectacles, was dressed in a discreet dark suit and black brogues, but was as dashing as ever and, despite trying, it was impossible to hide how beautiful Cordelia was. She wore an inconspicuous black suit, black loafers, hazel lenses to change the shade of her violet-coloured eyes, and her mahogany shoulder-length locks were covered by a short light-brown hairpiece. Her habit of dressing up as Hollywood's Golden Age film stars meant she excelled at disguising herself. Whether it was Lana Turner, Ava Gardner, or Paulette Goddard, she had the wardrobe and the wigs.

'As he's a native French speaker will you do the talking. I'll try and get the measure of him, then psy-comm any bottles he shows us,' Cordelia said.

'If he says anything relevant I'll telepath,' Elodie replied as they walked into the hotel lobby. When they spotted Duvel, Cordelia exclaimed, 'Blooming heck, he could hide his lunch in it! If that can't be seen from space then the astronauts are looking in the wrong direction.'

With his walrus moustache, well-fed jowls, and receding hairline, Duvel resembled the nineteenth-century Grand Duke of a central European principality. He stood up, welcomed them to Luxembourg and shook hands. Cordelia held on longer than was customary in Europe so she could psychometrise him while enthusiastically pumping his arm, the way she had seen Zambians do. It gave her a great deal of useful information. Elodie, who was concerned about meeting him, telepathed, *Will he guess we're lying?*

He doesn't know us and we haven't claimed to be what we're not. We said we are collectors and that's not a fib. We collect shoes, Cordelia replied.

They sat in the bar, all heavy wood and leather furniture, lit by weighty multi-tiered chandeliers. Duvel was polite, attentive, and offered them a drink, recommending the Glen Balangie, a rare single malt he supplied to the hotel. Elodie preferred hers neat, no ice, and Cordelia added a drop of water to open up the flavours. Duvel handed them both a brochure showcasing the wine, champagne, and whisky he distributed and proudly emphasized the world-famous restaurants, hotels, and members' clubs that formed part of his clientele. He also boasted of the investment potential and how, during stock market fluctuations, his collectibles often outperformed traditional financial assets, even gold.

Cordelia asked to see one of the bottles of Bonheur Blanc de Noir 1962 listed on the menu and, while Elodie conversed with Duvel, she psychometrised it. With the aid of her chacruhana enhanced vision she noticed the label, made to look old, had been produced by laser printer, a non-existent technology at the time the wine was supposedly bottled. She requested a 1959 Chateau d'Yquem Y, the first vintage, and sensed it was younger. Not only that, but Duvel had inadvertently used the redesigned bottle label from 2011.

Yes, he's a crook, Cordelia telepathed to Elodie who, as a poker player, was able to keep her face from revealing her disdain.

Can you distract him so I can test the whisky, she replied, sipping it and concentrating. The chacruhana microdose taken that morning in London had honed her hearing and she was listening for an almost imperceptible musical note that signalled the liquid's age, high for youth and low for maturity. If the Glen Balangie really had been aged in a sherry cask for 64 years, as Duvel asserted, then it would register the low A0 note on a piano scale. This one was C8, the highest and so the whisky was probably little more than three years old, the minimum amount of barrel ageing required for it legally to be called Scotch.

Yes, definitely a crook. Je le déteste. I'm going to ask him where he sources the Bonheur, Elodie telepathed.

Duvel described how his grandfather started the family wine business and hundreds of valuable vintages had been acquired over the years. He told them he was also descended from a man named Henri Auclair, which made Elodie feel nauseous. Auclair was the person to whom Apolline Bonheur had been unhappily married. Their union produced one daughter, but no one knew how many children were sired from his numerous extra-marital dalliances. He'd gambled away the fortune Apolline had brought into the marriage, but fortunately died before her wealth was exhausted, so she'd used the remainder to establish the eponymous champagne house.

What a horrible shock. We have a tenuous link. More than two centuries have passed and the Bonheur name is still being exploited by an Auclair, Elodie telepathed. *I'm going to tell him who I am.*

Is that wise? We have enough proof of his skullduggery for Manon to take action. We could exit now, knowing that Globo Pol will come knocking.

Yes, it's probably unwise but I'm going to do it. I want him to understand the human cost of defrauding my charity. Would you mind leaving the two of us alone for a few minutes?

Cordelia stood up and said, 'Excuse me,' then went to other side of the room. Her chacruhana boosted brain enabled her to hear Elodie calmly and firmly speaking to Duvel. *I'd be unable to keep my composure and stop myself calling him a pillock.*

Unsurprisingly, he denied the allegation and became defensive. 'What are a few bottles to such a major establishment?' But after Elodie told him how the profits funded her charities and that she worked every few months for Rebâtir, he squirmed and lost his braggadocio. He did not apologise, but he did agree to her conditions for not pressing charges. He was to recall all the so-called Bonheur from his myriad clients and donate to the Bonheur Trust the value of the champagne he had sold over the years.

'As for the other brands and collectors you have deceived, I'll leave that to your conscience,' she said.

Elodie stood up to go, heart racing. Outside the hotel she held her forehead in both hands and said to Cordelia, 'That was awful, and he demonstrated no remorse. Thanks for helping to foil him. Now he is well and truly smote.'

'I couldn't have remained so serene. I'd want to parade him naked in front of the global media wearing a dunce's cap printed with "Greed" in large letters and disclose how his dishonesty had an injurious effect on the work of a medical charity.'

Days later, Elodie told Cordelia that she had briefed the Bonheur CEO on the Duvel conversation, and they had released a statement to warn of fakes on the market and to reiterate that the only way of guaranteeing authenticity was to purchase directly from La Maison.

'I want to trust Duvel to do what he promised, but if he doesn't then Globo Pol will be informed of his activities so they can close him down. You and I will need to travel the world pre-emptively testing Bonheur, and listening for the heaven chord. If we come across the devil's interval instead then we'll ask La Maison to intervene. Of course, wherever we go we'll visit all the dance halls and karaoke lounges. Do I hear a Botticelli?'

Chapter Seven

'There appears to be a pattern but we have no suspects and no evidence to link the crimes, so we are baffled. That's why we need your superpowers. Are you available for some investigation near Strasbourg?' Manon was speaking to Cordelia and Elodie on a video conference call and describing a spate of robberies at regional art museums in mainland Europe.

A batch of cold case files sent to Globo Pol's clandestine new department Project 273 – the number represented absolute zero on the Kelvin temperature scale, in other words, cold indeed – had been examined and similarities had been uncovered, namely, the brazen attitude of the burglars. Small town museums with lax protection and no cameras were targeted and some, routinely staffed by volunteers, were so higgledy-piggledy it was weeks until they realised anything was missing. There were no clues and no fingerprints, as if a phantom had pilfered the goods. At each site the burglars used one of a number of crafty methods to steal easy-to-handle pieces, for instance, claiming to be:

- sent by the trustees to role play a heist and check for gaps in security
- taking the work away to be restored by showing a bogus letter of authorisation from trustees
- transferring the artwork for loan to another gallery.

'In each case the thieves were so convincing in their motive for removing the work that staff members accepted it without question,' Manon continued. 'These people are professionals in a lucrative criminal niche. Art and antiquities theft ranks fourth in transnational criminality. Drugs, money laundering, and armaments are the top three. In the European Union art thieves take advantage of the Schengen area because it is simple to move goods between countries, particularly small pieces.'

'Why is it such big business?' Cordelia enquired.

'Organised crime gangs often use art as collateral for drugs and weapons deals. Its value converts to any currency. That's what Milton was doing with the Degas you located.' She was citing Cordelia's first experience of using psychomatricks to locate missing art. 'Sometimes, if gangsters have been found guilty of other offences, they use the whereabouts of a high-profile piece of art as a bargaining chip, in exchange for a reduced or quashed sentence. Then there is the art taken to order for collectors desperate to own it, even though their bragging rights are limited by the risk of being discovered in possession of illicit property.'

'We met someone who specialises in tracing stolen artworks. She's well connected and negotiates for its return. Her name is Valentina, no surname,' Elodie interjected.

'I am aware of Valentina and Rightful Owner. She has handled paintings in some of the cold cases we are investigating, but even so, we want to locate the culprits.'

'How satisfying if we can help you. Where do you want us to visit? And will they know we are coming or are we undercover?' Cordelia probed, hoping it was the latter because she enjoyed the subterfuge.

'Two places – one in Alsace and the other one over the German border. Both paintings are still missing and the museums are on their guard against irregular activity, so they have been briefed on your requirement to examine the location with no distractions. The raids happened several months ago so I hope there is still something useful to inspect. No pressure!'

'This will be my first visit to Alsace. I learnt a bit about it in school history – all that swapping between France and Germany throughout the years. I called them the Dog People cos they are Alsatians and that's an alternate name for German Shepherd dog,' Cordelia recollected. 'Where are we going exactly?' She scrutinised the map on her phone as the train sped eastwards. 'The towns mostly have German names. Do you reckon the locals would prefer French titles? Or are they not French?'

'They are culturally mixed, not quite French and not quite German. The architecture and cuisine are Germanic, so is *l'Alsacien*, the regional dialect.'

'I'm fascinated by liminal lands where it's a hodgepodge and TV and radio broadcasts seep from one country across to another because the airwaves are ignorant of borders. There's a spot on the Kent coast at the narrowest point betwixt England and France where French mobile phone signals override English ones and roaming texts pop up. Some people think they will need to pay extra charges and have a conniption and switch off their phone.'

The train slowed and came to a halt. A voice crackled on the intercom and announced the reason for the delay – a swan and her cygnets had strayed onto the line and refused to move. This made the agents late in arriving at their Strasbourg hotel, so they were behind schedule and had limited time to disguise themselves.

'We will be picked up in thirty mins. See you back here,' Elodie said as they waited for the elevator.

Cordelia chose a feminised Clark Kent look, black-rimmed spectacles, coloured contact lenses, a straight black wig scraped back in a loose bun, sober black suit, and light-blue shirt. 'It'd look better if I added a silk scarf as a cravat, but that will draw attention,' she contemplated, gazing in the mirror and applying nude lipstick.

Elodie was unrecognisable in a short brown non-descript hairpiece, grey skirt suit with black polo-neck sweater, and charcoal grey overcoat. '*Bonjour Madame Noire,*' she said, joining Cordelia in the lobby. 'Dressed this way we could get jobs as financial analysts.'

'And our employers would swiftly spot how rubbish we were and thankfully we'd be fired.' Cordelia shuddered. 'Can you imagine not doing what we love?'

'We'd die of misery.' Elodie's phone dinged. 'Our taxi is here. *On y va.*'

Forty minutes later they were in the small town of Berlesheim. The driver dropped them at the museum, a yellow half-timbered structure with a steeply pitched roof, stepped gable, and decorative terracotta tiles lining the arched entryway.

'If their tongue is *l'Alsacien* will they understand you?'

'Yes, everyone speaks French too.'

'You do the talking and I'll be your shy work colleague.'

Monsieur Durand, the museum manager, was waiting for them and rigorously checked their Globo Pol ID cards bearing the pseudonyms Cordelia Brown and Elodie Moreau then accompanied them to the room where the painting of Berlesheim's medieval church used to hang. A printed sign on the wall proclaimed, "This missing item will soon be reinstated".

'We are so happy because the painting will be back here tomorrow after a parade through the town in admiration of the woman who found it,' Monsieur Durand said excitedly.

Cordelia and Elodie glanced at each other and concurrently telepathed, *Valentina*?

'How marvellous. What time is the parade so we can witness this fortunate occasion?' Elodie asked.

'It will be here at 12pm. The church bell will peal in celebration.'

Notwithstanding the imminent homecoming of the painting, news of which had yet to reach Globo Pol, the special agents still wanted to apply their investigative procedures and Monsieur Durand left them alone to do their work.

'If we place our hands on the wall where it used to hang we might feel something,' Cordelia instructed.

They splayed their hands, little fingers touching, closed their eyes and meditated. Despite having downed chacruhana microdoses on the train they felt nothing. So they tried again. Still nothing.

'Frustrating and not unexpected. There were no prints and the painting was nicked months ago, so that's too long for any quintessence to remain.' Cordelia sighed, 'I feel rather deflated.'

'We'll have more success at the German museum,' Elodie said in a consoling tone.

'Yes, this is a blip. How far away is it?'

'Over the border, roughly 20 minutes from Strasbourg. An hour in all if traffic is good.'

'We must come back tomorrow and see Valkyrie in action, if it's her. Although who else would it be?'

'Definitely. Let's eat lunch in that café in the square so we have a good view. We'll be in disguise so she won't spot us.'

'I like this plan. I want to be acquainted with Alsatian cuisine and we need to nourish our psychic talents.' She snapped a photo of the wall where the painting had been. 'Have you ever noticed that James Bond never eats? Big on cocktails but no grub. What do you think he has for brekkie?'

'I can't see him eating porridge or a bagel. He has to maintain muscle strength and stay lean, so I'd say scrambled eggs and a protein shake.'

'Low carb diet? How dull. Imagine never gorging on buttered toast and marmalade.'

More disappointment for Cordelia was coming down the *strasse* when they visited the German village of Hesselstätt, where the museum was in a medieval hunting lodge used by the rulers of a fiefdom within the Holy Roman Empire. A small and crudely rendered fourteenth-century painting had been seized. It was a depiction of a mythical wild boar said to host the spirit of Tamfana, a deity who protected the town. It had no monetary value but was priceless to the citizens of Hesselstätt. In the ensuing weeks the river flooded, damaging dozens of buildings, then a block of ice fell from an airliner and smashed the roof of a greenhouse. Some residents said it was a coincidence, others assumed it was because the loss had left the town susceptible to bad luck.

'Good job we've only been showing off to Rexicles about our past triumphs. I wouldn't want to admit to anyone else we are not infallible,' Cordelia said as their psychomatricks experiment yielded no results.

'If only we could arrive quickly to read the thief's energy. But we are not giving up. I can feel that we'll have a breakthrough, so we must not be disheartened,' Elodie replied.

'You're right. We just need the robbers to make a little mistake, such as scarpering from the museum's barking dog and losing a shoe. All that quintessence imprinted inside it would lead us right to their doorstep. Anyway, I will not be downcast. We're having a jolly time and I can't wait to mock Valkyrie in her full pomp tomorrow.'

When they arrived in Berlesheim the following morning the town centre was closed to vehicles. People were already lining the square and the café was busy. Fortunately, Elodie had booked the last available table on the terrace with a direct view of the museum.

'What do you want to drink *chérie?*'

'Something local please – an aperitif or a glass of fizz.'

'Try the Crémant d'Alsace. Crisp and dry, it will awaken your palate.'

'Just what I need. And I cannot visit Sassy and not taste G-Tram at some point. I'm big on wine that reminds me of rose petals.' She meant the Gewürztraminer for which Alsace was renowned.

'*Bien sûr*. We are not leaving the region without ordering a bottle. It will go well with smoked herring, and we must eat choucroute garnie too, it's an exalted dish in this area.'

Suddenly the atmosphere began to buzz, the church bell started to ring as the procession, led by a band playing Alsatian tunes, entered the square. Children were strewing flower petals ahead of an open-top horse-drawn ceremonial carriage in which Valentina sat, unsmiling.

'Have we wandered into North Korea? It's the cult of Vampire Val and it shivers my timbers,' Cordelia commented.

As the carriage stopped outside the museum, a school choir sang a specially composed song of gratitude and Valentina was ushered to a stage built especially for the handover. There was prolonged applause as she presented the painting to the mayor. To reciprocate he awarded her the freedom of the town and placed a gilded chain around her neck, from which hung the emblem of the municipality, a goat-shaped medallion. He also pointed to a table where a large Berlesheimer cheese, a gastronomic signifier of the area, was on display. Then he bowed and tried to kiss her hand, but she yanked it away.

GOAT stands for Greatest Of All Time, so she'll appreciate the goat motif seeing as she considers herself to be at the zenith of her profession, Cordelia telepathed, having stopped speaking because she was struggling not to snigger at how fulsomely the town had delivered

Valentina's ludicrous demands. Elodie managed a poker face that gave no indication of her mirth however once she saw that Cordelia's expression resembled a death mask her shoulders started to shake as she attempted to swallow her giggles.

You look like the Mask of Agamemnon, she telepathed.

Stoppppp or I'll start again.

Picture a sad subject and dig your fingernails into the back of your hand, that always works for me.

After they calmed down Cordelia wondered aloud what benefits freedom of the town bestowed.

'That concept is unfamiliar. Free parking maybe?' Elodie suggested.

'Being able to push ahead in a queue would also be useful,' Cordelia mused.

Elodie had a quick conversation with the couple at a table opposite and turned back to Cordelia. 'The mayor is their neighbour and he told them honouring a person in such a manner does not exist here, but Valentina insisted on it as a condition for the return of the painting.'

'Cheeky bint, that's extortion.'

Suddenly there was a tumultuous cheer in the square as the painting was solemnly carried through the museum doors by two children who had won the opportunity because of good behaviour and consistent high marks at school. With the formalities completed the crowd dispersed and the streets reverted to their usual tranquil state.

'How nauseating to behold Valkyrie's gargantuan vainglory,' Cordelia said, rolling her eyes.

'She's auditioning to be the next Italian dictator.'

'If I was a dictator I'd always smile to make people feel good as a way to distract them from my totalitarian intentions.'

'Can I be your Director of Policy?'

'Of course. What are you thinking?'

Elodie contemplated for a few seconds. 'Definitely a tax on beards, and mandatory music lessons in schools.' She picked up the menu. 'We need to complete our visit by drinking a glass of the nearby estate's Riesling and match it with the local chèvre of the type the mayor gave to Valkryie.'

'Bet she throws it away, seeing as food rarely passes her lips.'

'What a waste! She does not deserve it. The goats who sacrificed their milk would concur,' Elodie remarked, catching the waiter's eye. 'When is she at HoT for another fitting?'

'She hasn't booked it and is not in a hurry for the shoes to be finished. Too occupied being deified in towns across the continent. Hope she cancels the order. I'd happily not see that disagreeable piece of work again in my beloved lair.'

Cordelia was speaking to Rex on the phone after she arrived back in London from Strasbourg. 'I'm back babe. Empty handed as far as success is concerned. I've become used to winning though it was worth the trip for the Valkyrie story I have to tell. What are you up to later?'

'I'm on my first befriender meet-up. His name is Osbert but goes by Bertie. I'm taking him to the pub.'

'Fill me in tomorrow and I'll spill about capital V.'

The next morning Rex joined her for Blanche's walk.

'Bertie's a dear. Worked for years as choreographer at the Talk of the Town and knew Judy Garland. Lives in an old folk's sheltered living home where he's the only 'mo. Says most of the tenants are cordial but they can't relate to that aspect of his life and the fellas avoid him cos he's camp. His best friend Barbara is in the flat above and she gets it cos she used to work in a theatrical agency.'

'Do you think he'd want to come out dancing with me sometime? I'm always in need of men who can move.'

'I'm sure he'd L.O.V.E. that. He's 85 and very spry. Used to host Bertie's Tea-Dance at the Café de Paris.'

'Aren't you lovely to be his new pal. He must be glad of the male company. And if he wants to gaze at a young, ripped man perchance he'd like to go to a drawing class where Basti has his kit off.'

At six foot five inches and resembling a clean-shaven Neptune bristling with chunky muscles and long hair in a vibrant shade of Titian, Sebastian was a coveted model for life-drawing classes.

'He'd probably enjoy that. If the home has a programme of activities the females might relish holding a pencil and ogling. Barbara's bound to.'

As they strolled in the park Cordelia described in detail Valentina's narcissistic appearance in Berlesheim.

'If you'd been there your eyes would have rolled so far back you'd have seen your brain. She-She was quaking so much trying not to laugh that the café table wobbled.' Cordelia stood and threw Blanche's ball, then told Rex how maddened she was to have failed in the latest mission. 'We need your intellect to solve the mystery. Manon says there's a pattern to the robberies. Perhaps you can see a pattern within a pattern.'

Rex, who felt left out when Cordelia and Elodie went away for Globo Pol adventures, responded brightly, 'Reporting for duty.'

Chapter Eight

'Rolling.'

Cordelia looked into the camera and smiled.

'Good day and welcome to The Footwear Chronicles. I am Cordelia Tanner and my co-presenter is Doctor Elodie l'Archambeau who is a living encyclopodia. That's not a mispronunciation, it's the most accurate description of her extensive knowledge and if anyone from the Oxford English Dictionary is watching, the word is now yours.'

Cordelia and Elodie were recording new material for House of Tanner TV in a series that focused on shoe history by highlighting their remarkable collections. That day's episode focused on heels and Elodie enlightened viewers by explaining:

- Persian cavalry men, as early as the tenth century wore heels, not to increase height, but for the practical purpose of securing their feet in stirrups and to balance themselves on horseback as they fired arrows from their bow
- European aristocratic males adopted heels in the sixteenth century to symbolise their virility and social status
- France's Sun King, Louis XIV, passed an edict in 1670 that permitted only those of noble birth to wear heels
- Height through heels had a sociological meaning; as heels restrict mobility only the wealthy who had leisure time wore them, whereas poor people who had to work wore flats or went barefoot
- When heels became the fashion for European women in the eighteenth century men ceased wearing them because they

were no longer the symbol of masculinity
- High heels change the wearer's posture and by accentuating breasts, hips, and backside, make women sway as they walk, all reasons for the heel's connection to sexual allure.

'Cowboy boots with Cuban heels are direct descendants of the Persian version,' Elodie said pointing to her own Cowbike boots.

'Everyone shoe-ey should read the Doctor's PhD thesis,' Cordelia recommended to viewers, then said to Elodie, 'I'm fascinated how, depending on context, heels for women have an association with sex and power. Take stilettoes for instance, some men consider them to be aggressive and predatory but simultaneously erotic. Fetish wear for women is heels all the way. Flatties may be comfy, they just aren't titillating.'

'Yes, and there's also the danger factor. Stiletto is the Italian word for a thin dagger. A spiky heel potentially causes damage and explains the link with dominatrices.'

'Doctor l'Archamboots, I'd like to hear you talk on this subject forever but it's time to unveil the favourite heels of your collection.'

'These are hard to resist. They are practical and so inventive.' Elodie held up a pair of scuffed brown leather boots. They had belonged to Obadiah Waters of Dymchurch who, in the 1780s, transported contraband over Romney Marsh in Kent and managed to evade the vicious thugs who competed to control the lucrative smuggling trade. His simple ruse was to wear boots with the heel built beneath the toe so his trail of footprints implied he had walked in the opposite direction.

Obadiah ran the village's Lamb Inn and his occasional nocturnal occupation involved unloading illicit brandy, tobacco, and tea from his brother's fishing boat. Most coastal smugglers were also fishermen who sailed to meet French vessels in the English Channel and transfer the goods. Under-resourced government excise men had extensive territory to police, so the odds of them being spotted were low. Even so, Obadiah always wore his special boots to bamboozle anyone hunting for suspicious activity.

'Judging by the design, Obadiah stood at a rear-leaning angle to the perpendicular. They must have been so clumsy to walk in,' Cordelia said, giggling at the image of him picking his way along the beach.

'It's not the only cunning way to disguise footprints. Smugglers were also known to attach carved wooden blocks that resembled cow-hooves to the soles of their boots.'

'So ingenious. Now, let's do the lucky dip of viewers' enquiries.' Cordelia pulled several strips of paper out of a cavalry boot and chose one. 'This is for you Elodie. Malcolm in Edinburgh is asking why so many old buildings in Britain conceal shoes in their walls or chimneys.'

'Hello Malcolm, thank you for your intriguing question.' Elodie gazed at the camera with a come-hither smile. All her smiles were come-hither, not purposely but because that was how her face expressed itself and she was unaware of the swoonful effect it had. A coterie of viewers tuned in specifically for her and there were numerous fan pages on My Bit Of Web, including one called El's Belles and Beaus. Cordelia thought it was sweet and referred to them collectively as Elbows.

'In an era when people believed in supernatural threats, hiding a shoe in a wall cavity or chimney served as a protective amulet. Footwear moulds to the shape of the feet and imprints the wearer's essence, so it acted as a lure for evil forces to attack, assuming a human was attached and caused the demon to be trapped.'

'Did it only happen in the UK?'

'No, the phenomenon has been reported in the USA, Canada, and Australia. Probably due to British immigrants importing their superstitions to those countries.'

'Thanks doctor. Now then you shoe-ligans, before we finish this is a reminder to please send in any queries for our upcoming episode on footwear in literature and art. Until next time, farewell.'

'Cut,' Gail, the director said. 'Fascinating content. I love working on this show. Almost finished. Just require some over the shoulders of you both please.'

'Always ready for my close-up. This is my best side, and so is this one.' Cordelia pointed to both cheeks, then to Elodie, 'Fancy lunch at Bonatti's? We can discuss our women's day spectacular. I'll text Rexicles to check if he's free.'

He replied swiftly, *Yes, yes, and thrice yes. I walked past earlier and noticed Spam fritters are on the specials board.*

Oh good, and She-She is unaware of Ant's new menu item, so it'll be a surprise, Cordelia replied, referring to a dish devised especially for Elodie by Antonio, the café owner.

The TannerBeaus were planning an extravaganza to mark International Women's Day with themed exhibitions at House of Tanner and Worship, plus new Left To Their Own Devices works. Rex was temporarily moving paintings of unacclaimed female mathematicians from the walls of his office (named House of Hypatia in tribute to the fourth-century Greek polymath) to the gallery. 'I'd like to call my contribution "The Language Of The Universe" seeing as maths underpins everything.'

Visitors would learn that in the eighteenth century Marie-Sophie Germain assumed a male persona in order to study at Paris's l'École Polytechnique, where females were not permitted to enrol; they would be introduced to Ada Lovelace, mid-nineteenth-century pioneer nicknamed "The Enchantress of Numbers" and regarded as the first computer programmer; and see a triptych of Mary Jackson, Dorothy Vaughan, and Katherine Johnson, three African-American women who worked for NASA in the 1950s and whose calculations were the foundation of the USA's successful space programme.

For the exhibition at House of Tanner, Cordelia and Elodie were highlighting footwear from their collections, but with so many extraordinary characters to choose from Cordelia found it impossible to pick only three. 'I need a theme. I'm thinking notable firsts but how do I whittle down my potentials?'

'They all have such interesting stories so could you choose the pairs you dream about?'

'Yes! I know just the ones. Want to see them?'

Cordelia showed her some kitten-heeled knee-length purple kidskin boots laced with mauve satin ribbons. The hand-tooled leather inlay of golden acanthus leaves made them glow.

'These stunners were the property of Ottoline Loosvelt who, in the 1880s was the first woman to own a professional baseball team. She refused to marry, shocked Chicago polite society by smoking cigarettes in public, and kept a pet snake called Persephone in her handbag.'

Next, she held up a pair of green satin embroidered evening shoes with oversized rhinestone buckles and flared Louis heels. 'Don't these make you want to contemplate them for the rest of your life? They belonged to Constance Markievicz, Irish politician, suffragist, revolutionary, and nationalist. In 1918 she became Britain's first elected female parliamentarian, even though she never took her seat, then as Minister for Labour in the breakaway Irish Republic government, the first female cabinet member.'

'Exquisite. And in honour of Constance they should be the motif for all women politicians.'

Then Cordelia moved on to pink leather crystal encrusted strappy sandals, with heels cut from a piece of Ethiopian amber, worn by Cressida Kensington, beloved comic actress. As founder of Sea Kay Studios she was the first woman to be sole proprietor of a film and TV business.

'Her post-Depression-era productions were pure escapism. She's revered for the screwball comedy series where she played Dandy, a socialite who was also a fairy godmother, able to make anyone's dreams come true.'

Dandy's native tongue was Fairish and although she spoke English fluently she did not comprehend idioms so took everything literally. This caused mayhem when granting the wishes of: the man who had requested animal magnetism, not specifying for humans only; the woman who wanted to dance like a demon; the child who longed to fly like a bird. Audiences loved Dandy, and her catchphrase "Time For A Cheeky Cocktail", inspired The Cheeky, a concoction of naval strength gin, peppermint tea, and crème de menthe.

'*Délicieuse* and good as a digestif. Now, do you want to see my choices?' Being a swashbuckler Elodie went for the daredevils in her collection. 'Meet Queen of the Mist, Annie Edson Taylor who, on her 63rd birthday in 1901, became the first person to survive the plummet over Niagara Falls in a barrel. She was wearing these sensible black leather lace-up boots, which were typical of the era.'

'Let's psy-comm them later.'

'Definitely. Let's psy-comm them all, especially Gladys Ingle, doyenne of wing walkers. In the 1920s she was one of the first females to have a pilot's licence and the only woman in an aerial performing troupe of 12 men. I repeatedly watch a film clip of her undertaking an unbelievable stunt where she fixes the landing gear of a biplane by standing on the wing of a rescue plane, spare wheel strapped to her back, then transfers to the stricken plane, climbs to the underbelly and replaces the damaged wheel. All in mid-air!'

'Extraordinary, can I see the footage?'

Elodie pulled out her phone and handed it to Cordelia who was unable to believe her eyes as she watched a video of the tousle-haired young adventurer in white shirt, khaki jodhpurs, and brown leather knee-length aviator boots, executing the improbable repair with no harness and no parachute.

'Unreal! Are the boots she's wearing the same one's as these?'

'Not sure. They are similar, and this pair was definitely hers.'

'Have you tried them on?'

'Yes. They are a bit tight, so I loosened the laces and managed to force my feet in and now I have the urge to wing walk. There's an aerodrome in Sussex where I can do it.'

'I'll ask the production team to make you some boots similar to these. When you're up on that wing you'll resemble the figurehead on a ship's bow.' Cordelia lifted up her hair and held it behind her making a swooshing sound effect. 'Why aren't women called Gladys any more – it's such a good name. Your jet doesn't have a moniker and she's definitely a Gladys.'

'*Parfait!* Now, shall I reveal my third choice? Bessie Stringfield, Motorcycle Queen of Miami. She's close to my heart.' Elodie held up a baby-blue leather cowboy boot. 'Bessie was the first black woman to drive solo on a motorbike, coast to coast in the USA. She earned a living doing stunts in carnival shows and throughout World War II worked for the US Army as a dispatch rider on her Harley. Not only that, but she knew how to weave a makeshift bridge using rope and tree limbs for crossing swamps. She is so renowned the American Motorcycle Association confers an annual memorial award in her name.'

'They should give you a Glam Bam Thank You Ma'am award for the way you remove your helmet and shake your hair like in a slow-mo shampoo commercial. No one does it as fabulously as you.'

Rex was already at the café drinking builder's tea, seated at a table by the arts and crafts wooden panelling in the corner.

Antonio, all smiles, greeted them. 'Elodie, I have a treat for you.' He went on to describe Croque Madame Le Docteur, composed of creamy Lancashire cheese, rare breed Tamworth ham, an egg from his backyard chickens, and organic apple slices for a crunchy contrast and as a nod to an apple a day keeping the doctor away, even though that was most definitely not his intention for Elodie.

'Thank you for this lovely gesture. I feel so privileged and can't wait to try it.' She hugged him and he felt as if he had won the lottery jackpot and top prize in the Premium Bonds on the same day.

'Sounds delish and I want to sample it, but corned beef hash is also calling me,' Cordelia said, looking at the special's board.

'I must have Spam fritters, it's the law. Let's me and you get a Croque to share,' Rex proposed.

Orders placed he took out his notepad and said quietly, 'Oh, nearly forgot, I've been looking at GPol's files and spotted a couple of things. The data set was small, only fourteen cases, so nothing conclusive, but this is what I have to show.' He pointed to his annotations. 'Works by unknowns were returned quickly – on six occasions. Pieces by artists anyone has heard of were never returned. That implies the unknowns have no resale value. I also spotted that returns never occurred in winter. Valkyrie was involved in all of them, so she probably waits for spring cos, being skinny, she has no layer of body fat to keep her warm in cold weather. And people are less likely to turn up in chilly temperatures to applaud her, which is the whole point isn't it?'

'Who needs AI for data analysis when Rex Tanner is on the case? There is nothing artificial about his intelligence!' Cordelia exclaimed.

'He's our very own mastermind.' Elodie waggled his left earlobe.

'Oh go on then, if you insist.' Rex preened. 'So, what did you decide on for the exhibition?'

Cordelia passed him her phone and told him of their choices as he looked at the photographs.

'It's going to be increddy! Cressida is my fave. If only I could travel on one of your psy-comm journeys I'd go for a cocktail with her. What a pair we would make, her in those gorgeous sandals and me in my even more gorgeous two-toners.' Rex pointed to his periwinkle and royal yellow co-respondents.

'Cressida is a total ledge. And you'll love Gertie Grayson, although I haven't chosen her for this exhibition. She's cocktail-ey too and I have a pair of her dancing shoes. Each heel has a secret compartment for storing a miniature of booze. Her parties were something else and made Jay Gatsby's funereal in comparison. I described them to Oscar and he's planning a modern-day version of her Prohibition Repeal bash in homage.' Its wild celebrations to mark the end of restrictions on legally buying a drink, ensured the shindig had gone down in American folklore.

Cordelia described how she and Elodie "met" Gertie during a psychomatricks session. They had knocked back a double dose of chacruhana infused eau de vie and held one of Gertie's shoes. The alcohol rapidly delivered the hallucinogenic into their bloodstream, sending starbursts of light across their vision. It felt as though they were catapulting around the Solar System and bouncing off planets like pinballs, then spinning down a wormhole and gently landing in 1931. They were at Gertie's nightclub, Nine, situated in the warehouse complex she owned on the Brooklyn waterfront. It was a citadel of entertainment that tempted Manhattanites to traverse the bridge to the Badlands, with amusements including dancing, a water tank featuring synchronised swimmers, burlesque performers, and show girls choreographed by the one-and-only Jack Ventura, who went on to rule Hollywood musicals. However, the biggest draw was the quality of Nine's liquor.

'Gertie's preferred type of person was the one who answered, "Here!" to the question "Where's the party?". Prohibition was ruining her social life so she started dealing in bootlegged liquor. The Mafia had the monopoly on that activity, so they demanded a cut and refusal was a one-way journey to the bottom of the East River,' Cordelia explained.

While most racketeers supplied bathtub gin so poisonous that it was the last thing hundreds of poor soaks drank, Gertie specialised in top shelf vodka from her parent's Polish homeland. She heeded the legal stipulations on the sale of alcohol and exploited a loophole that meant although buying was a criminal offence, imbibing it was not – an ambiguity that existed to avoid the Government being accused of criminalising church communion wine. Drinks were free at Nine, subsidised by the high entry fee. Despite technically being within the law Gertie resented the inevitability of being hauled downtown if the place was raided. In that event an alarm sounded, and customers were instructed to knock back whatever they were drinking then fill the glasses with iced tea from jugs on the table. Family heritage was not the only reason Gertie chose to trade in vodka. Unlike highly aromatic gin and bourbon, which promiscuously revealed themselves, vodka's barely-there flavour and subtle aroma were imperceptible in a smoky atmosphere. Federal agents taking a test sip of iced tea would suspect nothing, particularly as the innocent refreshment contained a sprinkle of nose- and tongue-numbing cayenne pepper to mimic the burn of alcoholic spirits.

'We arrived at the same time the off-duty Chief of Police and Mayor of New York showed up as punters. They started chatting and invited us to join their table,' Cordelia told Rex. 'Mr Mayor was – how should I describe him politely – a rambunctious, thirsty chap who smoked a huge cigar. Then Gertie dragged the four of us onto the dancefloor to show off the Rumble, a sassy dance she'd invented in her days as a flapper. Kick steps, hops, slides, standing back-to-back rubbing bottoms with the nearest person, then mooching to the right and left. A complete hoot.' Cordelia demonstrated it for Rex, who did his superstar-on-the-red carpet pose as he stood, chin-out, hands on hips, and ready to rub. 'After our cosy encounter Mr Mayor hired me to be his Chief of Staff.'

Elodie giggled. 'And the Police Chief offered to deputise me, said I was bound to suit the uniform, and that he'd drop everything to personally pin the badge on my chest.'

'How handy, you have careers lined up if you decide to go back,' Rex said with a sarcastic edge, trying but failing not to feel miffed about the fun they were having without him.

Cordelia continued, 'Then there was a commotion and dozens of federal agents swaggered in, cleared the dance floor and ordered everyone, including us, to sit down and place our hands on the table. They moved throughout the room picking up glasses and sniffing them. The senior agent recognised the Police Chief, who poured some iced tea and invited him to sit and have a drink. Poor bloke was thoroughly thwarted. Hope he was not dependent on commission for the number of arrests made because he left empty handed.'

Rex changed the topic. 'Are we having pud?' He glanced at the menu. 'Ooh look, pear crumble and a choice of ice cream or custard. I'm going for both.'

'Baked Alaska. Haven't had that in an age,' Cordelia said.

'What's jam roly-poly?' Elodie asked.

'If food was eligible for state honours it would be "arise Sir Suet Pudding." Dough spread with jam then rolled up, steamed and deluged in custard. If I wasn't in a crumble frame of mind I'd go for it,' Rex replied.

'Mmm, I'll order that and you can help me eat it.'

Bonatti's was always packed at lunchtime, so people often had to share tables. As their desserts were served a middle-aged man sporting a cheeky expression and spiky hairstyle held in place by masses of sticky product approached and said, 'Is this anyone's seat?'

'No, you can take it,' Cordelia answered.

'Shift up then treacle,' he replied and sat next to her, bringing an overpowering cloud of aftershave with him.

Cock of the walk. Full of himself but I quite like the attitude. Cordelia thought.

The man listened in as the others nattered. Then, realising they were the owners of Worship, said with a pronounced glottal stop typical of Estuary English, 'I'm keen on that Left To Their Own Devices lot. Any new works on the 'orizon?'

'Come and visit the gallery on 8 March and you might be pleasantly surprised. And when I say might, I mean definitely,' Cordelia responded teasingly.

'Wonder who they are. Must be difficult to remain anonymous.'

'Yes, they're clever in keeping up the secrecy.' Cordelia turned back to the others and with furrowed eyebrows sent the visual message they should be going in case he posed additional questions on the identity of the collective. They swiftly finished eating and stood up to leave.

'8 March, don't forget.'

Chapter Nine

For Women's Day the TannerBeaus created new Left To Their Own Devices works on the theme of XX for the female chromosome, a choice that Rex found satisfying because of x having a starring role in algebra. For his creation he wrote XXtraordinary within an image of earth from space. Cordelia's contribution, 'X Marks the Spot', was two enormous Xs formed of hundreds of multicoloured dots to represent baby girls who had never been born due to pre-birth gender selection in countries where boys were preferred. Elodie drew her Xs as vermicelli pasta because chromosomes in the cell nucleus are thread-like structures.

'Porkin' Dorkin will be scathing,' Cordelia said. 'Each year he posts on soshe "So when's international men's day then?" even though he knows the date is 19 November. He only does it to be annoying and cos it always trends with thousands of retorts saying, "That would be every day".'

After the news that three new LefDev canvases were to be unveiled on International Women's Day a queue formed outside Worship the evening before and people camped overnight in the quiet private street.

'Can't believe the size of the throng,' Rex declared on the morning of the big reveal. 'I had to fight my way through. A couple of queuers accused me of pushing in and told me to get to the back.'

'Astonishing isn't it. Some of them had a party last night. It was really noisy and I couldn't sleep, so I went and joined in. A group of Manchester lasses were on the way to watch their women's footy team play Brighton and had come a day early specially for the exhibition. Such a laugh. They're campaigning for their city to be renamed Womanchester.'

'What a good idea. If I was a Manc I'd support that. It makes such sense because the word "woman" contains "man". It's not only men who live in the city, so why should they have naming rights?'

'Think if all words beginning with "man" were swapped. Then we'd go on womanoeuvres and visit Womanitoba.'

Rex tittered and said, 'Womanufacturing and womanagers. And while I'm at it, why isn't the Brighton women's team nicknamed "Shegulls" instead of "Seagulls"? That's a missed opportunity.'

'Babe, if I did not already love everything you are, I'd love you for your feminism.'

'Cheers sissy.' He held up in his left fist in the Power to the People symbol. 'All this LefDev hype is good for the caff isn't it. I popped in for brekkie, but it was mobbed so couldn't get a seat.'

Bonatti's was not the only small enterprise in the area to benefit from the Worship bounce. Mrs Gupta, who supplied luxury fabrics to House of Tanner, was now a social media star, thanks to her shop window displays being so vibrant that almost everyone who passed by on the way to the gallery snapped them and posted on Visuality.

A few weeks after the new works were unveiled Elodie called Cordelia to say Sandrine Rivera had been in touch to ask for an early morning viewing. 'She has a lay-over in London for several hours on Monday and wants to make the most of her time. She's keen to see HoT operations too. It'll be 7am-ish. Any good?'

'Of course. Hope our pet critic is as eager as she was at the beginning.'

On the day of Sandrine's visit Cordelia came back from Blanche's walk as Elodie was parking Nike. The dog, backside waggling in excitement, launched at Elodie. '*Bonjour ma belle*, what a delightful welcome.' She petted her and, pointing to a hot-pink glittery high-heel in Cordelia's hand, asked, 'What's that?'

'Blanche found it near Dragannini's. I did a swift psy-comm and it belongs to a queen who stumbled barefoot from the club holding her shoes. She must have dropped one.'

'This is familiar. Was the owner wearing a wig that resembled a walnut whip?'

'Yes, quite edible looking. Do you know her? If so, I can hand it back. Blanche's mouth is so soft it isn't damaged.'

'I do. Her stage name is Chocca Holic. Dragannini's has a karaoke parlour and we once duetted on "You're The One That I Want", with her singing Olivia's part and me as John. She's a vicar in the day job.'

At that moment a taxi drew up and Sandrine alighted. 'So good of you to meet me this early. How has the new work been received?' she said, kissing them both.

'Very positively. Lots of excitement and it's been so busy the gallery staff don't take all their breaks because they'd rather chat and enthuse with visitors,' Cordelia replied.

'It also has a helpful side effect of introducing my collection to people who do not normally seek out that type of art, so I am content,' Elodie explained as they entered the gallery. 'Do you want to be alone so you can concentrate?'

'How thoughtful, yes please. Normally at an official visit I get no chance just to 'be' with the art. It is hard to judge properly if the gallery owner is hovering and waiting for me to comment.'

'We will be lounging in the armchairs by Louise Moillon's still life of the basket of plums.'

Forty-five minutes later Sandrine joined them. 'Inspiring. Relevant. Now. Whoever the members of this collective are, and I don't want to know because I enjoy the mystery, are empaths, understand humanity and care deeply. I see them as revolutionaries changing the world one canvas at a time.'

Virtual high-five hon – I'll do a real one when she's gone, Cordelia telepathed to Elodie, then said to Sandrine, 'Many thanks for being so enthusiastic.'

'Can I also send a verbal bouquet to your brother for championing an unexpected niche. His portraits of dead mathematicians are so engaging. And Elodie, I find your collection even more significant now I have seen it again.'

Elodie beamed. 'Thank you so much. For a person of your standing to say that means everything. I just wish the directors of major museums shared your view. There is more art by women in this one room than in all the European national museums combined.'

'I may be able to help. I am acquainted with most of the directors, so I'll discuss the subject. And if you agree, we'll make a documentary on Worship for the Art Is Life TV Channel. It will be a calling card for women's art.'

Returning the high-five, Elodie telepathed to Cordelia, then replied to Sandrine's offer, 'That is so generous. What a magnificent ally you are. It will make all the difference.'

Sandrine's advocacy of Worship excited Cordelia and she had a feeling her guest would also be keen on House of Tanner. 'Are you ready for shoes?'

They crossed the street and into the lobby of House of Tanner.

'We'll start in the archive,' Cordelia said as they climbed the stairs up to her treasure trove of shoe designs.

Sandrine was awed by them and had no words other than, 'Oh my.'

'Each model is inspired by a bird. This is Red Cardinal and is based on the male's plumage.' Cordelia passed her a scarlet velvet mule, trimmed with black feathers rising above the toe in recognition of the creature's assertive quiff. 'Some of our clients wear theirs purely in the bedroom.' She grinned.

'And what's the story of these?' Sandrine pointed to black and orange velvet ankle boots, with heels covered in mirrored panels.

'I have such a soft spot for Northern Red Bishop, our eternal best seller because the mirrors are so useful in case lipstick needs reapplying.'

Every element of House of Tanner impressed Sandrine – the Boudoir of Pulchritude, Cordelia's glorious designs, and not least the grand architecture of the building itself. Something had happened to the cool and reserved art critic who never normally gave clues to her opinions. She'd become effusive, excitable, and overwhelmed by what she saw.

'So that's contemporary shoes, now you're in for a treat in the historic collections,' Cordelia said as they went to the second floor and through a glimmering gold doorway. It led to a magical realm, with a woodland of gilt-painted trees, the joyous recorded songs of forest birds trilling from speakers in the boughs, and soft green moss underfoot that, when stepped on, released mind-altering essential oils. This was Shoeseum, a combination of museum and amusement park, which was the ultimate "let loose in a sweet shop" fantasy. It had a "cannot-be experienced-anywhere-else" element called *If the Shoe Fits* in which, courtesy of what Cordelia had learnt from her psychomatricks activity, the story of the footwear was brought to life. It entailed entering a pod where augmented reality, video game technology, and kinaesthetic communication applying motion, touch, and smell all combined in vignettes starring actors portraying the original owner.

'Here's a pair that always makes me smile.' Cordelia led Sandrine to the jewel-encrusted embroidered slip-ons worn by an eighteenth-century Ottoman Sultan nicknamed the Rock of Constantinople.

Their lengthy corkscrew curled toes curving above the upper part of the foot had surely been the inspiration for every cartoon genie. 'Come and have a look at my favourite historical figure, Lancelot "Beau" George, the best-dressed man of his era and master of ceremonies to high society during Britain's early nineteenth-century Regency period. I have a massive crush on him and his shoes.' They went to an exhibit where ultramarine velvet slip-ons with carnelian-ornamented buckles sat on a plinth.

Sandine was flabbergasted with Shoeseum. 'This whole place is extraordinary.'

'Thank you. It was my guardian, Celestine Priestley, who translated my imagination into what you see. It's one of my fave places to be and I'm often tempted to abandon real life and move in with my virtual friends.'

'Please don't *mon coeur*, we all love you too much to lose you to Lancelot,' Elodie begged.

'Back at you hon. In that case I'll only do it part-time. On a Tuesday afternoon. I've never been keen on Tuesday afternoons, they have a whiff of half-day closing.' She turned to Sandrine, 'Elodie also collects historic shoes, that's how we met, both wanting the same pair in an auction. She has honoured House of Tanner by donating her exceptional collection. If you want to drool then have a look.'

Elodie's collection was in a separate area called L'Archambeau Bequest and exhibited in individual glass and chrome pyramids hanging from the ceiling of a grotto rendered in papier-mâché and painted gold to look like iron pyrite ore.

'This pair belonged to Gabrielle, Duchesse de Polignac, one of the great beauties of pre-revolutionary France.' Elodie picked up an eye-catching white and pink embroidered mule with Louis heel bejewelled in diamonds, a type of shoe coquettishly termed *venez-y-voir* (come and see). 'The placement of the heel under the vamp made walking so precarious that fashionable French woman of the era had to use a cane for balance.'

'I've worked in the art sector for years but did not realise the depth of artistry involved in shoes. You two have opened my eyes,' Sandrine declared.

'It's funny you should say that because at the Worship opening party Vance Dorkin questioned what I knew of art, seeing as I am a cobbler – his word.'

Sandrine tutted and shook her head. 'He's clueless. I hope you enlightened him.'

'Did I ever!'

Cordelia continued to show her round and, after pointing out Gladys' and Bessie's boots and the other footwear highlighted at the women's day exhibition, asked if Sandrine was peckish and fancied breakfast.

When they were in The Weasel Cordelia spoke of its initial purpose as a coaching inn during the eighteenth century, and then as a gin palace after its nineteenth-century refurbishment with a polychromatic tiled exterior so striking that passengers on buses trundling past on the adjacent main road regularly alighted to take selfies. The resplendent interior décor of mosaics, marble columns, and stained-glass windows bestowed its Grade I listed status as one of the country's most renowned heritage pubs. 'The woodwork was carved by craftsmen responsible for the interiors of transatlantic liners. What year did your ancestors emigrate to the US?' she asked. 'There is a chance they travelled on one of those very ships.'

As they took their seats at a table in the saloon, chosen specifically for its unobstructed view of the Royal Doulton tiled mural of the goddesses Calliope and Euterpe, Elodie said, 'I endorse everything on the menu, in particular the hot smoked salmon and scrambled eggs with truffle butter. It's divine.'

Sandrine cooed, saying that ordinarily she would order a plain egg-white omelette. *That's not an omelette, it's a lette. What's the point?* Cordelia thought just as her guest went on to say, 'Instead, I will have what Elodie proposes. I don't know what's come over me. I'm under some sort of spell and am the opposite to the usual me. I feel like that person in photos who jumps for joy and touches their feet together while they are off the ground. As a critic I need to be impartial, but I can't stop loving everything I see and experience here. I was the same the first time I saw Left To Their Own Devices. Normally, I give no indication of liking, being indifferent, or even hating a work. That evening I was gushing. I will revert to the familiar opaque hard-headed me, but for the moment it's as though I'm on vacation from myself.'

'I'm so pleased you are feeling it. Our little street contains a mystical ambience that elates all who visit. I can't explain what it is or why, I just know it's there. Your reaction is proof,' Cordelia responded.

'What you have created with House of Tanner, Worship, The Weasel, your personal style, and overall outlook makes you the living expression of Art Is Life and Life Is Art. It is in my gift to recognise one exemplary person who personifies art and you more than anyone deserves it. Will you accept the accolade?'

Cordelia heard a blast of the Hallelujah chorus playing in her head and was momentarily stunned. *'Chérie, c'est incroyable!*' Elodie, flung an arm around Cordelia's shoulder and kissed her cheek. 'You are the equivalent of Marianne, the symbolic embodiment of the French Republic, who represents liberty, equality, and fraternity, but in your case it is beauty, originality, and creativity.' Then she said to Sandrine, 'There are busts of Marianne across France, perhaps you could commission someone to sculpt Cordelia for global distribution to art venues.'

Sandrine considered the suggestion for a moment. 'That is such a fitting way to acknowledge the prestige of this award. Cordelia, what do you think?'

Cordelia, normally so articulate, found herself at a loss for words. Then she recovered and answered in an excited jumble that would not win a prize for eloquence, 'A greater honour there is none and my magnitudinous gratitude is massively massive.'

'You are an inspiration. Where will you display your bust?'

'On a womantlepiece which I shall acquire from Longton. Have you ever been there? Stunning architecture. When you are next back in the UK we'll go. How are you on Knickerbocker Glories?'

Rex was elated to hear the news of Cordelia's Art Is Life and Life Is Art distinction. 'Babe, it's impossible for me to be any prouder. If I ever wore T-shirts, I'd have one printed bearing the slogan, "I Shared A Womb With Cordelia Tanner". And as the last three letters of your name are l i a, it's handy that the acronym for Art Is Life and Life Is Art is AILALIA. I baptise you Cordailalia. Ooh, that sounds similar to Dalai Lama. Cordalailamia, spiritual leader of the Church of Creative Expression.'

'Does it make me a holiness or an eminence?'

'More of an irreverend.'

'Accepted my child. Seriously though, I feel ecstatic and I'm sharing it with you, She-She, Vulpy, Cel, and everyone who works for us. That sounds like an Academy Award winner who dedicates their win to all the people who helped them get there. I mean it though, and I want you to be recognised too. House of Tanner would collapse if it weren't for your behind-the-scenesery. Is there an award for spreadsheets? I'm aware my eyes glaze over if I'm forced to look at them, but the way you speak about the formulas is poetry. And no one, but no one, can make the word logistics sound so saucy. It's the look in your eyes and way you enunciate the L.'

When the news was announced, congratulatory greetings and flower deliveries inundated Cordelia. Sebastian was kept busy addressing thank you cards and checking social media. 'Look at this, Vance Dorkin is boasting of being your dear friend,' he said pointing to Dorkin's Visuality account and a selfie he had posted of him, Cordelia, and Sandrine at the Worship launch. 'He also claims to be close to Sandrine Rivera and that he's the reason you have been distinguished with this award, because he lobbied her for it.'

'He's such a berk and can't breathe without lying. Surely no one takes him seriously do they?' Cordelia grimaced.

'It's hard to tell what's the truth and what's not these days.'

Cordelia, who some might say was Hoodwinker-in-Chief due to her covert connection to Left To Their Own Devices, quickly changed the subject. 'Could you remind me what date the PM is coming?'

'On the seventeenth, mid-morning, so the footage is ready for the lunchtime news.'

Cordelia's newly elevated status gave her a platform to champion the creative industries, so she had invited the Prime Minister to House of Tanner to meet some apprentices and to state a case for art provision to be improved in schools. 'It's not only good for the soul, it also nurtures talent and inspires the next generation. Good design improves society – product, engineering, the built environment, and all the rest. It's no overstatement to say that Britain is an art and design powerhouse and that will only be maintained by governments recognising the importance of art education,' she had said to the Prime Minister's adviser as they reviewed plans for the visit.

'Are you taking your hols soon Basti?' In gratitude for their role in the Art Is Life and Life Is Art award all the staff of House of Tanner, Worship, and The Weasel had received a cash bonus and extra paid holiday.

'I was going to go next week but I don't want to miss the do, so I've delayed for a while,' he replied.

The 'do' was a celebratory bash being produced by Oscar. 'Where and what my gorgeousness?' he had enquired and felt sentimental when Cordelia replied, 'A jollification at Tivoli Gardens please,' referring to a vintage ballroom in south London, the location of their first meeting several years earlier at Latin dance lessons. The teacher encouraged class members to swap partners regularly and as there were always fewer men some women were forced to take on the male role. That was what Cordelia had had to do until a tango, when a tall, striking man with green eyes and a perfect chin strolled up to her and said, '*Buenas tardes señorita*, fancy a dance?' and holding out his arms in preparation for the first position.

'*Por supuesto Señor Zorro*. But where *were* you for the foxtrot?' she'd replied, gazing into his eyes as they started to dance.

He gazed back. 'I wanted to save myself for this and give you my best performance. And by the way you're leading, but I quite like it.'

Both their hearts were beating so fast, beta blockers would ordinarily have been prescribed. If the doctor had measured the torrent of dopamine and oxytocin hurtling through their bloodstreams, she might have concluded they were experiencing a formidable coup de foudre.

'I don't want to dance with anyone else but you,' Cordelia had murmured, by now following.

'Me neither. Ever,' Oscar had replied. So they'd excused themselves from the class and left to embark on an epic romance.

'And what are we drinking and eating?' Oscar asked as they continued to plan the party.

'Bonheur, Cheeky cocktails, and will Daisy brew a celebration beer too? As for food, it always makes me titter that somewhere so glam has such down-to-earth grub.' She meant Tivoli Gardens' bar snacks – a choice of cheese and pickle or ham and tomato crusty cobs. 'Let's have what the venue provides and ask if they can also do salt and vinegar crisp sarnies.'

'Are we going big or keeping it medium to small?'

'I prefer to keep it fairly intimate, so let's invite close friends, fam, and everyone at HoT and Worship. And can we close The Weasel so the staff can come too?'

On the night of the party, Cordelia knew the ballroom itself was the star of the show, despite her fierce attire of a sleeveless body suit embellished by marigold and bronze sequinned tongues of fire, fringing, orange marabou tail feathers, and golden-heeled, winged, strappy sandals worthy of Mercury. With its red velour padded walls, French chandeliers, Chinese lanterns and crimson leather banquettes bordering the sprung dance floor, Tivoli Gardens was the definition of flamboyant.

Oscar engaged the head judge of the hit TV ballroom dancing show to come and teach guests a few moves and professional dancers to partner them. Cordelia, a keen amateur needed no tuition. Clips of Hollywood musicals played on a big screen and she and Rex astonished everyone by competing admirably with Eleanor Powell and Fred Astaire in the "Begin the Beguine" number from *Broadway Melody of 1940*. Celestine had taken them as children to Saturday morning cinema and they loved classic musicals. They had begged for tap dancing lessons, which they'd kept up for years.

Whoops and whistles at their routine were suddenly augmented by amplified applause and Cordelia glanced up to see her headshot on the screen and the words "Art Is Life and Life Is Art Laureate of the

Decade". The photo dissolved to a live feed of Sandrine surrounded by her employees in the boardroom of the organisation's Manhattan headquarters. They were all clapping. 'Cordelia, we can't wait to welcome you to New York and officially present the award, but in the meantime have a look behind you for a preview of your bust.'

Handel's *Arrival of the Queen of Sheba* struck up and Cordelia peered towards the door to see Blanche, resplendent in a sparkling cape, trotting into the room. On her back she was wearing a saddle upon which a likeness of Cordelia's head and shoulders was balanced.

'Waggy darling.' She rushed over and kissed the dog's forehead. Oscar carefully removed the bust and presented it to Cordelia at the same time as Elodie placed a wreath of tuberose on her head and flower petal confetti sprinkled from the ceiling.

'It's edible,' she exclaimed.

Elodie explained it was choux pastry filled with coffee and hazelnut cream, encased in dark chocolate and made by Madame Pelletier, her favourite pâtissier.

'Speech, speech, speech,' the guests bellowed. Cordelia was joyful beyond measure and tears prickled in her eyes.

'What a delightful view my sole brethren. Everyone who makes each day so special, and the four most divine humans and dog who I love more than anything.' She waved at Sandrine and her team. 'I am so grateful to you all for this astounding honour. See you in person very soon.' As they said farewell and the screen went dark, Cordelia said to the guests, 'Without you all this award would not have happened. I may have the ideas but you inspire me or make them a reality, so the accolade is yours too. Anyway, enough of me blathering on, we need more dancing and afterwards the filthy kebabs are on me for the journey home.'

Choon, The Weasel's resident DJ, had compiled an irresistible playlist starting with Barbara Tucker's 'Beautiful People' and for the rest of the evening no one left the dancefloor, a flawless finale to a flawless night out.

Chapter Ten

Cordelia's increased profile promoted all aspects of her professional life, Worship in particular, in no small part thanks to the Art Is Life documentary. This in turn gave a boost to Left To Their Own Devices and the bids for borrowing rights were even more generous.

When Cordelia realised that the highest bid for a canvas in the Women's Day tranche came from singer-songwriter Shantina, Britain's first black self-made billionaire, she said, 'I feel a bit guilty. Shantina's married to Wilbur and I made her wedding shoes. It seems a little cheaty that I know her, but she doesn't know I'm involved in LefDev.'

'I'd feel peculiar too, although we're not exploiting her, she wants the piece, and can afford it,' Rex replied.

'You're right. Which one did she choose?'

'Yours.'

'In that case I'd better not attend her birthday party cos she might show the canvas to guests and grill me on the collective. Shantina's a lavish host and the cocktails keep on coming so the Lemon Drops will loosen my lips. Oh, hang on, the date will clash with our trip to the US so I won't be able to go anyway. That's handy.'

She was referring to the presentation ceremony for the Art Is Life And Life Is Art award. Rex, Elodie, Oscar, and Celestine were accompanying her to the inauguration, and staying on for a couple of days because Sandrine wanted to introduce the TannerBeaus to the players in New York's art sector. The Classenheim Gallery director had invited them to discuss his invitation for Left To Their Own Devices to produce an exclusive new work for an upcoming exhibition focusing on rule breakers. They planned to decline on behalf of their client because rejecting an offer by one of the world's leading contemporary art institutions was more newsworthy than accepting, and it fit the collective's attitude of being outsiders. The director felt anything but snubbed and said he would use it to his advantage by reserving a blank space on the wall where the canvas would have hung. When the exhibition opened that void became a must-see with visitors taking selfies of what the gallery had titled, *The Emperor's New Clothes.*

'Will you be eligible to add letters to your name now you're a laureate?' Sebastian asked on Cordelia's return to work from the swift New York visit.

'Yes, and there are so many it could be a random selection of Scrabble tiles.'

'Dozens more bouquets were delivered while you were away. We ran out of places to display them so they've gone to hospices as you requested. Have a look at the photos. Some right stunners.' He held up his phone. 'Now there's a pile of thank you cards to sign. I've filled your fountain pen with purple ink.'

'Oh Basti, how am I so lucky to have you keeping me in order?'

Sebastian felt special and answered, 'Because you told me at my job interview you didn't believe in hierarchy and would never expect me to do any work tasks you'd be unwilling to do yourself. And you called me darling without any sense of being patronising. I didn't want to be anywhere else and still don't.'

Working at House of Tanner felt like being part of a family and he was deeply fond of Cordelia and the loyalty she engendered. Now she was often away on adventures and able to cogitate and sketch anywhere, she was not physically in the studio as often and he greatly missed being in the same room as her.

'I'm off to Paris imminently – not sure which day, it depends when Elodie is back. You'll be on your hols so I'll book my ticket. Where are you going?'

'Cumbria, to work on a peat bog restoration project for the local wildlife trust.'

'You're so good. Is that why you asked the production team to make you those wellies?'

Sebastian had such large feet he had difficulty finding things to fit, so free bespoke footwear as one of his employee benefits was a godsend. 'Yes, and I'm guaranteed to be the only person wearing rubber boots adorned with the image of a Wilson's Bird of Paradise.'

Cordelia arrived early at London St Pancras station for her train to Paris and strolled past the cathedral-like redbrick façade of the Gothic Revival fantasy where pinnacles, arches, and a prominent clock-tower competed for attention. She always made sure to visit the statue of Sir John Betjeman, who led the campaign to save the station from the redevelopers' wrecking ball in the 1960s, to rub his chubby tummy in gratitude.

In the departures lounge she tried to picture how it had looked, sounded, and smelled in the late nineteenth-century, when it had been a storage warehouse for beer. She told a stranger sitting next to her about its initial purpose and how the distance between the roof-supporting iron columns was measured by the number of beer barrels that could be packed into the space. 'Did you make that up?' he answered, to which she replied, 'No, one of my mates is an accredited beer sommelier who writes history books and she told me.'

'Beer sommelier, I didn't know that was a thing. What a job! I'm keen on trivia. Did she tell you anything else beery?'

'Yes, India Pale Ale existed as a style in the mid-eighteenth century when it was known as October Ale. The India connection relates to it first being exported from London's East India dock.'

'Is this friend of yours married? If not, does she want a beanpole of a husband with thinning hair who's quite good at snooker? I'm available and looking for a beer wife.'

Just then Cordelia heard an announcement for her train, stood up and said, 'That's mine. Cheerio.' The man replied, 'Beerio.' She laughed and swung round, 'Nice one! I'm partial to a pun. Never mind my sommelier pal, if you can make a 147 break at snooks *and* 180 at darts then you and I have an aisle to walk down. Ale be seeing you.'

Elodie was standing at the end of the platform as Cordelia alighted at the Gare du Nord. '*Bienvenue à Paris ma chérie*,' she said, hugging her. They were in the city for a reception at the Élysée Palace to celebrate the anniversary of the Entente Cordiale, an historic treaty signed by Britain and France in 1904 to end centuries of antagonism.

'We've been invited for lunch by a couple of my friends who live in Le Marais. They collect the work of an artist I want to consider for my collection. Let's go on Nike. I can arrange for a taxi to drop your luggage at my apartment.'

Cordelia never said no to a ride on the superbike. As usual, roads surrounding the station were congested but that was no problem for Elodie, who wove her motorcycle in and out of traffic so swiftly they reached Rue du Temple in no time. She pulled into a parking spot and said, 'Madame Pelletier's shop is nearby, and I need to pop in to collect the special macarons I ordered as a gift for our hosts.'

'Madame P's macarons are a thing of glory. What flavours did you choose?'

'Violet and clementine, for their first name initials.'

Vincent and Clark lived in a sprawling apartment on the top floor of a nineteenth-century block. As they waited for the elevator, Cordelia said, 'I highly recommend these cramped old lifts for snogging in. This I know cos me and Oscar spent part of our honeymoon in Paris and visited his elderly godmother who lived in a building with an even tinier one. We were a bit early so took several round trips …'

'Did you end up being late?'

Cordelia gave a naughty smile and raised her left eyebrow.

Elodie laughed. 'I'm impressed you managed to make the visit at all!'

Cordelia instantly warmed to her hosts, not least because Clark, an American in Paris, greeted her by saying, 'Welcome to Château Clarcent where the fridge is always full of gorgeous nibbly bits.' He was not kidding. 'Elodie told us how disappointed you are about the dearth of omelettes in Parisian restaurants, so I'll be cooking one and it will include girolles, chanterelles, and cèpes from the local farmer's market. Matched with Sancerre of course.'

'Clark, the moment you opened the door I liked you and now that's been promoted to love. If you're not careful I shall refuse to leave and will take up residence in your spare room.'

'Wait 'til you see what we're having for dessert, I'll need to hand over the spare key without delay,' he replied, cheersing her with a glass of Bonheur rosé. Crème brûlée was on the menu and he had dusted off the flame thrower to give the caramelised sugar an extra powerful nuking.

'Can't wait!' Then, looking out of the window she said, 'What a perfect, view of the Pompidou Centre. Does it give you both 'appiness?'

She sniggered because she had purposely dropped the H and given it a French pronunciation by stressing the P.

Everyone chortled. 'Please move into the spare room immediately. I promise breakfast will always be Viennoiserie. Our favourite boulangerie is around the corner and sells the best croissants aux amandes, which I hear you are keen on,' said Vincent.

'If it were possible to award more than five stars on Trip Report you would get them.'

'What an honour, much more desirable than a Michelin star,' he replied appreciatively then asked Elodie if she wanted to look at the art they had recommended and went into the sitting room where works by printmaker Helen Peyton were on show. Her speciality was lino-reduction printing, a complicated format that required great skill.

Elodie moved from piece to piece, 'Excellent. So colourful. I've read up on this technique and it's very difficult. She's so accomplished. I don't have any printmakers in my collection and looking at this work I hope I soon will.'

'You must visit Helen's studio in the Yorkshire Dales,' Clark suggested. 'Such picturesque countryside. Her work is hand done and low tech, using a cast-iron printing press made in 1885. The counterbalance is an eagle holding an olive branch in its mouth and clutching a cornucopia in its claws. It's astounding.'

Cordelia was examining the bookshelf and picked up a paperback title *La Visitation*. 'I'm not familiar with this author.'

'Goliathus is very handsome and writes thought-provoking magical realism,' Vincent explained. 'Once you are settled into the spare room, I'll read it to you as a bedtime story. Actually, I don't need to read it, I know the words by heart because I am Goliathus. It's my pen name. *La Visitation* won a literary award and I've been invited to the Élysée Palace tonight as one of France's emerging writers, so I'll see you there. I'm very excited.'

'And I'm going too, not merely as Vincent's plus one, but cos I'll be singing in the Mélo'Men choir,' Clark added.

'Ooh, what are you performing?'

'Wuthering Heights. Three reasons. We love the song; Emily Brontë spoke French as well as English; and the choir's favourite dinosaur is a brontësaurus – yes, we know that's a typo.'

'Have you heard the ukelele orchestra version? Bonkers. What genre are you doing it in?'

'Swing.'

'Love a bit of swing. I'll be jigging along.'

'*Monsieur le Président* is a swing dancer,' Elodie interjected. 'If you ask him to join you on the floor, he'll be unable to resist. Did you bring dancing shoes?'

'Botticelli!'

The Elysée Palace reception was as grand as grand could be. Its purpose was to highlight shared values and the soft-power factors both countries had in common, so guests included luminaries of literature, music, architecture, and other cultural professions. Cordelia had been invited as a representative of design. As for Elodie, she was a regular at state occasions, not only in recognition of her humanitarian work and her link to one of the great champagne houses but also for the fact she was enchanting, and every occasion was immeasurably improved by her presence.

The President welcomed everyone warmly then Anne McDonald, the British Prime Minister, made an amusing speech in which she repeated Oscar Wilde's aphorism on the UK and USA – *We have really everything in common with America nowadays except, of course, language* – and went on to say, 'In the case of language the same is not true for Britain and France, well not for almost half of it.' She was alluding to the fact so many English words derived from French ones. 'Meaning that if a Briton visiting France does not speak French, all they need do is speak English, probably loudly, and they might be understood approximately 45% of the time.' The audience laughed. 'Britain and France are two maritime nations that some say are separated by a narrow body of water, while others consider they are connected. That's why Britain's Choir of Heavenly Voices will be singing "La Mer". Our connections run deep, not least under the Channel with the Euro Tunnel.' She lauded the presence in London of one of the world's largest expatriate populations of French citizens. 'They contribute greatly to our society, and it means we can find a decent croissant.' Then she raised a glass and invited guests to toast, '*Vive l'amitié franco-britannique*! Unbreakable bonds.'

After the ceremonial element of the evening was complete the entertainment began. The President immediately said yes to Cordelia's invitation to dance. She was relieved to discover he had rhythm, so she asked whether, if the rendition of 'La Mer' was danceable, he was in the mood for a further spin and he answered emphatically, '*Oui, bien sûr,*' It transpired he was also nifty at the cha-cha-cha.

'*Monsieur le Président,* you deserve to win the next election for your ronde chasse alone,' she exclaimed.

Afterwards, Cordelia was besieged by guests keen to meet the person who had introduced a welcome relaxed element to the stuffy formality of an official reception.

On the way back to Elodie's apartment, she described the people she had met. A notable one was Mathilde Lenoir, producer of Calvados apple brandy, who had enlightened her on how seventeenth-century cider makers in England had experimented with secondary fermentation in the bottle decades before wines of the Champagne region underwent the same process. Elodie was fascinated to learn that cider was the original, purposely sparkled drink and said they must take a trip to Little Pomona, a Herefordshire cidery recommended by Mathilde. The guest who'd made the greatest impression was Guillaume, Duc de Roches-Villeroy, the soon to be appointed French Ambassador to the United Kingdom. 'My family owes your country so much for giving our ancestor Joséphine refuge. Her husband Hercule, my ducal predecessor, was executed during the Reign of Terror. She was welcomed so generously to England and lived there in contentment for the rest of her life.' When Cordelia told him Elodie owned a pair of Joséphine's shoes, which were displayed in Shoeseum, he confessed to feeling emotional and said his priority upon arriving in London, after submitting his credentials to the King, was to see them. 'It will be my pleasure to invite you and then we'll go to the pub and I'll buy you a pint of real ale. You can't live in Britain and not become acquainted with the boozer,' Cordelia declared.

Guillaume nodded his head enthusiastically. 'How delightful. I suspect my time in London will be memorable.'

The following morning Elodie was drinking tea as she watched Cordelia pack her suitcase.

'How long will you stay there?'

'A day and over-nightie, then back to London.'

Cordelia was on her way to Le Musée de la Chaussure in Romans-sur-Isère, in south-east France. She'd visited it previously and its collection of historic shoes made her heart race.

'It should be twinned with Shoeseum.' Elodie paused. 'Actually, that makes total sense. I sometimes do consultancy work and know the management. Why didn't I think of it before? Am I a plonker?'

Which she pronounced as *plonkare*.

'I've never thought of you as a plonker, but now I know that's your pronunciation I shall ask you to repeat it every day.'

'Only if you promise to say *le prestidigitateur* back at me.' That was Cordelia's favourite French word, which she always enunciated with a flourish and extra 'r' rolls to make Elodie smile.

Romans-sur-Isère had special significance for Cordelia because, due to the area's tanning and leatherworking heritage, it was the historic capital of France's footwear production. She thrived on her solo trips because they gave her time to please herself, wandering round exploring alleyways, entering any open door to see what was behind it, and chatting to everyone she came across. She spotted a tourism poster publicising a village called Gervaliar and wondered why she knew the name, then remembered reading of the world-class sculptures in its small museum. *How thrilling, I'll visit tomorrow.*

Early the next day Cordelia strolled through the town centre so she could quietly appreciate the urban scape above eye-level and to sketch its architectural features. She ate breakfast in a café opposite a twelfth-century stone tower that reminded her of the Rapunzel fairy tale, after which she returned to the hotel to wait for her taxi. The driver, Matis, greeted her and then did not converse. She was relieved because she wanted to daydream and watch the countryside turn from green to purple as the taxi drove past countless fields of lavender. She was tempted to ask Matis to stop so she could pluck a flower and crush the spikes to release the aromatics. But she did not want to break the silence so she opened the window to breathe in the scent and closed her eyes.

Gervaliar was a tiny medieval village on a plateau, with a

defensive vantage point as it clung to the side of a cliff in a gravity defying manner. The museum, La Maison des Fleurs, was the former summer home of perfumier Madame de Verdier, whose fragrances had been worn by France's most glamorous women. She'd bequeathed the house and its contents to the commune as a gift to benefit the area and had left instructions for it to operate as a cultural centre for her art collection.

As the taxi stopped outside Cordelia said in French, 'Thank you Matis. I will call you when I am ready to go. If you have refreshments, please add them to my bill.'

Walking through the decorative gates she experienced a familiar thrill of anticipation. She had purposely done no research beforehand, so to be met by a grand neo-classical house inspired by Versailles's Petit Trianon made her happy. At the entrance she was welcomed by a dapper man in his early seventies modelling a purple rinse bouffant reminiscent of the raconteur Quentin Crisp. 'Hello, hello, our colour scheme matches today,' he cried, pointing to Cordelia's purple and pink houndstooth check tailored skirt suit then to his hair. Monsieur Fouché was a museum volunteer and local coiffeur, although some of the men referred to him as a coiffeuse. They were jealous of his friendship with the women of the village, who appreciated the quality of his gossip and his skill at teasing their locks into the equivalent of spun sugar.

I hope his first name is Touché. 'Well look at us two. I was drawn to this museum and now I know why – it was you.' Cordelia beamed as she spotted a large chestnut-brown dog snoozing in the sunshine. It was a barbet, a popular family pet because of its amiable, loyal nature. Unlike most barbets, which were shaggy, this one was neatly coiffed, the hair on his head plaited in side-buns so he resembled Princess Leia. It appeared that Monsieur Fouché doubled as a dog groomer.

Cordelia, always helpless in the presence of dogs cried, 'Who is this beauty?'

'This is TiTi my best friend. Say hello my love.'

The dog jumped up and nuzzled Monsieur Fouché's outstretched hand.

'TiTi you darling.' Cordelia stifled a laugh as she pictured Rex's reaction when she sent a photo of the dog with clues to guess its name. Ever since childhood they had been inordinately fond of words that sounded slightly vulgar. They regularly asked Elodie to say, 'yes' in French and as she did one of them would reply, 'Down the corridor, first on the left,' and chortle. She always pretended they were saying it for the first time, like an adult acting as if they are unaware the child is hiding beneath the table.

'Now, should I propose a route or do you want to do it freestyle?'

'Freestyle please. I am unaware of what treasures are here so it will be a revelation.'

'You are in for a treat so I shall let you encounter them for yourself.' Monsieur Fouché went back to his position by the front door.

Cordelia's eyes grew wide with astonishment to be met by the works of Antoine Bourdelle and Jean-Baptiste Carpeaux. 'Hallelujah, a female sculptor too', she muttered, examining a work by Marie-Anne Collot. There were several flower paintings on the walls, so she took a few photographs to send to Elodie. Around a corner, two entwined recumbent nudes in bronze had heads united in passion. She was unable to move as she contemplated Camille Claudel's proficiency in representing each element of her subjects' form so realistically. Then her silent reverence was interrupted by a man saying in English, with a pronounced Russian accent, 'It is a masterpiece. She specialised in figurative art. You should see her *Perseus and the Gorgon*.'

I have actually.

'She and Rodin had an affair. I am convinced she took some of his ideas,' he continued.

Yes, thanks Dickipedia. Cordelia internally rolled her eyes and scrutinised her interlocutor. Stocky, average height, short dirty blond hair, and dressed in what he considered to be Riviera chic (it wasn't) – cream trousers, white polo shirt bearing the crocodile logo, sweater tied to his shoulders, and deck shoes. She responded with, 'Camille Claudel's a marvel. I studied sculpture at art school and wrote a thesis on her work.'

He was not listening. Or he was choosing to ignore the comment to continue telling her what she already knew. 'Some of her work is autobiographical. She is renowned for its powerful representation of the human condition.'

Cordelia, marvelled at his gall at passing it off as his own knowledge – she'd just read those same words on the exhibit plaque.

'Is sculpture your speciality?' she asked.

'No, I am just a fan, but I doubt there is anyone more passionate about Camille Claudet,' he boasted, not realising he had pronounced Claudel's surname incorrectly.

Try me.

'Prince Dmitri Nikabolokov.' The man bowed and kissed her hand. 'Are you English? I go weak at the knees if I hear an English accent.'

He doesn't look very princey. 'Yes, I'm a born Londoner, but don't have an accent that identifies me as such.'

'Oh, the King's English?'

'Not quite, he speaks RP, received pronunciation, whereas I have a neutral cadence. I can do a good Lincolnshire though. 'ey up babby duck.'

'I am in love with you. Please tell me your name.'

'Lauren, how do you do?' She was having a Screen Goddess Veneration Day, outfitted as Lauren Bacall in *The Big Sleep*, a navy-blue beret worn jauntily over a tawny-blonde wig.

'If you do not join me for lunch I will die,' he implored, now on his knees.

'Thank you, I must decline as I have other plans. Do you want me to call an ambulance?'

Dmitri sighed in a way that convinced Cordelia he had done hundreds of times before when using the same line on other women.

'Are you leaving me alone with only these statues to talk to?'

'Yes, but they are very good company. So is Monsieur Fouché. Ask him to have lunch. Now I must go. Goodbye.'

Cordelia walked out, giggling at her encounter. The awful thing was that his technique probably worked sometimes.

Monsieur Fouché was standing in the entrance hall and knew by her rapturous expression that she was elated.

'Heaven. I want to live here. This is a short visit so I will return when I have more time. May I look in the garden before I leave?'

'Of course, TiTi will join you. He can sense your love for dogs so he is your friend.'

'What a privilege. TiTi, I am the human of a dog called Madam Blanche Wagstaff. You'd like her.'

He wagged his tail and followed Cordelia as she wandered around the sensory garden planted with gardenia, lily of the valley, jasmine, frangipani, and lilac, all varieties used by Madame de Verdier to create her perfumes. She rested for a while on a bench, tickling the dog under his chin as he sat looking adoringly into her eyes. 'Dearest TiTi, if only I could stay a while longer, but my taxi is waiting.'

As the car drove away she blew a kiss to the museum, thinking to herself, *Au revoir you totally unexpected delight. I'll be back.*

Chapter Eleven

'Darling! Are you still in Paris?' Cordelia said cheerfully to Elodie, who was video calling her.

'Yes, and look who I bumped into.' Elodie moved her phone to include Sandrine Rivera in the frame. 'Howdy laureate, how ya doing?'

'Good evening guru of the arts, I'm very well thank you,' Cordelia replied.

'I've had dinner and am a little tipsy so I'm probably being very indiscreet in saying what I did to Elodie and now I'll tell you too. What have you done to Valentina? I saw her recently at Basel Art Fair and mentioned you and the laureate accolade. She tutted and scowled and that gave a lot away cos she's notorious for being inscrutable and never voicing opinions.'

'I have the feeling she's envious of Worship being the LefDev representative, so that must be it.'

'I've known her for years and she's used to being the top woman dealer, so that's probably the reason. I wouldn't want to be on her bad side though.'

'Oh dear, are we talking horses' heads in beds?'

'No, but she is a spiteful character. The type who spreads damaging rumours that cannot be traced back to her. It's all to maintain her superior status. She keeps her enemies close and has a working relationship with them. Oh dear, I shouldn't have said anything. I hope you're not upset?'

'Not at all. I'd rather be aware so my defences are primed.'

'Good, I won't feel guilty then. Is that my cab? Yes. So lovely to see you both. We need to get together soon somewhere in artworld.

Mwah!'

After Sandrine's taxi had left Cordelia said to Elodie, 'To think I let Valkyrie become a HoT client. Cow.'

'She was frosty in Rome and I assumed that's because she was speaking English and not including emotion. We conversed in Italian at the Berlin Art Mart and she is more animated in her native language.'

'Maybe she's a Scorpio. All those negative traits. Or it is jealousy? And if so, why?'

'Because you are a high-profile creative woman and that is confirmed by the AILALIA recognition. You also have loving family and friends, which I doubt she does. And nobody is more personable or amusing. Valentina is none of those.'

'Bless you hon. I really don't care for her but try to hide it.'

'You conceal it well.'

'Phew. Surely she must sense my dislike. She makes me shudder.' Cordelia gave an exaggerated tremble. 'Anyway, enough of Valkyrie. When are you back in the Smoke?'

'Friday. I have a fitting with Algernon for my special gown.'

'I've just seen him. He didn't mention it. Mind you, we were busy gossiping.'

Algernon was one of Cordelia's art school pals. His given name was Andrew, but he did not consider that distinctive enough for a fashion designer so had changed it upon arriving in London to start student life. Now he had an eponymous couture house and an international clientele and, being originally from Newcastle, called everyone pet or hinny, which they found endearing.

'He's adorable and my dress will be stunning. Where were you tonight?'

'A new cabaret club in Soho for the first night of Effie's residency. Fabulous décor. All dark green, old gold, and candlelight. Made everyone look alluring, even the mingers, although that might have been the cocktails. We'll go sometime. Not sure if you've met Effie. She used to work at The Weasel during the day then appear in comedy clubs in the evenings. Writes and sings comic songs and accompanies herself with a harpsichord. Last year she won a TV talent show and is touring the country. Vulpy has booked her for a week at the Lair.'

The Minoan Lair, to use its full title, was a small theatre attached to The Weasel, and, typical of its nineteenth-century provenance, was a fantasy of red velvet drapery, gilt trims, and friezes of Greek mythological scenes. Leading music hall acts of the Victorian era had entertained there and today it hosted a miscellany of performers, including stars who normally sold out stadiums but occasionally chose to play in an intimate spot.

'She sounds fun. Can we get tickets?'

'If only I knew someone who can make that happen …'

The next day, as Cordelia was walking Blanche, she replayed Sandrine's comments in her head, particularly the part about Valentina being spiteful. Then she reflected on some incidents that had occurred at Worship, House of Tanner, and The Weasel over the past few months. Someone had thrown paint over the gallery's exterior and it had taken great efforts with a high-pressure washer to remove; tacks scattered outside had punctured Nike's rear tyre; and fly tippers had dumped an old fridge and bags of building waste in House of Tanner's colonnade. Environmental health officers had visited The Weasel in response to an unwarranted complaint, and terrible reviews had been posted on Trip Report. Fortunately, anyone reading the hundreds of glowing comments by erstwhile customers would realise the negative ones were prompted by malice. *Were they anything to do with Valkyrie?*

When she saw Rex later she mentioned Sandrine's revelation.

'Seems as if the *vacca inutile* is spitting fire at the mention of my name. Apparently she enjoys punishing people. Those recent annoyances affected the three businesses in which I'm involved. Could be a coincidence but I reckon she's behind it.'

'I'm glad I haven't met her. That one time I saw her in Berlin I sensed she was the type of person who'd nail someone's pet cat to the door.'

'It started after I was AILALIA-ed. What does your mathematical genius have to say in terms of probability?'

'My gut says it's her and my brain will no doubt concur. Should we erect lockable gates at the end of the street and have cameras installed for night-time viewing?'

She frowned. 'I hate gated communities and anywhere in the public realm that keeps people out unless there is a good reason.'

'We could trial them.'

Cordelia fiddled with a pencil as she mulled over the proposal. 'Yes, let's give them a go. Shall I develop a concept for pleasing as well as functional designs? Something reminiscent of the Gates of Paradise, like the ones in Florence cathedral. We'll need a blacksmith – are there any in the area?'

'Such a coinco, cos yesterday I read a profile in the *Guardian* about a young woman who recently finished an apprenticeship and has opened her own forge in Theydon Bois.'

'Is that how its pronounced? Boys? You should move there. I've always said bwa, as in French for wood, cos it's near Epping Forest.'

'Deffo not bwa. I hope it's not pronounced boyce but even if it is I'll still say boys.'

'You know how psychiatrists refer to "having their own couch" if they start a practice? Do blacksmiths get their own anvil?' she pondered, scribbling doodles of ornate gates on her notepad. 'Anyway, she sounds ace. Let's visit her, even though Theydon Bwaaaaa is the penultimate stop on the Central Line so we will be frozen by Londoner-born-terror at the certainty of falling down a chasm at the end of the civilised world if we go any further.'

'*Bonsoir les copains.*' Elodie climbed into the taxi and kissed Cordelia, Rex, and Oscar. 'Tonight we are the TanTonBeaus.'

'Such pleasing alliteration of the Ts,' Rex replied.

'And my sliver of surname being the filling of a Tanner and l'Archambeau sandwich is also pleasing,' Oscar said.

The four were on their way to the Imperial Theatre for the inaugural Karaokeverse, a singing competition conceived by Oscar as a belated 'welcome to the family' gift for Elodie, veteran karaokista. He was executive producer in collaboration with the International Singing in the Shower League. Audience tickets had sold out in minutes and the anticipation was frenzied. Ten amateur acts, representing themselves rather than their countries, had made it to the finals. The panel of judges was to select the winner for overall impression, stagecraft, and audience connection, the latter to be measured by a clap-o-meter.

I'm sure heaven could not look as glorious as this, Cordelia contemplated, as they arrived at the theatre, crossed the lavish foyer and walked up the monumental staircase to their box in the dress circle, where Bonheur was on ice. Everything about the theatre's grandiose Byzantine architecture was sumptuous. Extensive Carrara marble glowed with its celebrated luminosity, mosaics and gold leaf flame palmettes glittered. The vast proscenium arch was flanked by lion-drawn chariots driven by Roman charioteers sporting impressive six-packs.

Inside the auditorium the atmosphere was electric. Everyone in the crowd, almost exclusively members of the Royal Society of Pub

Singalongsters, and the Sisterhood of the Hairbrush Microphone, was noisily celebrating the staging of their passion in London's largest theatre.

The set was a simple painted backdrop of the Austrian Alps because, as every singer knows, the hills are alive with the sound of music. To open the show a live big band played an instrumental medley of the most popular karaoke songs, including 'I Will Survive' and 'Sweet Caroline', and the decibel level of the unsolicited singsong was ear-splitting. The host, Georgie Michaelson, beseeched the audience to listen instead of joining in so the judges could evaluate the upcoming acts. They ignored her plea. Thousands of voices added to the cacophony from the first act, a Czech Republic band *Duchové Na Stromĕ*, a name that translated roughly as ghosts on the tree, with a building-shaking rendition of 'Ace of Spades' complete with head banging and top-class air guitar solos.

'Why is it always a guitar that gets the air treatment? There's even an air guitar world championship,' Rex remarked as the band left the stage.

'Guitars have an effective publicity manager,' Oscar replied.

'I believe the triangle deserves to shine in the instrument miming sector. We need to give others a chance. I know, let's organise an air orchestra tournament.'

'I'm definitely a contender. What's this.' Oscar stretched his arms to look as if he was grasping an object to his chest, puckered his lips then blew.

'So easy, a tuba,' said Rex triumphantly.

'Close, it's a euphonium.'

'Cheeky tactics.'

'My turn.' Cordelia wiggled her fingers and moved her arms sideways back and forth.

'You want us to think it's a piano. That's a bit obvious so it's not. It's either an organ or a spinet.'

'You've got to be spinet to win it. What tune was I playing?'

'Hmm, would you do it again?'

She repeated the actions.

'Poulenc's *Organ Concerto*,' Elodie stated confidently.

'Not quite.'

The others made incorrect guesses.

'Wasn't it obvious with the ardent chords I played? It's "Chopsticks".'

'A virtuoso in our very midst.'

'*Chérie*, we should go backstage now,' Elodie said to Cordelia who was her stylist, boot designer, and dresser for the evening. 'I'm nervous and want to give the audience a performance they will enjoy.'

'Darling, it's a foregone conclusion you will enthral everyone. *Bon courage*.' Rex kissed her cheek.

They had no inkling of what Elodie was singing. All she disclosed was that the song belonged to a bejewelled diva beloved of both Cordelia and Rex, an entertainer like no other who put the ooh ma'am into glam. 'Diana Ross? RuPaul?' they speculated.

Back on stage Georgie said, 'That woke you up didn't it. Now, are you ready for a complete contrast?'

'Yesssssssssss.'

'Direct from Pitcairn Island, the world's most secluded inhabited outcrop, give a rousing welcome to The Christians.'

The audience applauded warmly as three middle-aged men took their places on the stage.

'Are they a religious group?' Rex asked Oscar.

'No, it's their surname. The most common one on the island. They're descendants of Fletcher Christian, who hid there in the company of other HMS Bounty mutineers.'

The men shifted nervously behind the standing microphones and one of them said, '*Whatawey ye* – that's a greeting in our dialect.

We're here to sing our unofficial anthem, but first let me introduce you to my neighbours.' He pointed to the video screen showing a couple of dozen people waving at the camera. 'We live on a spec of volcanic rock in the south Pacific and there aren't many of us Pitkerners so that's almost the entire population.' One of the others started strumming a guitar and they sang, 'We from Pitcairn Island'. They were modest in their stage presence, but the reception was enthusiastic, largely due to them having travelled so far and because their mash-up of Polynesia meets Country was a genre no one in the Imperial had ever heard.

Several acts later Rex looked at his notes. He was comparing the audience response as each finished and working out their odds of winning. His non-scientific analysis suggested *Duchové Na Stromě* was ahead.

'Who's been your fave so far?' Oscar enquired.

'The Beignet Boys were adorable, and their supporters back home deserve an award.' He meant the hundreds of raucous fans, well-oiled by Hurricane cocktails, dancing and singing in New Orleans' French Quarter as a squad of cheerleaders chanted the groups' initials. Then everyone scoffed the doughnutty delicacy after which the group was named. 'Puerto Rican Javier was sassy, and the way the Kazakhstan entrant sang "No Limit" was the epitome of shipboard entertainer. But where's Chocca Holic? Her name is in the programme.'

'The Bishop instructed her to withdraw cos he was anxious in case of negative reports in the tabloids looking to invent a scandal. They'd be relentless in destroying a man of the cloth whose secular hobby is a karaoke-singing drag queen.'

'Honestly, those rags are deplorable. You can just picture them in editorial conferences with their pallid faces, long yellow teeth, and vicious claws deciding which innocent person they are going to destroy. She's not hurting anyone nor breaking the law. What was she planning to sing?'

'"There Are Worse Things I Could Do" from Grease, which in the circumstances is most apt.'

Rex ceased his rant when Georgie said, 'I don't want this evening to end but now for our final routine please give it up for Doctor Elodie l'Archambeau of France!' Even before she finished the introduction there were screams of delight as many in the audience recognised Elodie from two years earlier when, as a gift for Rex, she'd hired the same venue and engaged the London Symphamonia orchestra as an opportunity for him to apply what he had learnt in conducting lessons. Back then, she'd performed a playlist of lounge classics. This time she'd chosen a movie theme and strolled on stage to the opening bars of 'Goldfinger', looking ravishing in Algernon's figure-hugging, ankle-length dress, dripping with ultra-rare red beryl crystals. On her feet she wore gold bugle beaded knee-length platform boots, the soles and heels fashioned of Bonheur corks.

The deafening welcome made it impossible to hear her backing track, the original orchestration minus Dame Shirley Bassey's vocals, so she paused for it to quieten and the music restarted. Elodie waited for her cue, the growly muted trumpet, then began to sing. To choose such a dramatic song so indelibly associated with one of the world's greatest entertainers was daring but she sang it her way and cast a spell. Cordelia had once described Elodie as being Puck from *A Midsummer Night's Dream*, sprinkling love potion wherever she went. That night at the Imperial Theatre she had extra potency, and everyone was enraptured. The exuberant cheers as she sustained the note at the song's crescendo made it obvious who the winner was. She bowed, smiled, waved, and left the spotlight to cries of 'Encore!'

Only the winner could give the encore, but Elodie did not have long to wait as the judges unanimously agreed she was the champion.

All the artistes were invited back on stage to receive a medal from chart-topper Millie, a popular young singer discovered busking in front of a betting shop in Belper. Elodie's prize was glory (priceless) and a trophy bearing the letter K carved of oak, a visual reference to the karaoke perennial 'Tie a Yellow Ribbon Round the Old Oak Tree', secured on a plinth fashioned in the shape of Mount Everest. Oscar, certain she would succeed, had arranged for her piano accordion to be backstage for the encore and he supplied the sound engineer with a selection of compositions she enjoyed playing.

'Now I understand why Oscar is a showman without peer, he thinks of everything,' Elodie declared when the producer asked her to choose another song. 'I'm going for an upbeat tune to match my elation.'

She returned to the stage, accordion strapped to her chest, and waited for the cheers and whistles to hush then sincerely thanked everyone for choosing her. As the pulsing beat of '(You Make Me Feel) Mighty Real' started playing and she sang the first line, the audience did as the lyrics directed and "were out there dancing on the floor". When she finished there was prolonged stamping of feet and demands for more, so the producer said yes to another song. Elodie decided to calm the atmosphere and quietly started to sing 'Dream a Little Dream of Me'. Everyone sat enthralled as if each word she sang was for them alone. At the end there was a collective sigh as she left the stage blowing kisses. Georgie came back on to say goodnight and safe travels, but the audience was shouting 'Ellodee, Ellodee', ignoring all pleas to vacate the theatre. Only after 'Elodie has left the building' boomed from the speakers did they file out, euphoric as only karaoke zealots can be.

Normally after a full house at the Imperial the local bars and restaurants were packed but that night they were inexplicably quiet. Staff, aimlessly standing around, said, 'Surely not everyone has already gone home?' and 'Have they been kidnapped?' A waitress sauntered down the street for a crafty cigarette and saw where the clientele was – outside the Symphony pub lining up for a selfie alongside the object of their karaoke crush. Elodie did not want to disappoint anyone and kept going until the queue had disappeared, refreshed by Cordelia bringing her glasses of beer.

Oscar had booked the entire pub and was hosting a celebration for everyone involved in the event. With his typical charm he was ebulliently thanking each member of the production and stage crew and congratulating all the participants.

Ayana, the Kazakh competitor who, as Rex had joked, was imminently starting a professional job as an entertainer on a cruise liner on the Caspian Sea, chatted up Oscar in a corner for so long he had to politely extricate himself. Across the room Rex was surrounded by all eight Beignet Boys, who were in hysterics as he related a tale of mistaken identity that had included himself, the Prince of Wales, a Pot Noodle, and an escaped Komodo dragon.

Cordelia was asking *Duchové Na Stromě* to help improve her air guitar technique, in case Oscar ever did stage an air orchestra contest, thinking it would be a transferable skill for the air double bass played pizzicato-style. When Elodie finally joined the party Cordelia and Rex hugged her tightly and told her the only other person who had ever performed 'Goldfinger' with such verve was Dame Shirley herself. Everybody was in a buoyant mood, socialising, swapping contact details, and eagerly discussing where the next contest was to be staged – London again or perhaps Las Vegas?

'I feel bad and hate to disappoint the other acts cos they are all so eager, however I've decided Karaokeverse was a one-off so then Elodie will be the champion for all time,' Oscar explained.

'Dearest Oscar, thank you, thank you,' Elodie said with tears in her eyes.

'Elodelightful, a worthy victor. Where will you display your trophy?' Rex asked.

Elodie pondered for a few moments, 'Somewhere that always makes me happy. It has to be The Weasel.'

'What an honour. I shall build a shrine for it in the Pleasure Gardens,' Oscar said.

'Move over Cecelia, there's a new patron saint in town, this one for aspiring karaoke wunderkinds. The Weasel is sure to become a pilgrimage site.' Cordelia genuflected and made the sign of the cross.

'Come here *mes chéris*.' Elodie gazed fondly at her family and pulled them towards her in a huddle of arms around shoulders, '*Je vous adore*.'

Chapter Twelve

A few days after Karaokeverse, Rex opened an email alert about Left To Their Own Devices. It wasn't the usual 'Call That Art?' in the letters page of a conservative newspaper or a glowing review by a culture writer, it was a throwaway line concerning a man called Daniel Tredd in the satirical, *Tuesday, Wednesday And Thursday* (a publication that skewered people in public life – the first initial of each word in the title signalled the magazine's editorial attitude). The alert read: 'Dimwit Danny Boy has proved what a dullard he is by being duped into paying an arm and a leg for a scribble that a blind howler monkey would do better.' The photo was a screenshot from Tredd's social media feed, which the magazine captioned, 'Left Your Commonsense At Home To Consider Paying That'.

Rex had never heard of Daniel Tredd and was horrified to learn that the former professional boxer was now an influential weaponeer of misogyny, enriched by a worldwide fandom of marginalised young men. He titled himself The Man, and his brand How The Ruler Rules. He produced videos and books that brainwashed his followers to despise women with directions such as: Consent Is A Con; You Own Them; and Don't Let Them Out Of The Kitchen.

Repellent, Rex thought and picked up his phone in disgust to send a text to Cordelia.

Free for a chat?

Not at the mo – with the design team. An hour yet. Weasel for a cuppa when I've finished?

Will you come to Hypatia? It's sensitive.

Yikes. Should I be worried?

No, just a blooming annoying LefDev development.

I'm coming now.

Within a minute she was on the sofa in Rex's office. He was glowering. 'I've upgraded blooming annoying to fee-oooming. Have you heard of Daniel Tredd?'

'No, who is he?'

'Have a look.' He showed her Tredd's Visuality account and a post of him smoking a fat cigar and wearing a satin dressing gown embellished with dragons. He was sitting in a black studded leather winged armchair in front of a canvas bearing the title *National Park*, depicting a pile of yellow sticks splashed in red paint. On the wall behind him were the mounted heads of a lion and a hippopotamus. The caption read: 'Only the wealthiest men can own one of these. #LeftToTheirOwnDevices.' In another post he cradled a rifle, motioned to the canvas and snarled, 'This cost me more than the entire GDP of the country where I shot that lion.'

Cordelia was aghast. 'Those poor animals will have been doped and unable to run away before he murdered them. And if that's how he stands, imagine how he walks. It'll be like an ape. Evolution was on holiday in his case. Bet he says chop-chop and capiche too.'

'It gets worse.'

He scrolled endless pictures of the unsmiling Tredd posing beside superfast cars and stopped at a cartoon of a man's booted foot on a woman's neck and the slogan, Teach Them The Rules, which linked to his latest book and video, *The Player Birthright*.

Cordelia shuddered. 'Nauseating. And worrisome that he's influencing youths to believe that masculinity means hating women. If only they'd revere men like you and Vulpy rather than that loathsome creature.'

'My inner armchair psychologist concludes that he has never had a girlfriend cos he's so awful and now he detests females and wants to punish womankind.'

'How dreadful being him. No joy, no laughter, no levity. No one to call him my love. No one fondly tweaking his chin or jiggling his nose. Vulpy loves it when I do that to him. If there was any justice he'd have been trampled by that hippo. I can't bear him taking LefDev's name in vain. We must shut him down. Ideally, we'd kill him. Unfortunately that's not an option, so what do we do?'

'I'm on it. We need a natter with Doctor Love. Where is she?'

'Toronto, doing some consultancy for the BATA Shoe Museum.'

'Let's arrange a call.'

That evening they were oohing as Elodie took them on a video tour of her hotel suite.

'That bed looks to be the size of Wales,' Cordelia observed. 'Have you checked to see if there is anyone else in there, cos you'd never know.'

'Yes, the population of Cardiff could easily fit and all have a good night's sleep.'

'We have some LefDev news,' Rex said, coming to the point.

They chose to shield Elodie from having to see Tredd's posts and instead outlined his pernicious influence peddling.

'What a grotesque man. How do we stop him? It will damage LefDev's standing to be associated with such an individual.'

'Exactly. And I'm really annoyed that our attempt to create forgery-proof art has failed. I don't like losing.'

'Someone is making big money, but they don't get the LefDev ethos cos if that pile of sticks is supposed to be ivory then the work would be called *An Elephant Never Forgets* as a statement against hunting. Tredd is too moronic to realise he's forked out for a dud,' Cordelia remarked.

'Whoever sold it to him is probably supplying others and our charities will receive nothing. That makes me unhappy.' Elodie frowned.

'He's risking it by being so mouthy, cos anyone can check the website to identify the current guardians, so they'll see his name's not on the list. That means he's either unaware of Worship being the only authorised dealer or, for the sake of boasting to his gullible fanbase, he's willing to chance being rumbled.'

'Should we talk to the lawyers as a start?' Elodie proposed.

'Yes, and if that doesn't work I have another scheme,' Rex disclosed.

'Ooh Rexicles, are we talking the dark arts?'

'Obligatory.'

'Dark arts, how mysterious. What are they?' Elodie asked.

'You don't want to know. It might change your opinion of me and that will never do.'

'One word She-She. Ruthless.' Cordelia nodded in agreement with herself.

'Rex is incapable of being ruthless. He's *ma colombe*.'

'Even doves can have an unexpected side,' Cordelia replied cryptically. She was having a flashback to a similar scenario when an infuriating character who'd called himself Melchizedek fraudulently claimed to be in partnership with Footloose, an ingenious wearable 3D holographic technology secretly developed by her and Rex several years previously. Footloose had given a person the appearance of being shod in incredible and improbable footwear, while underneath the holograms, unseen by others, they had on their comfy old trainers. The customer chose from a database of designs in a smartphone app, then digital data was sent to bracelets around the wearer's ankles and a hologram surrounded their feet. However, virtual footwear was contradictory to the luxury bespoke brand pillars of House of Tanner so they'd resolved to be clandestine in their Footloose association. Naively they had not anticipated its popularity and millions of people, spurred on by Melchizedek's Foot Freedom Liberation Front, downloaded Footloose, temporarily causing a meltdown in the shoe industry and associated businesses. His crusade was sustained by activists of the opinion that forcing one's feet into shoes was the equivalent of chickens being reared in tiny cages. They approved of holographic footwear as the solution and were avid supporters.

Melchizedek's insistence that Footloose had begged him to collaborate on a holographic version of the Jesus sandals he customarily wore had been a lie. When he'd refused to retract the assertion Rex had unleashed his formidable computer skills and seeded the internet with the truth about the cult leader – he was not the socialist eco-warrior who eschewed money and lived in a bender in the woods, as he maintained, but was a wastrel called Hugo Spencer-Lottway who lolled in a luxury home supported by his rich parents. Rex had prompted social media to do its worst, which it had with steely efficiency and when Spencer-Lottway's bogus existence had been exposed he'd abandoned his gullible supporters and scuttled away to oblivion. Now Daniel Tredd was making false declarations, Cordelia and Rex had a precedent for action.

The following day Rex instructed Worship's law firm, Jeffrey and Joffrey, to send a cease-and-desist order to Tredd advising him that as his artwork had not been acquired from the only official broker it was a forgery and he must stop claiming it as authentic. Several weeks passed and Tredd continued to post images crowing over his ownership of a Left To Their Own Devices. He did eventually reply to the letter but would not accept the canvas was an imitation and ranted nonsensically about 'a bunch of feminists who cannot bear that I'm rich enough to afford the art'. He also stated that he had millions of admirers who defended everything he did. It was a veiled threat and so Rex monitored Tredd's social channels and saw how he was bad-mouthing Worship and Jeffrey and Joffrey, and encouraging his disciples to do the same. They obliged their master with mostly juvenile insults verging on the illiterate and with a distinct lack of grammatical understanding, particularly in the use of possessive apostrophes. As neither Worship nor the law firm had social media accounts they did not have the intended effect and fizzled out, so the pile-on was little more than a handful-on. More worrisome was a couple of Tredd's more obsessed acolytes, who left death threats on the gallery's voicemail. These were referred to the police.

Right, he's asking for it. Rex bristled as he called Cordelia. 'Time to shred Tredd. We need to move quickly. Drinkie in The Weasel in an hour?'

'Ooh, plotting. Yes!'

Cordelia was first to arrive and petted Blanche's ears as she waited, singing 'Shaggy Waggy Wonder Dog of House of T' to the tune of 'Boogie Woogie Bugle Boy of Company B'. After Rex joined her they ordered drinks and sat in a quiet area of the garden.

'Men like him have no sense of humour and need to control everyone and every situation. They cannot bear people laughing at them. His absence of a funny bone is his weak spot. So that's what we'll do, make him a figure of mockery,' Rex said, revealing his plan.

'Approve. What do we need to do?'

'Are you still in touch with the freelance journalist who did that Observer magazine profile on you?'

'Mary Ball? Yes. I saw her at a party last month. What are you thinking?'

'Of giving her a world exclusive by "leaking" Worship's legal letter and telling her Tredd's claims to have a LefDev are lies. One of the tabloids will be interested. They exploit his notoriety as click bait and jump on any excuse to feature him. This is a big story. They'll be rats fighting in sacks to be the ones to report it. And yes, I am a total hypocrite to be encouraging the type of dirty work I usually deplore the rags for.'

'He deserves it. I'll ask her out for lunch.'

'I'll also drop a humiliation bomb on soshe and get it trending. If we make an example of him then it's a warning to anyone else claiming possession of an unauthorised LefDev.'

'Soshe is a growth hormone of hatred but it can be useful, so I'm a hypocrite too. If I had the inclination, I'd start a social media platform where people were funny, cheeky, and kind, but had a bit of edge. Cute animal photos yes, cute baby photos no.'

'You've just described your life, so you don't need a channel cos you're already living it.'

'Why haven't I been here before? Food of the goddesses, and the name alone deserves endless praise.' Cordelia gazed approvingly around Fish & Chip Off The Old Block restaurant near Marylebone station.

'I'm from a fishy family. Dad has a trawler out of Fleetwood, Mum is boss of a fishmongery, and my brother operates a late-night chippie in Blackpool. This is our flagship, run by my sister,' Mary Ball replied.

'Punnery in your DNA is beneficial if you're a journalist. What are you working on at the mo?'

'My latest is a piece on yarn bombers who creep out at night and try to beautify the towns voted ugliest in the land. They do things like attach knitted flowers to lamp posts and hang crocheted multicoloured dreamcatchers in bus shelters. They told me Slough was a hopeless case so they left eye masks in public places embroidered with the truism, Drink Ale, Beer Goggles Make Everything Look Better. I won't win a Pulitzer but it was fun to write. Nowadays, the number of clicks influences editorial decisions and believe it or not, that was a hugely popular story. The crafting community is vast. Anyway, enough of that, I'm dying to know why you called.'

'I have a scoop for you that will be click-massive.'

'Joy to a journo's ears – I've never had one.'

They stopped talking as the waiter brought their drinks and asked if they'd decided on what they wanted to eat.

'I have. Cordelia, anything taken your fancy?'

'How could I not choose the fish and chip tapas?'

'It's the bestselling item on the menu. I'll have the tapas too so should we go for the sharing platter? It has all the menu items in mini form, except for the mushy pea fritters which cannot be miniaturised so they come in standard size, which is as big as a giant's fist.'

'What a scrumptious sounding delicacy. Why can't they be small scale?'

'They're fiddly. Peas are formed into an orb to dunk in batter – the tricky bit is getting an even coating so it remains solid and does not break apart as it cooks. I was taught how to do it as a teenager. Took me a week to master the technique. It's like those Japanese chefs who train for years to prepare puffer fish and to extract the poison so their customers don't die. Feral peas floating on the fat won't kill anyone but they will make the fryer really annoyed cos they are difficult to remove. That's why so few places sell them.'

After the waiter left with their order Cordelia clarified the reason for the meet-up. Mary tutted and said, 'Urgh, hate everything Daniel Tredd stands for. I hope it's something that'll ruin him.'

'Yes, done right it might. It'll certainly make him a laughing stock and that will destroy his macho status.'

Cordelia detailed the lawyer's letter, Tredd's unreasonable attitude, and the aggressive threats to let his supporters loose.

Mary shook her head, 'Why am I not shocked at his hostility, that seems to be his default position. Dave Bringer, editor of the *Herald* will eat his own hand to splash this story. And the online edition is one of the world's most visited websites – huge in the USA. Plus, they have the digital radio and TV channel and a very active social media presence. This story will be everywhere.'

'That's what I'd hoped. It's yours if you want it. Someone will leak the lawyer's letter and if you need a Left To Their Own Devices comment I can arrange it. As long as your source remains confidential.'

'Of course. My lips are sealed. Some journalists have a code of ethics and I'm one of them. I'd do anything to help the sisterhood and if this story douses Tredd's malign influence, then I'll have an achievement to be proud of. Thank you for trusting me. Can I see the letter as soon as possible then I'll contact Dave and offer him the exclusive. If he declines, which is unlikely, there are dozens of others to consider.'

Mary Ball was right to assume the *Herald* would snap up the proposition and, given Daniel Tredd's widespread recognition, the paper and its parent media corporation went big. They splashed it for a Sunday edition as a world exclusive with the front-page headline 'Wrong In The Head Tredd Scammed For Multi Millions'.

Current event TV and radio shows discussed it and hundreds of online news outlets reported the story, pretending it was their original journalism. Within hours the story was everywhere. The *Herald* had contacted Tredd beforehand to give him right of reply but he'd told them to sod off, except he'd used a four-letter word that had the same sentiment, so the *Herald* led on that, in asterisks, for the Monday edition.

Social media did what social media does best and memes devised by Rex to ridicule Tredd went viral: Tredd claiming to own the Venus De Milo, but one bearing complete arms; Tredd wearing Tutankhamun's mask and the caption 'chilling in my home spa with a face mask on'; and an AI-generated image of Tredd dragging an intransigent ostrich on a lead and the speech bubble, 'Me and my pet Dodo'.

Each time anyone posted in Tredd's defence other users responded by lampooning his self-styled soubriquet, The Man, sharing cartoons of him painting a woman's nails in his guise as The Manicurist; wearing a white Ku Klux Klan head-covering as The Manhood; and a Photoshopped picture of him as The Mannequin in a department store window, dressed in a foofy ballgown and striking a pose.

All the relentless derision was highly damaging to the furious he-man personality cult Tredd had built. He craved attention and publicity on his own terms and people jeering at him was beyond his control. His relegation to buffoon status was celebrated by the media because he was even more valuable as click bait with countless people who despised his misogyny gorging on schadenfreude as they watched Tredd being served his just desserts.

The final factor that sealed his transition from humourless bully to caricature was the report that he was booked to appear in the Christmas pantomime of *Snow White and the Seven Fruits*. His role was The Mango, dressed in budgie smugglers and go-go dancing in a tree. Even though it was a tale concocted by Rex's Rumour Mill, it appeared everywhere online and was even reported by a trusted news organisation, which did stress it was not verified and that they were not commenting on the story but on how rapidly it was spreading. The absence of verification was not clear in the headline, 'Tredding The Boards?', so those who scanned news feeds and did not bother to read whole articles were convinced that, come Christmas, The Mango would be entertaining families in a church hall in Kidderminster.

But Rex was not finished with Tredd. Left To Their Own Devices had yet to comment, and comment it did, on a global stage. A video narrated by God in the form of a Public Service Announcement was projected onto Sydney Opera House, the Tower of London, l'Arc de Triomphe, and the Empire State Building. It showed visuals of a cartoon mango clumsily jiggling in front of the canvas Tredd claimed was by Left To Their Own Devices and the dialogue boomed a warning, 'How to ruin a reputation, spend millions on a counterfeit artwork and be unwise enough to flaunt it. Remember, unless you rent a Left To Their Own Devices from Worship Gallery, which Tredd did not, it *is* a fake. God sees everything, so Tredd carefully.'

Naturally, the video was played repeatedly by news outlets around the world and only hours later, T-shirts proclaiming the slogan 'God Sees Everything, So Tredd Carefully' were being flogged by entrepreneurial street hawkers.

'How amusing it would be if The Mango tried to sue God for slander,' Rex said to Cordelia during their daily business update.

'It wouldn't surprise me. He's like a livid bluebottle relentlessly thrashing against a closed window. And he's missing an opportunity, cos if he had any humour he'd start marketing God Sees Everything merch and exploit his notoriety.' Then she pondered for a moment and said, 'Hang on, why shouldn't LefDev do that and then donate the profits to women's rights organisations?'

'Brilliant notion. I'll source a womanufacturer. Now, what are his latest tirades?' Rex scrolled his phone for Tredd's Visuality page. 'Nothing new. I'm sure he can't bear it that his opponents are waiting to respond with lolz if he posts anything.' He continued to scroll. 'Oh look, he's removed the LefDev posts. We've won!'

Cordelia raised her arms in the air and swayed in *We Are The Champions* style.

'Implementing this project gave me a massive brain chemistry climax. Quite addictive,' Rex continued.

'It's had a bigger impact than I expected. Were we a bit harsh? My conscience is a bit raddled.'

'Well, we had no clue it'd blow up the way it did. We set it in motion and he destroyed himself by his bellicose reaction to our reasonable request to stop claiming to have a LefDev. And he did embolden his followers to make death threats. And one of them sent the photo of a gun to J and J. Plus, there's all the misogyny he has encouraged, normalising it for young men.'

'Good points, but we can't let on to She-She the degree of input we had in his downfall. She'd feel sorry for him and possibly hate us if she discovered her siblings are schemers. What if she wanted a divorce? Is that the terminology when it's a non-legal, verbal-only adoption? I can't bear the thought of us not being a family anymore, not playing our daft games, and feeling sad each time I saw a bottle of Bonheur. And who would get custody of Worship?'

'Don't! Too hideous to contemplate our tripletism reverting to twinage – no offence – so yes, hush-hush it will be then, between us two and no one else.'

Chapter Thirteen

'Oh, it's so sexy, all those sculptural shapes and that sensuous ornamentation,' Cordelia commented as she carefully scrutinised the façade of a mansion in Brussels.

'It makes me think of music. The repetitive patterns give it rhythm.' Elodie pointed to wrought-iron vine tendrils. 'That one is the swans' passage in *Le Carnaval des Animaux*.' Then she started humming the melody to Saint-Saëns' acclaimed composition.

'I see what you mean. From now on I shall think of music whenever I look at art nouveau.' Cordelia snapped some photos of the detailing, as she did wherever she went in order to create mood boards for inspiration. 'I adore this place. If I wasn't happy living in a platform boot on top of an Italian Renaissance Revival palace I'd want to live here, but only if I could transport it to London.'

'What do you hear with that one?' Elodie motioned to a tiled panel ornamented with curvaceous female forms.

'"Bohemian Rhapsody", especially the line on doing the fandango.'

'What *is* a fandango?'

'A Spanish and Portuguese courtship folk dance with lots of castanets and stamping of feet. In the Philippines it evolved into the pandanggo, much statelier. Females hold lit candles and balance one on their head. Just imagine if the hot wax leaked. Much worse than chewing gum in your hair.'

They were outside Lommel House, one of Brussels' art nouveau superstars, where dozens of people were standing around, gossiping or looking at their phones.

'What do you reckon she'll be after? Better not be the shoes,' Cordelia whispered, gesturing to a stylish woman in a flamboyant hat.

'She looks to me as if glittery jewellery boxes are her passion.'

'I've just realised this is the first auction we've been to since we first met. What a pleasing memory.'

'It is impossible to forget.' Elodie linked her arm with Cordelia's.

'How miserable if we hadn't met and then passed each other numerous times throughout life, unaware the best friend we never knew had gone by.' Cordelia squeezed Elodie's arm. 'Although what if we weren't sisters previously but we are sisters now in a parallel universe?'

They animatedly chit-chatted about how idyllic that parallel universe would be – no litter, no loud mobile phone conversations on public transport, and everyone would have good manners.

'I wonder what our professions are. I'd want to be a peace envoy uniting warring factions by making them join a choir. People who sing together do not fight,' Elodie said.

'You're all heart and I'm a beast in comparison because, as you know, I have dictatorial inclinations, so I'd be President of the World.'

'And of course you will rule by decree. What are you planning?'

'I'll start by sending all the tax evaders, nasties, and people who spit in the street to a remote island where there are no means of communication or escape so we'll never hear of them again.'

'Wouldn't you get bored of having absolute power?'

'I'd only do presidential things part-time.' She handed a catalogue to Elodie. 'Do you want to look at this?'

It was the inventory for an auction of the personal effects of Thilde Goossens, a legendary name in Belgium, founder of the eponymous Brussels department store. In the late nineteenth century, department stores represented freedom through consumerism because they were socially acceptable places for women to go alone, without a male chaperone. Miss Goossens recognised the importance of that and, in addition to frocks and furbelows, she provided services and activities so her customers could spend the whole day there if they desired. And they did desire. Goossens' became *the* destination, a luxurious home-from-home with restaurants, tea salons, and comfortable lounges. There was a lending library, musical recitals, and a packed schedule of educational talks. On the roof, outdoor entertainment included boards for playing *vogelpik* (Belgian darts) and a sand pit for *krulbollen*, the local variant of pétanque. Unknown to all but her trusted associates, Miss Goossens was a radical and within her store there was a secret clubhouse for *De Beweging*, which translated as The Movement. Courtesy of its status as a founding branch of the International League of Suffragists, *De Beweging* was active in the campaign for women's right to vote. Affiliation was by invitation only and came via a nod and a wink from existing members to female acquaintances who shared the same desire for equality. At lively meetings they smoked cigarettes, used language euphemistically referred to as 'ripe', and sipped cocktails in contravention of societal opinion that women who drank spirits were morally suspect.

'Thilde is a goddess,' Cordelia exclaimed upon learning the story. 'Why is the house being sold? This should be a museum to celebrate free thinkers.'

The reality was that since Thilde had never married and had no living descendants no one had an emotional link to her. Distant relations had leased out Lommel House as a residence for decades and were now selling it for conversion into a boutique hotel. Her possessions had no place in their plans and were to be sold, hence the auction that afternoon.

The queue started to move and Cordelia and Elodie shuffled into the lobby, excited to see Thilde's treasure house where her collection of Venetian glassware, decorative boxes, maiolica ceramics, and more were displayed. Cordelia was intent on buying a pair of her shoes and Elodie coveted a painting by Eva Gonzalès.

'*Chérie*, look here, it's by Leonardo.' Elodie pointed to a small, framed drawing of the Virgin. 'I believe it is a study for a painting.'

'Are you going to bid for it?'

'No, I do not feel it in my soul and that is an essential consideration in my decision to buy a piece.'

Cordelia thumbed the catalogue. 'You're right Doctor, it was a study for a work called *Virgin on the Rocks*. Sounds like a non-alcoholic cocktail.'

They spent a couple of hours admiring Miss Goossen's belongings and dodging the crowds, some of whom were there purely to ogle the spectacular building. Built as a dwelling in 1895, public access to Lommel House had been limited, so this was an occasion not to be missed.

'Wish we were here on our own to fully appreciate the interiors,' Cordelia said. 'All these peeps make it impossible.'

'If you buy the shoes and we psy-comm them after a big dose of chackalacka we might be lucky and end up here with Thilde. She'll show us round.'

'Even more reason to get them then. I feel quite confident cos I doubt many people will be interested. They only have value to obsessives like us.'

The organisers had underestimated how popular the preview would be and were forced to implement a one in, one out policy, even so, the place was congested. Winded from yet another elbow in the solar plexus Elodie said, 'Should we go for refreshments before the auction begins? One of my favourite Brussels spots is in this neighbourhood. If you think art nouveau is sexy, wait until you see where I'm taking you.'

No matter where Elodie travelled she always knew the notable places to eat and drink so, despite arriving at an unprepossessing slate-grey box-like structure, Cordelia had confidence in her recommendation.

'Prepare yourself for curves.' Elodie pushed open the swing door and suddenly they were in 1933. An oval room in muted marine-green was dominated by two chrome-girded central columns standing sentinel to a grand piano. 'Cole Porter played a taster of *Anything Goes* on it prior to its Broadway debut.'

'How perfect, *Anything Goes* was set on a ship and this resembles a cruise-liner. It is more than sexy, it's downright seductive.'

'This was popular as *une maison des rendez-vous d'amoureux* when it first opened. The booths against the perimeter wall were separated by wooden screens and provided a discrete location for a private romance.'

'Fabulous. There are no straight lines, even the bar is undulating. And look at that serpentine silver beer pump. This place is GatBat's stunningly gorgeous cousin.'

'I agree and now you can see a theme in my architectural aesthetic.'

'It's soignée and wildly sophisticated, like you.'

'What a lovely thing to say. Where do you want to sit?'

'Always a banquette, if only because the French pronunciation makes it sound a little bit hor hee hor.'

'I don't understand what that means but as its you it is bound to be amusing.'

They chose a booth opposite the bar and Cordelia picked up a menu.

'One thing I love about Belgium is a beer list as long as a bible and equally as heavy.' She turned the pages, looking intently at the listings. 'One of my all-time fave beers is Belgian. I'm checking to see if it's here.'

'Let me guess. Knowing you it will be distinctive and have a sense of place.'

'Impressed.'

'And it will be something not available everywhere.'

'Go on.'

'A sour taste?'

'You know me so well. It's a particular brand. Picture an aristocratic title and a French wine region.'

'La Marquise de Languedoc-Roussillon?'

'Not quite. I'll tell you. La Duchesse de Bourgogne – Red Flanders Ale. Once you're acquainted with her, you'll never forget. She has a hint of balsamic vinegar in sherbet form, which sounds bleurgh but is extraordinary. I regularly have dreams in which I am drinking it. And now I am full of joy because they have it here. Do you want to try one?'

They placed their order and two chalices containing the beer of Cordelia's dreams were placed in front of them.

'This is the one for people who say they do not drink beer cos they assume it's all bitter. It's also a bridge for wine and cider drinkers to cross into Beerlandia. Chin chin!' She sipped and sighed. 'Heaven.'

Elodie was an immediate fan. '*Délicieuse.* I shall always associate her with Streamline Moderne – and that is a very good thing.'

Just then a waiter approached them holding two glasses of rosé wine. 'These are from the man sitting at the bar.'

A highly tanned, stocky man was staring at them, so they nodded in thanks.

'I don't want to be an ingrate, but I can't stand rosé unless it is sparkling. He's bought us what he thinks we should be drinking not what we actually want to drink.' Cordelia studied their benefactor and said in disbelief, 'Oh crikey, I've met him before.'

It was Prince Dmitri Nikabolokov.

'I was dressed as Lauren Bacall in a houndstooth suit, wig, and coloured contacts, but even so, he might recognise me. He chatted me up at the La Maison des Fleurs and mansplained me about Camille Claudel, even though I told him I'd studied sculpture and she was the subject of my thesis. Then he said he'd die if I did not join him for lunch. I see he's still alive.'

Dmitri took their acknowledgement as a summons to join them. He swaggered over and said, '*Bon après-midi mesdames. Goedemiddag dames*,' unsure of their native tongue.

'Good afternoon,' they replied.

'Good afternoon lovely ladies. Prince Dmitri Nikabolokov at your service. Are you English? I go weak at the knees if I hear an English accent.'

Cordelia telepathed, *He said exactly the same thing to me last time. It's one of his lines.*

Dmitri peered at Cordelia. 'You remind me of someone. Have we already met?'

'I must have a doppelgänger,' Cordelia answered, attempting a higher pitch than her normal mellifluous tone.

'She had green eyes and yours are an even more extraordinary shade I want to gaze at all day and get lost in.'

Elodie changed the conversation. 'What are you doing in Brussels?'

'I was at Lommel House. I have a weakness for beautiful women so I followed you here.'

Stalker, Cordelia telepathed. *I wish he'd stop staring at me, but I'm intrigued that I have now seen him in two places, so I don't want him to go away. Not yet. If I speak I'll draw attention to myself so will you do the talking?*

'Are you an antiques collector, or a devotee of art nouveau?' Elodie said pleasantly.

'I am both. And more than anything I am an art dealer. In fact, I'm a mover and a shaker.'

'What type of art do you specialise in?'

Go on, give him your fascinated look. He'll be unable to resist, Cordelia telepathed.

Dmitri, already unable to resist, said boastfully, 'Masterpieces, Old Masters. Only the best.'

Elodie replied telepathically, *That's a vague answer. Anyone who really did trade in art would be more precise. I have a feeling about him and don't believe he's an expert.*

Elodie often had feelings and she never ignored them. She probed the depth of his expertise. 'What a privilege for you to be in the presence of great art. Do you represent any works we have heard of?'

He reeled off a list of paintings that almost anyone could name and then surprised them by saying, 'Have you heard of Left To Their Own Devices?'

'Of course, who hasn't.'

'I am responsible for their major sales to important collectors.'

Cordelia glanced at Elodie in alarm. *That's a shocker. We need to psy-comm him. I'll get another drink for us all so we can delve*, she telepathed, then went to the bar and returned with a glass of rosé and two more Duchesses.

'Thanks but I was drinking beer,' Dmitri said when she handed him the wine. 'Cheers anyw …' His telephone rang. 'That is mine, please excuse me.' He stood up and exited the room.

Quick, we should do his man-bag, Cordelia telepathed. They linked little fingers and concentrated. *Oh flippers, we don't have enough time. This is naughty of me, I'm going to look inside.* She unzipped it and pulled out a small frame. *What's this then?'*

It was a pencil drawing of a woman's head, eyes cast down, at a three-quarters angle to the viewer.

'*Sacrebleu*! It's Thilde's Leonardo,' Elodie exclaimed out loud.

'The dirty beggar has nicked it. Oh heck, he's coming.'

Cordelia hastily stuck the frame back into the bag. They smiled innocently at his return.

'Forgive me for ignoring you,' he said and sat down.

We need to know more about his LefDev claim. I don't want to miss the auction so let's invite him for dinner and we can discover more, Elodie telepathed.

Good suggestion. He's definitely dodgy but he makes me laugh with his clumsy playboy act. He'll be all excited cos he's scored a brace of babes.

Dmitri felt a shiver of desire as Elodie asked him to join them that evening. 'I cannot bear to leave you but reluctantly I must refuse your invitation because I have a flight booked,' he said plaintively, taking a mouthful of wine which Cordelia could tell he was not enjoying. She sipped her beer and telepathed. *Darn, we must arrange another meeting and uncover what's going on.*

Yes, but what will entice him to meet up again?

Us being us.

Unlike worldly Cordelia, Elodie never noticed when someone was hitting on her, despite it being a constant occurrence. She telepathed, *We could ask his advice on starting an art collection.*

Have you ever walked alongside the railings of Green Park at the weekend? There are dozens of inexpensive artworks for sale – mostly chocolate-box type prints that would not offend anyone's grandmother. That's a good place.

Then we can invite him to lunch afterwards and do the psy-comm.

We'll be near to Mayfair. Plenty of restaurants there and he'll feel at home cos it's full of international people who waft around the globe spending their laundered dosh. I'll pretend to be a palm reader so I have a reason to hold his hand. He'll like that.

Dmitri accepted enthusiastically. 'London is one of my favourite cities. And if it is the home of you two lovely ladies it is even more special.' He bowed and kissed their hands, satisfied he had wooed them.

Once he'd gone Cordelia said, 'Cor, he's keen. Let's ring Rexicles after the auction and give him the scoop on our Russian boyfriend.'

Elodie looked at her watch. 'It starts in 30 minutes. *On y va*, I have a painting of peonies waiting to be welcomed to Worship.'

Later that afternoon, following their successful bids, Cordelia stood with Elodie outside Lommel House and called Rex, who answered after a few rings. 'Bonj' and Gut'tag,' she said. 'We're in Brussels. Back tomorrow. We've met a geezer who's claiming to be a LefDev dealer.'

Rex frowned. 'Oh, is he. What was your response?'

Elodie moved her head into the frame. '*Bonjour ma colombe*. We arranged to meet him and will try to uncover what he is up to.'

'There's a chance he's lying cos he was trying to impress us, so I will be psy-comming the skin off Prince Dmitri Nikabolokov's hand. I also reckon he's telling porkies vis-à-vis being a prince. I know they are ten a penny in eastern Europe but he has no aristocratic airs. Perhaps his middle name is Dmitri and Prince is his first.'

'Well, as the ne plus ultra of regality with my very own monarchical moniker, I recognise authentic royalty when I see it.'

'Oh yes, soz your majesty, silly of me to forget. Will you come too and observe him from a distance to give a second opinion?'

Cordelia and Elodie were by the entrance of Green Park station to meet up with Dmitri. He arrived punctually. They greeted each other and talked pleasantries about the weather and how London sparkled under blue skies.

'What have you done?' Cordelia gestured to his hands, both bandaged. She was genuinely concerned because she did like him, even though he was a thief who spewed out eye-rolling chat-up lines.

'I tripped as I was boarding a yacht and now they are sprained,' Dmitri explained.

'Oh dear, I hope you are not in pain,' Elodie said.

'It is uncomfortable, and maybe I should not have come, but I did not want you to be disappointed because I know how important my art instruction is to you.'

Damn, if his hands are wrapped up I won't be able to pretend to read his palms when really I'm psy-comming them, Cordelia telepathed.

We need a change of strategy and I have an idea. If Rex causes a diversion it will give you the chance to examine one of his possessions.

Good thinking, I shall give him a quick ring. He's waiting in a caff nearby. You walk on with our princey pal. I'll catch you up.

She and Rex made a plan for him to sit at a table next to them at lunch and listen in, not making it apparent he knew who they were, and then to join the conversation. A few minutes later she rejoined them and they wandered down Piccadilly, past hundreds of works pinned on the railings. Dmitri kept stopping by paintings of bowls of fruit, misty Scottish Highlands, and clones of well-known Impressionists and expounded his opinion that the core of any collection should include still lives, countryside views (he had forgotten the word for landscape), and portraits by familiar artists. As they suspected, his art knowledge was basic, at the level of any generally cultured person, and he did not question Elodie's purchasing intentions. Was it to buy pieces that touched her heart, to build a collection for investment, or to acquire art for showing off to others, whether or not she liked it?

If I have to look at any more herds of horses running free on a sandy beach, I will have to sigh very loudly. Should we go for lunch? Cordelia telepathed, then, noticing a gap in the traffic, she cried, 'Come along Dmitri.' She grabbed his arm, Elodie the other one, and they dragged him across the road and up a lane that led to the Mayfair district of Shepherd's Market, a quiet pocket of London tucked away from the bustle. Laid out in the eighteenth century as a fashionable townhouse development, its narrow thoroughfares were now a mixture of residential and commerce. Cordelia had booked an informal restaurant so he could not assume it was a date.

'Dmitri, what do you want to drink?' Elodie asked as they settled into their seats on the patio and studied the menu. It had a limited and unimaginative selection of global brands.

'Go on, have a glass of rosé,' Cordelia teased.

He declined and plumped instead for a vodka and tonic. Cordelia and Elodie chose the bottled pilsner lager from the beer selection of one and asked for it to be served in wine glasses.

'We're posh birds doncha know,' Cordelia said, tongue in cheek. Once the drinks were served they asked Dmitri to describe his work. He started to brag, using references that made them even more certain he was role-playing being a broker. At that moment Rex was shown to his table. He acknowledged them politely and then browsed his menu.

'Dmitri, please remind us of your connection with Left To Their Own Devices,' Elodie said airily. 'We are intrigued.'

'As you know, it is the world's most exclusive art brand and I sell the works to people who know good art when they see it.'

'I hope you do not mind me interrupting but I cannot be silent,' Rex interjected. 'Left To Their Own Devices is utter garbage. Which sane person even considers acquiring such tat?'

This pre-arranged intervention worked. Dmitri became defensive and demonstrated aggressive territorial behaviour. He did not appreciate being challenged by such a good looking, well dressed, polished man while he was bragging to his harem.

'Well you obviously have no appreciation of art because the post-cubist-Dadaist-impressionist works painted by the Left To Their Own Devices artists are masterpieces. I'll tell you this for nothing, I earn so much in commission from my wealthy clients that I live in Monte.'

Rex stifled laughter. 'Monte Carlo, that pokey shanty town?'

This made Dmitri even more angry because Rex was making him

look silly. 'I make deals for major art works with major people,' he bristled. 'Van Gogh, Monet, Picasso.'

Other diners stared, disturbed by the hullabaloo and the restaurant manager came to check that the situation was not getting out of control. Rex placed his right hand over his heart and mouthed sorry to everyone on the patio. And all the while Dmitri was blowing his top Cordelia and Elodie were psy-comming his telephone.

Earlier that morning they had microdosed chacruhana and their consciousness and senses were so primed they were able to read his texts and see the recent calls log without the telephone being unlocked. Most were rather dull, the *running late*, and *get me some milk if you are going to the shop* type, but the ones sent to someone listed as T were more interesting. One discussed the delivery of a Leonardo da Vinci, and gave the date and time of a flight arrival.

That was the day we met him in Brussels. He must be on about the drawing he nicked from Thilde's. Who is this T person? Cordelia telepathed.

Would it be terrible to check the voicemails? Elodie wondered.

Well, as the saying goes, in for a penny in for a pound, we've already snooped without a warrant so let's go for it.

They managed to block the noise of Rex and Dmitri's argy-bargy and listened to the first of T's messages in their heads. Upon hearing the voice they had to stop themselves from reacting.

Bloody hell!

It was Valentina.

T for Tina.

She knew it was stolen. But why does she have it?

We need to say goodbye to Prince Dmitri NikaLeonardov and confer with Rexicles.

Yes, and we should keep him on our side, so he is unaware that we know.

Plan! Will you do the talking again? My high-pitched attempt to disguise my voice is not even convincing me.

'Dmitri, thank you for the art advice but we feel uncomfortable because of the argument and have to go now,' Elodie said.

He was chastened and scowled at Rex, who had spoiled the cosy date with his acolytes.

Rex gave them an apologetic look. 'I am *so* sorry, I hope you are not leaving on my account.'

'I'm afraid we are,' Cordelia squeaked. 'We were here to consult with Dmitri, not to be subjected to a public quarrel.'

'Please permit me to pay for your drinks. It's the least I can do to make up for ruining your meeting,' he replied smoothly, winking at Cordelia. The others did not see so she mouthed, 'Pub now.'

Cordelia turned to Elodie, 'Should we go hon?' They bade farewell to Dmitri and left.

Dmitri glowered at Rex for a few seconds then stood up and walked out in a huff.

Cordelia and Elodie disappeared into the warren of streets and when they were sure Dmitri had not followed them, Cordelia sent a text to Rex. *Come quickly, we have newssssss. Horse & Groom asap. I'll get 'em in.*

She stopped by an alleyway with its entrance blocked by a metal T-bar and asked Elodie, 'Can you guess what that bar is for?'

'Hmm. Probably not pole dancing. Is it to prevent something passing through?'

'Ooh, you're good. Carry on.'

'It's too narrow for a car.' She examined the buildings on either side. 'They are eighteenth century so that's prior to motorised vehicles. Is it to stop someone riding a horse in?'

'Is the right answer. This is why we are such detecting dynamos. Deductive reasoning, psy-comm, and Rexicles' brain power.' They high-fived their perfectly manicured hands and sauntered down the passageway to a tiny pub, originally built for the domestic staff from Mayfair's grand homes. Typical of its era, it had an understated interior of pared-down plain wood panelling, high-backed benches, and an open fire in winter.

Rex arrived a few minutes later, out of breath. He had dashed from the restaurant after apologising to each diner. The other two were standing at the bar and applauded as he entered. Cordelia handed him a pint of brown ale and they went to sit in a small side-room.

'Well, that kicked off didn't it? I was a bit worried he'd stand up and wallop me when I said Monte was a dump.' Rex sipped his beer and took a few crisps out of a bowl on the table.

'I would have come to your rescue *ma colombe*. Remember, I specialise in reconstructive surgery,' Elodie reassured him.

'Babe, you were brilliant. Very convincing.'

'I mentally auditioned a list of obnoxious men and decided to channel the winner. It had to be Porkin' Dorkin.'

'Method acting of the highest order.'

'It's the first time I've been in a macho altercation. Dmitri had a distinct "stay away from my women" vibe didn't he? You poor darlings, having to put up with that type of possessive attitude. Does it often happen?'

Cordelia gave a resigned look and nodded, then said, 'While Dmitri was scratching the ground in readiness to charge at you, me and She-She psy-commed his phone and you will never ever guess what we discovered.'

'He's a champion at Candy Crush Saga? Not really a prince? Cos according to my highly tuned instinct on aristos, he's most definitely not,' Rex replied.

'I'll give you a clue.' She ranted in Italian-inflected English. 'Signora Tanner, how dare you even consider being a woman and interloping on my realm. Doctor l'Archambeau, I don't mind you, it's your cocky friend I cannot stand.'

'What, he knows her?'

'Not only knows her, we reckon they are in league.'

'We listened to his voicemails without physically listening,' Elodie said excitedly, then realising that did not make sense, described how the chacruhana microdose had made it possible.

'Valkyrie said she had a buyer for the drawing. She must be aware it was filched,' Cordelia added.

'Unfortunately, we cannot prove it.' Elodie went quiet so the others debated whether Dmitri was truly selling phoney LefDev canvases until she interjected, 'I have a plan. Do you recall Valkyrie sold me a companion piece to my Glenora Richard's miniature? I shall ask her if she can source a specific painting, then we warn Globo Pol of our suspicion that someone might attempt to steal it.'

'Ooh, a sting!' Rex cried.

'I want to psy-comm Val, although I fear that spiky exoskeleton makes her immune to my skills. I need a psychic power drill to reach inside,' Cordelia sighed.

'I want to know what Dim-itri is up to with his LefDev claims. Could you bear to meet him again?' Rex asked.

Cordelia had on her ruminating face and did not answer immediately. 'I don't mind at all. You'll think I'm unhinged to like our little prince, but his silly swanking and inept flirting are quite endearing. Yes he's a light-fingered larcenist, nevertheless, I feel bad that we are setting him up.'

'If he's selling LefDev fakes then he needs to be stopped,' Rex said sternly.

'I am convinced he is not selling LefDevs, because he did not even know what genre they are,' Elodie opined. 'And not only that, I don't believe he's an art dealer at all. Did you notice which artists he mentioned? Such high-profile works are sold by prominent auction houses, not by small-time individuals.'

Cordelia leant back in her armchair as she pondered. 'Oh flipping heck, we forgot to do due diligence. I didn't check him out on the web, did you She-She?' Elodie shook her head, so Cordelia pulled out her phone and searched for Dmitri. 'No results. So, is that even his name?'

'Told you he wasn't a prince,' Rex said, rather pleased with himself.

'How apt that he is probably not who he claims to be and so he declares an interest in an undercover art brand that is also fooling the public. And not only that, he has been consorting with us – two people who occasionally use false names and IDs.' Elodie giggled.

'I doubt he's even Russian. He speaks fluent English and his cartoony accent is the Slavic equivalent of Inspector Clouseau. And all his texts were in English. Isn't that a bit suspish?'

'Please tell me he's really Gary from Gravesend, and just a low-level tea leaf.' Rex threw back his head and laughed.

'Why is he a tea leaf?' Elodie enquired.

'Cockney rhyming slang for "thief". It's a cryptic lingo. You don't have to be cockney to speak it, we're not. There's a lot of rhyming slang in vernacular English English,' he replied.

'You may have heard me use the term porkies. Pork pies = lies. And you might hear people being referred to as treacle. Treacle tart means sweetheart.' Cordelia placed her hands to her heart.

'I want to learn how to speak that way! I will combine it with French and start a whole new jargon. Will you coach me?' Elodie said.

'Absolutely. Now then, we didn't eat lunch.' Cordelia pointed to the chalkboard where the bar snacks were listed. 'Mmm, Scotch eggs. Anyone in the mood for a nibble?'

'Beware the English mustard,' Rex warned Elodie. 'It's so fiery it will lift your barnet right off your loaf.'

'Are they cockney words?' He nodded so she said, 'Let me guess what they mean. Anything connected to taste buds?'

'Indirectly, but it's actually Barnet Fair = hair, and loaf of bread = head.'

'How clever it is. We need our own covert language for Globo Pol projects.'

'Try Welsh, it's impenetrable. I use it for some of my online accounts and they send emails addressed to Dear Betws-Y-Coed or Dear Ynysybwl. It always makes me laugh,' Rex said.

'I like the notion of inventing our very own dialect. I shall work on this and report back.'

Cordelia ordered Scotch eggs and a round of drinks and they discussed whether or not Valentina was involved in a steal-to-order scheme or if the Goossens' Leonardo da Vinci was a one-off. They decided Cordelia should arrange Valentina's final shoe fitting and that Elodie should be there to ask about a painting in a particular museum. Rex, keen to ensure he never had to meet Valentina, said he intended to hide for the duration of her visit. 'I shall be snoozing in The Weasel garden, recharging my brain cells, so come and give me the goss once she's gone.'

Chapter Fourteen

Rex chuckled as he typed a text to Cordelia. *You'll never guess what's happened. In fact don't guess, get yourself to Hypatia toot sweet!*

Within a minute she knocked her knock – four swift taps to represent the syllables of the song title 'Mamma Mia' then threw open the door to his office and flung herself onto the sofa.

'Enlighten me, grey eminence.'

'This'll tinkle your tankles.'

He handed her a letter from the Turnaround Trophy director to inform Worship that Left To Their Own Devices was shortlisted for the prestigious contemporary art prize. The citation praised the collective's use of art as a campaigning tool to highlight important issues and its success in inspiring hard-to-reach demographics to appreciate art.

Cordelia looked dumbfounded. 'That's bonkers!' She read further, 'Did you see this bit in the terms and conditions that awardees must be at the ceremony?'

'Oh trossocks.'

'Perhaps they will let us represent the notoriously camera-shy LefDevs.'

'I'll ask the organisers. We must tell E. Where is she?'

'Reims, for a project with Bon-Bon.'

Elodie video called them the moment she received Rex's telephone emoji and several exclamation points. Her reaction was the same – disbelief and mirth.

'Let's create a special work to acknowledge the news. I'll be back in London tomorrow. Can you come to GatBat in the evening and we'll quickly do it?'

They accepted eagerly.

'Start thinking of a theme.'

'I've been reading a biography of J.M.W. Turner. Hard to accept now but at the start of his painting career his work was deemed to be controversial,' Cordelia explained. 'One critic commented that it was "the product of a diseased eye and a reckless hand", which is how the dreadful Pauline Westwich would describe LefDev.'

'She's a hater so that's a great accolade,' Rex remarked.

'What a perfect title for our next work. See you at 7pm,' said Elodie.

Diseased Eye and a Reckless Hand was an instant hit as a statement against bigotry. Its intense sharp and angular shapes were in a deep shade of red that Cordelia termed 'merciless' and believed should be the name of a Pantone colour. 'Who knew LefDevving could be such an effective channel for proclaiming our womanifesto on how life should be.'

'Propaganda,' shrieked the voices of commentators who chose unkindness over tolerance. They were furious that Worship welcomed school groups and accused the gallery of indoctrination. Elodie considered the visits an excellent initiative, so weekday mornings were dedicated to youngsters learning how to express themselves through art. Rex found a new role as an ambassador for mathematics by giving brief talks on the use of maths in art with linear perspective and symmetry. He taught his young audience a new word, fractals, and told them that even if they did not grasp the theory, they could see fractals in flowers, ferns, and snowflakes. Elodie supplied paper and coloured pencils for the children to draw an artwork that represented an issue for which they cared. Their choices included: *We Don't Have Pizza For School Lunch Often Enough*, made up of doodles that were meant to be broccoli, peas, and carrots and the words Healthy Food, Urgh; *It's Not Fair, Playtimes Are Too Short*, made up of stick figures and footballs; and *Danny Keeps Pulling My Hair In Class, Please Make Him Stop* and the face of a little girl with two plaits sprouting from her head.

Cordelia smiled as she examined the drawings. 'Future firebrands and politicians for sure.'

Following one visit the teacher asked her class to paint or draw the mysterious Left To Their Own Devices artists and sent the results to Worship. The depictions of angels, giraffes, and a dachshund-shaped balloon were so adorable that the TannerBeaus decided to clear an area of the gallery to display them at a later date.

'Hello. Did you run far?' Winnie, the Worship manager asked as Elodie arrived on the doorstep, panting. Even dressed in jogging gear and hair scraped back in a ponytail she still looked chic.

'Just from Fleet Street. I've returned from a long flight and need exercise. And now I'm here I feel better.'

She went inside, tilted her head, and sniffed the air. 'I recognise this aroma.'

'Awful isn't it. Some fella was here earlier wafting strong aftershave. He'd been smoking too and it clung to his clothes. That must be what you can smell. He was a bit annoying, very pushy and asked loads of questions about LefDev, including if the money really goes to charity. He was delving into you and Cordelia. I didn't say anything.'

Elodie felt anxious. Earlier that day she had noticed the same over-powering fragrance in the lobby of her home. Gâteau Bateau had a stellar reputation as one of the world's art deco masterpieces – particularly the lobby's gilt plaster reliefs, silvered pendant light fittings, and staircase with a chrome handrail in the form of a serpent. Design buffs clamoured to see it so Fabien, the housekeeper, had instructions to admit them for a brief look.

'You are so loyal. Many thanks for protecting us. I'm immensely grateful you are here, running the place with such care. I can speak for Cordelia and Rex too on that.' Elodie continued, 'You go early, I'll lock up.'

Winnie beamed and felt taller. 'I feel very special now, thank you. It's a blast working here. As for your offer for me to leave early, yes please. I have netball practice and I'm always rushing to get there on time. If you drop off the key at The Weasel I'll collect it tomorrow.'

Elodie secured the door and hung the heavy ecclesiastical key on the hook in the vestibule. Whenever she returned from a Rebâtir trip one of her first activities was to spend time alone with her art to transition from high intensity to serenity. She programmed choral music on the sound system, opened a cupboard in the storeroom and took out a thurible for burning frankincense, which she gently swung on its chain to spread the aromatic smoke. She slowly walked around the candlelit gallery, breathing deeply to relax her body, then sat in an armchair, closed her eyes and was so exhausted she slept to 7am, waking with a jolt, muscles aching. After a few stretches she went outside, squinting in the daylight, and locked up, hoping someone would be at The Weasel to take the key for Winnie. It was still closed but fortunately Cordelia was on Plumage Place with Blanche who bounded up, tail wagging in overdrive.

'Good morning adorable,' Elodie said, vigorously stroking the dog, and grinned as Cordelia approached, 'And good morning adorable. I spent the night among my art, although I didn't mean to.'

'Welcome home, hon. Do you fancy a cup of tea at the caff?'

'I badly need a shower so I'll say no. If you and Rex are free this evening come for supper at GatBat.' She did not want to mention her concern regarding the pungent man until she consulted her housekeeper to check if he had been at Gâteau Bateau.

'Most certainly will. How early do you want us?'

'Six o'clock for cocktails.'

Elodie showed Cordelia and Rex into her sitting room where generous curves triumphed over corners and two scalloped velvet love seats, one sapphire and the other emerald, dominated the space. She sluiced cognac over bitters-soaked sugar cubes in a line of three coupes, topped them up with champagne and added a twist of orange to each.

'*Santé*!'

They spent half an hour catching up then Elodie said, 'Veronique is on holiday so I've done the cooking. You are both so easy as you eat everything apart from baked beans and tinned spaghetti hoops.'

'I didn't know you were a cook,' Cordelia said admiringly as they went to the dining room. Neither she nor Rex had that inclination. Rex because his home was pristine and cooking caused fumes that overstayed their welcome; Cordelia because she lived in a shoe without a kitchen and considered life was too short to chop vegetables.

'The chef at Bonheur's Paris restaurant taught me when I was sixteen. And Veronique has worked with me for ages, so I've watched her. I focus on simple dishes and find it rather relaxing, but if you asked me to prepare multiple elements that need to be ready at the same time it would be different, and I would require tranquillisers.'

'I used to work in a takeaway breakfast kiosk and can confirm that a full English is one of the most stressful meals to assemble, especially when there is a queue of hungry, scowling builders,' Rex said, evoking his teenage Saturday job.

'I once tried to make bruschetta for friends. It didn't end well,' Cordelia confessed.

'How does crispy monkfish, capers, and asparagus, followed by crème de marrons vanillée sound?'

Her guests made enthusiastic noises in anticipation as Elodie served the meal.

'I'm such a capers devotee. How can a pickled flower bud be so flavourful?' Cordelia mused.

Rex waggled a spear of asparagus. 'Sparrow grass is my absolute favourite vegetable. As a child I felt quite rebellious scoffing it with fingers, despite that being the etiquette.'

'Do you recall how we used to eat bread and butter using a knife and fork and pretend that's what the Queen did?' Cordelia asked.

Elodie loved hearing her adopted siblings reminisce about their childhood. She tried to picture them as young versions of the people she knew now and the image that came to mind was two mischievous individuals who made every occasion fun. Nothing had changed.

When supper was finished she cleared the dishes and, as they drank coffee, said calmly, 'I have something to tell you.'

The other two were alarmed at her serious tone.

'We are being watched by someone who is investigating LefDev. Winnie told me he was at Worship asking questions. I smelled him here too. He wears strong aftershave and visited yesterday claiming to have an interest in the architecture, except he asked nothing of the design and instead interrogated Fabien, wanting to know if the LefDev studio was here, and how often you visit. I am pleased people want to see GatBat's beauty but resent someone prying.' She sighed.

'Stalky.' Rex shook his head and looked perturbed.

'Urgh. Who is he?' Cordelia said.

'You should be able to discover his identity. He lost a glove next door so you can psy-comm it.' Elodie was on such friendly terms with the people who worked in the neighbouring office that they let her park Nike in their loading bay. Earlier that day she had popped in to ask Solomon the security guard if anyone had been prying. He'd told her a fragrant man had wanted to know if large canvases ever went in and out and had offered a bribe (unsuccessfully) to check CCTV footage.

'Here it is.' Elodie passed a cheap black glove covered in bobbles to Cordelia.

'Nasty.' She held it at a distance, her nose screwed up. 'It hasn't been washed recently so it'll be infested by yuckerarmy. I'll psy-comm as quickly as I can.'

Elodie shuffled a pack of cards to play Blackjack with Rex. Cards were a shared passion and he hosted a monthly card salon, which she never missed if she was in town.

Suddenly Cordelia cried, 'We've met him! We were in Ant's reviewing our Women's Day plans and a bloke came and sat on our table. Spiky hair, loads of product. He listened in to our conversation and wanted to know who was behind LefDev. We left before he pried any further.'

'Oh, so that's why the aroma was familiar,' Elodie said.

'Did you psy-comm his name?' Rex asked.

'Yes, Terry Willerby. He's a tabloid journalist working on an exposé of LefDev,' Cordelia replied.

The TannerBeaus animatedly debated this development but knew there was no chance of him uncovering their identity because only the three of them knew the truth.

'He's been snooping here and at Worship, so I reckon he'll try Shoeseum and the pub too. I'll alert the staff to be on the smellout,' Cordelia said.

'What if he does?' Rex said.

'I'll ask them to call me and then walk in casually, see him, and say, "I remember you at the caff". I'll ask what his profession is and if he says he's a journo I'll propose an interview. He'll probably say yes so he can pump me on LefDev.'

'And what will you say?' Elodie asked.

'Haven't decided yet. Carry on with your cards and I'll take Blanche for a walk and mull it over.'

She returned twenty minutes later.

'How about this. We concoct some barmy story regarding the collective then I'll say Vance Dorkin knows them. In his TV report at Worship's launch party he claimed they were his pals and he's repeated it a few times since. Terry will go to him for a comment and ask who they are. The Dork will bluster as he always does and either have to confirm and make something up, or say no comment, which will show that he's been telling whoppers cos if he did really know he wouldn't be shy about showing off his association. The media is bound to be all over it. Hopefully they'll all accept his word and then Terry stops sneaking around us. Yes? No?'

The other two gave an emphatic yes.

'How delicious you've included the insufferable Dorkin in this wheeze. Let's dream up a ridiculous tale,' Rex said with a mischievous look.

'We need another drink to stimulate our imaginations. Bellini anyone?' said Elodie.

As Cordelia predicted, Terry Willerby was at The Weasel the following lunchtime, so she rushed from her studio to the pub. He was sitting at the bar sipping a pint of beer and trying to converse with the manager, who was purposely busying herself. Cordelia stood next to him, ordered a pot of Earl Grey, then said, 'Hello, didn't we meet at Bonatti's a few months ago? You said you were a fan of Left To Their Own Devices. Did you ever visit the exhibition?'

Terry greedily eyed her up. 'Alright mate? I did see it, yeah. Accessible. Sort of art I'd be good at. Wonder who they are.'

'As you can imagine I have made a pledge to keep the secret. You should ask Vance Dorkin, that fella off the telly, apparently he knows.'

'I'm a journalist so let's have a chat seeing as it's your gallery.'

'Why not. Do you want to do it there?'

Terry could not believe how straightforward it had been to inveigle himself in and was convinced it was his cheeky chappie persona, which in his opinion every woman found irresistible. They finished their drinks and strolled over to Worship. Well, Cordelia strolled, but Terry's cock-of-the-walk attitude made his gait more of a bounce.

'Can I get you anything?' Cordelia asked as they sat down in the café bar.

Terry declined, saying he wanted to focus on the interview. 'I'm going to record it. Saves me doing shorthand, although I still use it sometimes. I'm old-school. Learned as a cub-reporter. Those were the days. Started at the *Hornchurch Telegraph* in 'atches, matches, 'n despatches, then moved on to local crime reporting. Fancied myself as a bit of a gumshoe.'

'Who are you working for now?'

'*Daily Letter*. Few million circulation. More when you add the online version. This'll be good publicity for you. Might get some clients. You can call me Mr Business Development Manager, hahaha.' He leant back in his chair, feeling he was impressing her.

Cordelia tried, and failed, not to shudder. The *Daily Letter* was a scurrilous down-market rag, notorious for hounding people and passing judgements on lifestyles of which it did not approve.

Terry switched on his recorder and asked typical tabloid questions about her age, what her husband did, how many children she had, and how much money she was worth. But she refused to address personal or financial subjects. Then he wanted to know how the collective chose the themes, where they were based and their identity, all of which she ignored. He was not getting very far.

They'll make it up regardless, she supposed and stood up. 'Come this way, I have something to show you.' She led him to the Left To Their Own Devices precinct where a corner of the room had bare walls. 'We have a new show on the way. Small pieces, no larger than A4. We're finalising it with Blessed St Jude Primar …' then stopped, a vexed expression on her face. 'Gosh, I shouldn't have said that. Forget I did.'

Terry realised she had mistakenly made an important disclosure and his expression switched to that of a child who discovers that everything they touch transforms to chocolate. 'No need to fret. We're mates. You can trust me,' he assured her insincerely.

'Sorry, I need to finish now. I've said more than I should. Please don't report what I mentioned. Thank you for your interest, goodbye.' Cordelia shook his hand and went back to House of Tanner. *That was easy. Now I need to call Mrs Blenkinsopp and warn her he'll be in touch.* Earlier that morning Cordelia had spoken to the headteacher of Blessed St Jude Primary School to confirm the artworks produced by Year 4 were going to be displayed and that the media would want to know more. 'They can be insistent and may well make incorrect assumptions.'

'Don't worry, I can handle them,' Mrs Blenkinsopp replied. 'I have experience with school inspectors – that's equipped me for all eventualities. And because of my Brummie accent, people are always making wrong assumptions. I'm used to it.'

That evening Cordelia was on a video call, updating the other two on Terry Willerby. 'He's in a hurry. Perhaps the Daily Cat Litter wants this story to coincide with the Turnaround event.'

'Show us your "oops, I shouldn't have said that" face again', Rex begged. Cordelia had already re-enacted the scene twice but he found it hilarious.

Clayton Dandridge, the same Dandridge who owned the imitation Tintoretto's from Phyllida Rivington's early days in art authentication, had acquired the *Daily Letter* to join his extensive media holdings in Britain, which included the broadcaster of *It's Breakfast*. He had extended Vance Dorkin's contract and was looking for more opportunities for the loud-mouthed populist, who guaranteed audiences and clicks. Dandridge had grilled the *Daily Letter* editor on big upcoming stories and after learning that Willerby was hoping to expose Left To Their Own Devices he'd said, in his brusque newspaper baron way, 'Give it to Dorkin. He'll get the by-line. Hold it until I tell you to go.'

A few days after Cordelia's encounter with Terry Willerby, the TannerBeaus were walking in Myrtle Park with Blanche.

'Can I say something important *mes chéris*?' The others gazed at her in dismay. They did not want anything grave interrupting their happy-go-lucky life together.

'LefDev has been such fun, and our charities greatly benefit, but I did not like the sneaky journalist investigating us. We started it as a joke and we have achieved what we intended. Is it time to stop now?'

Cordelia and Rex were relieved. They'd been feeling similar sentiments.

'It's been on my mind for a while.'

'Too stressful to keep up the pretence.'

Rex picked up a stick and threw it for Blanche. 'Just think, we are soon to be the Art Collective Formerly Known as LefDev. How shall we announce it?'

'Do we need to go to that pub on the other side of the park and refresh our decision-making skills?' Elodie suggested.

'We certainly do. It'll be quicker to row across the lake than walk around it, so let's float,' Cordelia proposed.

'Yes, but I can't possibly exert myself, you'll have to do the work,' Rex advised them with a sorry-not-sorry expression.

'He was the same growing up. If we went skating he'd hold on to my jumper and I'd have to pull him along,' Cordelia explained.

'Tis true, but you see, my vitality is so much better employed on all the complicated brain work I undertake.'

'Do we need to provide a sedan chair next time we go out *ma colombe*?'

All the rowboats were booked so they hired a pedalo. Blanche jumped on board and Rex joined her on the rear bench. Cordelia and Elodie had to sit up front and pedal hard as he waved regally to any and every one watching.

'Will you have enough energy to walk to the bar Tyranno?' Cordelia said as they approached the jetty of the Swan and Her Cygnets. 'Oh look, grab that table so we can sit there and keep an eye on our luxury cruiser.'

Rex and Elodie went to order the drinks and came back with beer, nuts, and Twiglets to fuel them as they quietly deliberated on how to proceed. They decided that if Left To Their Own Devices won the Turnaround Trophy, they would make a valedictory speech at the awards ceremony. If it did not win, they would release a statement of farewell afterwards. All three admitted they were glad to say goodbye to the collective, that it had been a hoot, but the time was right.

'Welcome to Regent's Park and the Turnaround Trophy red carpet. It's a starry night of A-listers and the question on everyone's lips is "Will the Left To Their Own Devices collective be here so the world can finally see who they are?"' Letitia Falderole, ubiquitous presenter of outside broadcasts, was recording a package about the event for the ten o-clock news. Vance Dorkin walked by, looking even more smug than usual, then doubled back as he saw Letitia and sidled up, assuming he would be interviewed. He was on a high, due to his exclusive being splashed on the front page of tomorrow's *Daily Letter* and he would be live streaming from the event to unveil the identity of the collective. She saw him coming and quickly moved towards Jupiter (not his real name), the previous year's winner, to ask his opinion on the shortlisted artists. She was not avoiding Dorkin because he worked for a competitor, but because he was a complete twit.

Suddenly lights started flashing and camera shutters clunking as the photographers spotted the TannerBeaus, looking more fabulous than all the other attendees combined. Cordelia's status as the AILALIA laureate and co-owner of Worship made her a big draw. Shouts of, 'Who are you wearing?' were answered with, 'Algernon Couture and Algernon for Footloose.' She was resplendent in a calf-length purple silk taffeta opera cape, ornamented on the back with an elaborate sunburst pattern of golden crystals, which meant she had to turn away from the cameras to show off its splendour. This obliged her to give the 'peek over the shoulder' only a few could perform confidently, knowing that every photograph would be flattering. Then she pointed to Algernon's holographic Footloose design – high-heeled Roman sandals, straps embellished with golden zodiac medallions that wrapped around her legs and right up to her thighs.

As one of the event's sponsors, Sandrine Rivera was already at the drinks' reception to welcome her guests and was looking out for the arrival of the TannerBeaus. She relished their company and found them amusing and genuine, which could not be said of everyone with whom she hobnobbed.

'There you are – surely the most eye-catching trio in the place,' she said, admiring their wardrobe. It was not only Cordelia who looked swell. Rex was adorable in a pink jacquard velvet slim-fit tuxedo and Elodie dazzled in vintage Chanel, a floor-length cerise crêpe de-chine sleeveless sheath with trailing train. 'So pleased you were able to join us on the Art Is Life table. Will the collective make an appearance tonight, I wonder?'

They smiled beatifically and did not answer.

Rex said, 'Sandrine, thanks so much for inviting me. I hope you do not think me rude but I need to leave temporarily and may be delayed in rejoining the party.'

'It's hush hush for you know what,' Cordelia explained, tapping a finger against her nose.

'How intriguing. Now I want to know everything, but I'll resist the urge to cross-examine you.'

Elodie spotted someone she knew and crossed the room then, noticing Valentina was there, telepathed to Cordelia, *Prepare yourself, Valkyrie's heading your way.*

Urgh, I'd prefer not to talk but I need to see her for a fitting. Is the backing band in tow?

Valentina, guards in her wake, came by and said, 'Good evening Signora Tanner. What an achievement for your client, and you being so new to the industry too.'

She said with the sincerity of a hyena apologising for stripping clean a wildebeest carcass. 'Good evening. Thank you. The competition is stiff and even if Left To Their Own Devices does not win, they are honoured to be shortlisted,' Cordelia answered.

'Yes, they should be honoured and you should be too.'

So self-righteous. Can't stand her.

'I will be seeing you next week. Your shoes are looking fabulous.'

Sandrine saw them speaking and came over to rescue Cordelia. 'Valentina, we must talk about the Chinese art market now you are the go-to broker. I'd like to feature you for the magazine.'

'A cover profile will acknowledge the importance of China,' she replied, making it apparent it was the cover or nothing.

Cordelia took the opportunity to escape and joined Elodie, who was now conversing with a graffiti artist wearing a wolf mask. When there was a break in the conversation she telepathed, *Valkyrie has confirmed for next Thursday in the morning. Sorry, I should have checked first – can you make it?*

I am supposed to be writing a paper for a medical journal that day but I'd rather be sleuthing, so yes, I'll definitely be there.

Just then a gong signalled it was time to move into the main event space. The crowd ignored it because the networking was so good until the sound grew so frenetic they eventually filtered into a vast Spiegeltent, its baroque interior of intricately carved pillars, stained glass, and cut mirrors adding to the carnival atmosphere.

The focus of the room was a central display of work by the three shortlisted artists: Left To Their Own Devices' *Diseased Eye and a Reckless Hand*; Dimpy Fanshawe's *Superstitious*, a multicoloured glass ladder underneath which a real black cat was snoozing; and Maxwell Fulbright's *Slippy Sticky Dichotomy*, a huge banana skin sculpture made of chewed gum.

Rex discreetly slipped in and sat down at the Art Is Life table, nodding and mouthing 'all good' to the other two, before introducing himself to those on either side. The table was a who's who of art, but all anyone wanted to discuss was Left To Their Own Devices. The TannerBeaus tried without success to change the subject.

Once dinner was over the host quietened the crowd and introduced Jupiter, who was going to announce the result. Vance Dorkin, standing at the back, ready to go live, was feeling even more like the King of the World than he normally did, convinced his exclusive would win him an investigative journalism prize, ignoring the fact it was all Terry Willerby's work.

Jupiter asked the audience to watch a short film featuring recent works by the nominees, after which he opened the envelope and said, 'As soon as I reveal the winner I will be a has-been, so maybe I won't …' and pretended to walk away. Everyone laughed and then he read the card, 'This year's Turnaround Trophy goes to … Left To Their Own Devices!' Whoops and hollers resounded throughout the tent. Everyone was surprised by a group of Blessed St Jude Primary School pupils who assembled on the stage, plastic bottles attached to their uniforms. One held a stuffed gull with a six-pack plastic ring around its neck, and a tiny girl brandished a placard bearing the slogan 'Stop Polluting Our Water With Plastic'. The crowd cheered and Vance, self-importance oozing from every pore, started to speak to camera. 'Me and Left To Their Own Devices have been good friends ever since the collective was formed but I kept to myself the truth of who they are in order to play their little game. Now in a world exclusive I can finally tell you that the works were done by a group of kids at Blessed St Jude Primary School in east London. You heard it here first and you can read all about it in tomorrow's *Daily Letter*. Remember folks, it's my world exclusive.' The words had barely escaped his mouth when a child wheeled a frame onstage from which hung a green curtain. The curtain swished aside and out stepped Bertie, dressed in a teal-coloured tailcoat, hair slicked back. 'Good evening. The Wizard of Osbert in front of your very eyes.' He soft shoe shuffled up to the children, shook their hands, gave Jupiter a double cheek kiss, and turned to the audience.

'On behalf of Left To Their Own Devices, extravagant thanks for this magnificent recognition. And thank you to Blessed St Jude

Primary School for creating the fantastic art for the next exhibition at Worship. I wholeheartedly recommend you see it. And in case anyone was thinking that these youngsters *are* Left To Their Own Devices, they are *not*, despite what the media might assert.' Bertie's revelation penetrated Vance's eardrums with the force of a sledgehammer. It was too late to pulp the millions of printed newspapers with his false claims screaming from the front page. Public humiliation loomed. Miranda Jenkall, his *It's Breakfast* co-presenter who'd endured his arrogance, would now look at him with a "total loser" expression, although being such a narcissist he was unaware that was already her default position. Clayton Dandridge, not known for his delicacy in employee communications, was bound to be thunderstruck and demand reparations. It was a disaster.

Bertie struggled to be heard above the hubbub, but the place quietened after the children ran through the tent, fingers on lips, hushing the crowd. He continued, 'Left To Their Own Devices asked me to articulate that this accolade is the greatest thing they have ever experienced. However, the collective now intends to disband and their identity will forever remain a mystery, just like Shakespeare's Dark Lady.'

Vance was too angry with Terry Willerby to continue his live stream and to declare a real world exclusive about what Bertie had divulged. It was too late in any case because Mary Ball, tipped off by Cordelia, was in the newsroom of the *Herald* at that moment, holding up tomorrow's front page, bearing the headline, 'Left To Their Own Devices – Dramatic Farewell'.

Cordelia's phone buzzed and she saw a photograph of Mary with her thumbs up and the words, *I owe you big time.*

Mushy pea fritters for life? Cordelia replied.

And the afterlife.

Next day, the TannerBeaus met at Worship to discuss how to conclude the Left To Their Own Devices project. They decided that when the canvases were returned after their loan periods were over, a selection would be exhibited at the gallery to maintain curiosity. The pieces were never to be sold, which made them the definition of priceless.

'I'll miss Saturday afternoons at GatBat working on our magnum opuses,' Rex sighed. 'I still believe *Full English Breakfast* was my best.'

'I'll miss all the hurly-burly of running the world's most undeservingly glorified art brand,' Cordelia replied ruefully.

'We were exceptional at hyping it, so let's use our skills and your laureate status on another project,' Elodie proposed.

'I sense a plan brewing,' Rex said.

'You know me well,' Elodie responded. 'Worship now has a high-profile reputation as a contemporary art dealer. Why don't we take advantage and convert this area into a space for new artists and give them a chance for recognition?'

'Top idea. We can make it a place to discover emerging talent and have an annual show,' Cordelia suggested.

'Futurarta would be a good name,' Rex replied.

'Can we continue the school visits and keep a corner of the gallery for the children's delightful artworks?' Elodie asked.

'Botticelli!'

They were excited about the new plans but decided to have a rest from being art moguls. Then, once refreshed, they could revisit it. Each had other responsibilities, not least Cordelia who was completing the designs for House of Tanner's new season collection.

But first, there was unfinished business with Valentina.

Chapter Fifteen

On the morning of Valentina's shoe fitting Cordelia was sitting by Elodie in the lobby of House of Tanner waiting for her nemesis to arrive.

'I'm relieved you'll be there too. Don't you think she's very "stick pins in a voodoo doll" towards me?'

A vehicle drew up and bodyguards climbed out and checked the street was safe before their client alighted.

'Plumage Place, that notorious no-go area,' Cordelia murmured, rolling her eyes as the party entered the building.

'Valentina, welcome.'

'*Buongiorno* Signora Tanner.' She saw Elodie and gave the hint of a smile.

'I hope you do not mind if I join you,' Elodie said. 'I am keen to understand all aspects of bespoke footwear. I also have a private request to make.'

'Of course. It is always a pleasure to see you Doctor l'Archambeau.'

You'll be on her Christmas card list if you're not careful, Cordelia telepathed.

In that case we need to cancel Christmas, Elodie replied.

Cordelia led the way up the stairs, with Elodie making small talk and the bodyguards huffing and puffing behind them. All that bulk they carried was not conducive to exertion.

'Can I get you anything to drink?' Cordelia asked as she opened the door to the Boudoir of Pulchritude. 'We have decaffeinated espresso especially for you.'

'That is considerate. Yes, coffee for all of us,' Valentina said.

'As you may recall, the room is small so I hope your guards will be comfortable standing outside. It will not be for long. Now, if you wait in here I will initiate the most important task and ask my assistant to bring coffee, and what was that other thing … oh yes, and find your shoes.' She laughed, Valentina did not.

When she returned Elodie said, 'Coeurdelia, I asked Valentina to keep her eyes open for a painting I am keen on by Johanna Herolt-Graff. It is currently owned by La Maison des Fleurs. I dream it will one day be available for purchase. Here's a photo.'

Cordelia looked at it and said, 'How lovely,' then pulled from her pocket a pair of latex gloves, tweaked the fingers and let them bounce back with a noisy snap. She placed the shoes on Valentina's feet, who warmed up slightly at the sight of the black suede stilettos, decorated on the vamp with narrow orange and white patent strips to represent the colouring of a male Long-Tailed Widowbird.

'*Sono graziose. La ringrazio,*' she said amiably.

She's more dynamic in Italian. Perhaps she only dislikes you in English, Elodie telepathed.

You always see the best in everyone but I'm afraid I must disagree. She dislikes me in all languages and is having a temporary malfunction cos the shoes are gorgeous. I expect she'll be back to bee-atch in no time, Cordelia answered.

She was right and Valentina's abrupt attitude resumed. 'Contact my secretary to advise when they are finished.' She turned to Elodie and said, '*Cara dottoressa l'Archambeau, la contatterò riguardo a quel dipinto alla Maison des Fleurs.*'

Elodie telepathed a rough translation, *She dear doctored me and said she'll be in contact regarding the painting.*

Cordelia was relieved as the Italians swept from the building. 'Tranquillity returns and now I need to stroke Blanche, kiss her smiling face, and take her for a walk. Want to join me and afterwards we'll call Globo Pol?'

They ambled along to the park and sat on a bench chatting about what they would say to Manon and how to justify the set-up in the absence of any proof that Valentina was involved in the Leonardo da Vinci theft. Was it a coincidence that someone located in Rome, who sounded similar, had left a message on Dmitri's voicemail? They pondered why she would risk her elevated position in the art world for the sake of a drawing that, although prestigious, was hardly a rarity.

'We are doubting ourselves. Valkyrie's voice was immediately recognisable,' Elodie reminded her.

'You're right and WoManon trusts our instinct.' Cordelia paused, then said, 'But it is a major accusation to make and what if she's not up to any criminality?'

Neither was normally dithery but the seriousness of what they planned to do unnerved them.

Cordelia stood up, scanned the park for Blanche and called her to come then swung round. 'Ignore that last comment. Remember I told you of Blanche's response to Valkyrie when Oscar hosted a dinner? Miss Wagstaff is an infallible judge of character. Valentina's definitely a wrong 'un. Come on, let's go back to HoT and call WoManon.'

Manon was very interested to hear of Dmitri and Valentina's possible involvement and how they suspected she might arrange a theft from La Maison des Fleurs. 'Globo Pol will need to act quickly. Leave it with me.'

After the call ended Cordelia said, 'It's like having our very own police force.'

Elodie looked concerned. 'Have we solicited Valentina to commit a crime?'

'I'm not sure. Your wording was careful. You told her where the painting is, that you're a fan of the artist, and that you dreamt of it becoming available to buy. It came across as you being wishful. Anyway, she's a hard-faced cow who I doubt can be influenced to do something unless she wants to, so we need not worry that we have coerced her.'

Elodie nodded. 'Good. I am assured.' She looked at her watch and smiled. 'We still have the whole afternoon. Should we go flaneusing? I have some things I want to show you in the passages near GatBat.'

'Joy!' Cordelia exclaimed.

They left House of Tanner and ran as they saw a bus coming. 'Sitting on the top deck is mandatory,' Cordelia said as they climbed aboard and went up the stairs. 'Ooh, front seat, we've scored!' As the bus set off, Cordelia told Elodie how she often rode double-deckers to meditate and for inspiration as she gazed at the urban scape, scribbling words in her notepad and doodling the features that caught her eye. 'I'm really keen on that one.' She pointed at the dome of an Edwardian baroque building upon which a group of verdigris cast-iron cherubs stood, holding aloft a globe threaded with wires. 'It was the HQ of a telegraph company so that particular architectural detail is a visual clue.'

The bus approached their stop. 'Ready?' Elodie pressed the buzzer.

Cordelia, so used to being a leader, was looking forward to relinquishing that role and temporarily becoming a follower. Elodie did not disappoint, and they wandered into a dark alleyway in search of an iron grate in the pavement and listened for the sound of an underground river rushing on its urgent mission to join the Thames. Then they gazed at a clock where an automaton of two camp male figures in silver loincloths held weighty clubs and whacked a bell at intervals. They passed a topsy-turvy boozer behind the law courts where the pub cat wore a miniature white legal collar, then walked down a cobbled lane to the red brick Elizabethan hall where *Twelfth Night* was first staged. 'There is no public access, but one day I was passing by and it was open, so I went inside and saw an extraordinary hammerbeam roof.' Elodie pushed at the door. It was locked. 'That's a shame. Oh well, I have a treat for you around the corner.' They went to sit on a bench opposite a seventeenth-century church. 'Listen carefully.' The church bells started to strike a familiar melody. 'Can you tell its "Oranges and Lemons"? I had to research why it is played here. Any idea?'

Cordelia shook her head.

'This is the church of St Clement Dane and the opening line of the nursery rhyme is "Oranges and Lemons Say the Bells of St Clement's".'

'So that's why a blend of orange and lemon juice is called a St Clement's,' Cordelia exclaimed. 'If you ever decide to abandon your dual doctoring, you have a career ahead of you as the most glamorous guide in town. That was brilliant.'

Elodie looked pleased. 'I've been exploring this area. It has so many interesting sites. My favourites are the Egyptomania exterior of that building next to GatBat and the wedding cake spire of St Bride's church.'

Cordelia had a flashback to an epic day out with Elodie early in their friendship, as they strolled along Fleet Street looking at the architecture. 'Remember when you first saw GatBat and said how happy your eyes were?'

'I'll never forget. It made me want to move to London so I could admire it endlessly and now I live in that very place. I am so fortunate.'

'And as a resident of London you are eligible for the Freedom of the City, which offers something much more thrilling than Valkyrie's Berlesheim experience did and that is …' She sang the notes of a fanfare, 'The right to drive a flock of sheep over London Bridge!'

'Have you just made that up?'

'No, it's true, sort of. It was a privilege in the Middle Ages.'

'What an honour. Do you think they will let me gallop a horse across it instead?'

'Oh yes, that's much more you. Now, if you're ready for a change of atmosphere, I have something eerie to reveal.'

'Is it supernatural?'

'Not quite, but it might make you shiver a bit. It's in the West End, not far. We'll walk.'

'Do you know why it is called the West End?'

'Sure do.'

'I knew you would.'

'I wish I could say that born Londoners receive the keys to a red sparkly vault which gives access to all the information ever needed about their city, but the truth is that Celestine made sure Rex and I knew the important historical things. And each day after school we'd go roaming cos we're both inquisitive. Cel enjoyed hearing us describe what we'd found. I showed her sketches and Rex, with his photographic memory, recounted everything in detail.'

'What an idyllic childhood.'

'It really was. Our pals were envious because Cel gave us so much freedom. Their parents considered us to be feral and were worried we'd be a bad influence.'

'Please tell me that you were.' Elodie always encouraged mischief.

'Botticelli!' Cordelia smiled at the memory. 'Oh, I never explained why it's called the West End. It lies west of the Roman fortress of Londinium, which evolved into the original walled city, and conversely the east end is named for the same reason.'

'You will be the first hire for my tour guiding business. And with all your London knowledge you could provide the content for that red sparkly vault.'

Ten minutes later they entered a grand hotel near Trafalgar Square and Cordelia led the way to the bar.

'Fancy a cocky?'

They were shown to a table and Elodie looked at the menu. 'In honour of Gladys Ingle it has to be an Aviation. Not all mixologists include crème de violette but this one does. And the colour will match your eyes.'

'I'm having a beauticious Blood and Sand, which is deep red, so together they represent my tired eyes the morning after a big night out.'

Cordelia gave a friendly wave to a man at a nearby table. He did not reciprocate. 'I dated that fella for a couple of nanoseconds during my early twenties and he seems to still be sulking. He didn't like it when I tried to hang my jacket on his impressive hooter, despite me saying how amazing it was. We lasted a week until he realised my opinions were here to stay. He married a mousey creature who agreed with everything anyone ever said. And now, to paraphrase Scarlett O'Hara, they probably have a passel of mealy-mouthed brats.'

'He looks to be a person who insists his word is the law.'

'Spot on, he is now a Member of Parliament for the other side. I don't know what came over me. Well yes, I do know, I'm keen on noses and he reminded me of the Duke of Wellington, who was renowned for his aquiline features.'

'Is that the same Duke who vanquished Napoleon Bonaparte?'

'Yes, and apparently Napoleon thought the size of a man's nose was related to his brain capacity, so all his military officers had huge conks. The wars of the noses.'

'If the British and French had not fought at Waterloo ABBA would have needed another battle to sing about.' Elodie contemplated for a few moments then sang, 'Agincourt, I was defeated you won the war.'

'That's a better rhyme – good one.' Cordelia cheersed her and then said, 'This place used to be a piano bar where a professional singer regularly appeared. One evening the set had finished so I picked up the mic and started crooning "Feelings". I was with a musically illiterate pal who sat at the keyboard and plinked out a few bum notes. The manager rushed up and asked us to stop, saying they had no music license after a certain hour. Bless him for being polite and not inferring it was cos we were completely rubbish. And yes, in case you were wondering, vino might well have been imbibed.'

Elodie giggled. 'I wish it was still a piano bar so we could take up musical residence and convert it to a piano accordion bar.'

'We'd have a hoot. Anyway, so back then I came here regularly and kept noticing a group of businessmen in dark suits, all carrying the same type of briefcase, lurking furtively by that door over there. One night they disappeared so I went after them. Do you want to go and see what I discovered?'

They finished their cocktails, then made their way to the back of the room. Cordelia opened the door, which led to a staircase. 'I waited for the sound of the men's voices to fade then I crept down. Come on, I'll show you.' The stairs led to a heavy wooden studded double door with brass lion's head handles.

'I reckoned that's where they'd gone so I tried the door. It was locked. But I wanted to know what was going on, so I went to the passageway and it turned out to be access for the room, hidden behind a curtain.'

'Did you go in and look?' Elodie was hanging on each word.

'Yes, I peeked, expecting to see human sacrifice or devil worship, but it was worse.'

'What were they doing?' Elodie asked breathlessly, impatient to know more.

'Freemasonry rituals.'

'Urgh. Did you stay and watch?'

'No, because it gave me the heebie-jeebies, but I really wanted to see the room properly, so I went back a few days later.'

Cordelia had only ever been in the bar on a Thursday and assumed that was the evening the Freemasons met, so she'd sneaked in on a Tuesday using the same access.

'So there I was, having a nosy, and suddenly heard the door being unlocked. My heart was thumping then I noticed a tray of glasses on a table in the anteroom, so I darted over and grabbed it at the same time as a group of blokes entered.'

Elodie's eyes were wide as she cried, 'No! Then what?'

'They glared at me and one of them angrily demanded to know what I was doing there. I pretended to be a waitress and said casually, "Just collecting these", and walked past carrying the tray. I'm sure they weren't convinced cos I was dressed in a gold lamé bomber jacket and leather toreador trousers.'

Elodie chuckled. 'They probably supposed you had defiled their sacred space. And in gold lamé too …'

'Anyway, I legged it up the stairs. Next time I was in the bar the chap who had challenged me fired a volley of intense scowls my way.'

'Is the temple still there and can we see it?'

'Yes, fortunately it's no longer used for freemasonry. This is a listed building so the room's interior cannot be altered, but it has other purposes.'

Elodie followed Cordelia through the doors. The lights illuminated automatically to reveal a sky-blue dome on which the Masonic blazing star was rendered in gold leaf. Underneath, the empty room was lined by neo-classical Ionic marble columns and rows of high-backed wooden chairs, armrests embellished with carvings of the square and compasses. The chairs faced an ornate wooden throne on an altar-like structure.

'*Incroyable!*' Elodie gasped. 'What is it used for now?'

'A film set, private dining, and special events.'

'What a stunning spot for a tea dance. Is that something Oscar would produce?'

'Let's make a special request and if he does I'll be first in line. It's an unforgettable venue. I've been here on a few occasions for Monkey Business Ministries gatherings.'

She was referring to a members' club for people who wanted to be part of a congregation but had no religious tendencies. The MC was Drag King Wenceslas and it met on holy days, often in places with a former spiritual connection. Its irreverent format was loosely based on a traditional service, including readings, a non-sermonising homily, and "hymns" with racy lyrics. Afterwards congregants played games or visited somewhere that suited the club's attitude.

'Last time they were here we used the chequered floor tiles as a board for human chess. Wenceslas was the King of course and I chose the Knight, cos of the rebellious way it moves. Surprisingly, there was a clamour to be a feeble pawn. Turns out the ones who chose them were hungover and pawns are easily taken so it meant they quickly sat down again to rest.'

Elodie was about to expound on why she was keen on the bishop's diagonal moves when her phone buzzed. It was a text from Manon, *L'Opération Guêpe a commencée.*

'What is a *guêpe?*' Cordelia asked.

'A wasp.'

'Ooh, how thrilling. Let the sting begin!'

Chapter Sixteen

Manon was in touch a month later to arrange an update on developments in *L'Opération Guêpe*.

Cordelia said to Elodie, 'I'm glad it's named for a wasp cos they seem to sting people for fun. Most appropriate seeing as this concerns Valkyrie.'

They scheduled a call, Elodie in Paris, and Cordelia at home in her boot on the House of Tanner roof.

Manon quickly came to the point. 'The Herolt-Graff painting has been seized from La Maison des Fleurs and is now in the possession of Valentina. I cannot divulge details yet, it's an ongoing operation. Elodie, we believe she will make contact to sell the work.'

I hope Monsieur Fouché was not working that day, he'd kick himself if he knew something had been pinched on his watch, Cordelia thought. She was consoled to learn that the robbery occurred on a Friday, when Monsieur Fouché was absent, and the volunteer was the reviled Madame Barbier whose barbed tongue and holier than thou attitude reflected her name – and she was the most unpopular person in the village.

'So she did arrange the robbery.' Elodie shook her head. 'How do we proceed?'

'We want her to move the painting across an international border beyond the Schengen area so there is no doubt she is handling stolen goods and initiating the sale. Ideally, she will present it herself and Elodie you need to agree the purchase. Please do not worry, she will never know you collaborated with Globo Pol.' Manon paused, 'Are you sure you want to go ahead?'

Elodie took a few seconds to answer. 'Yes, I do.'

'Thank you. Please decide on a location to meet her then we will speak further on what to do next. We will not be arresting her at that point and you will be in no danger. Your co-operation on this project is known only to me and will remain that way.' Manon's reassurance comforted the sleuths, who were wary of Valentina's formidable retribution if she knew they were involved.

At the end of the conference call Elodie rang Cordelia for a conflab. 'Valentina is a scoundrel after all.'

'In an odd way I'm relieved because I want her to be like a film baddie and have a purpose to her nasty piece of workery and not be a cow for no reason, if that makes sense.'

'Sort of. I don't know what I wanted her to be. But now we are completing the operation I'm uneasy. I wish I knew what Globo Pol was planning then I'd visualise it.'

They spent a while speculating on what would transpire and then Cordelia said, 'Here's a suggestion. Her shoes will be finished soon and ordinarily we'd ship them. If she's in contact to sell the painting say you want to see it prior to making a decision. Then I'll get in touch and tell her that she needs to collect the shoes so I can do a final once over of them on her feet. That means she'll be in London and it makes sense to do your biz then.'

'Excellent plan, it will raise no suspicion. I'm leaving for Angola in a few days so she might call when I have limited ability to communicate.'

'Top excuse not to speak to her. Do you want me to do the enticing? If she leaves a message then you can text to say you are largely incommunicado and that I'll be arranging a date for when you are back in London. I will propose she collects the shoes simultaneously. She likes you so I can't imagine her being difficult.'

'Good plan. I hope Dmitri is not the thief. I don't want him to be in trouble. He's rather endearing.'

'Yes, he is a ninny but he's a dear.'

'So, do you want the latest?' Cordelia was sitting with Rex in Worship after the gallery had closed for the day.

'Botters!'

'Lock yourself in your office on Monday. Vampire Val will be in the house to collect her shoes, then she's coming here to do the dirty and flog the hot property.'

'Sounds like the name of a social media account for people who get off on looking in estate agents' windows,' Rex tittered.

'She-She's asked if we'll help her rehearse the scenario.'

'Ooh, amateur dramatics. Can I play Valkyrie?'

'You'll have to audition.'

'Do you want to come to mine? We can have a mucky curry on Brick Lane prior to roleplaytime.'

On the Sunday evening before V-Day Cordelia and Elodie arrived at Rex's home in Spitalfields, an early eighteenth-century terraced townhouse that had originally belonged to a wealthy silk merchant. The symmetrical brown brick façade was punctuated by tall broad windows. Inside, the oak panelling and floorboards contributed to an understated décor. A generous sense of space was maintained by a distinct lack of clutter.

'Babe, I do love your gaff, but "the Architectural Digest Photographer Will Be Here Any Minute" vibe always makes me feel as if I must be on my best behaviour, which I'm not very good at,' Cordelia teased.

'Tidy home, tidy mind.'

They settled down in the sitting room and Elodie pinged a glass with a pen to get their attention. 'This is what I will say to Valentina. I'll do it in English for you, but I'll speak to her in Italian, so she is conversing in her native language and there is no question of her answers being misinterpreted. I'm purposely going to be vague and not say much.' She stood up and took on a power posture – straight back, feet apart, and chin slightly lifted. 'Who's going to play Valkyrie?'

Rex shouted, 'Me!' then said, 'Oh hang on, I've never met her, so I'll be the acting coach instead and observe you two.'

'First, guess who I'm being?' Cordelia hunched her shoulders and moved like a gorilla, grunting as she went.

'Total dead ringer for Val's handbag holder at Berlin Art Mart – the one who probably sprinkles iron filings on his food. He's a modern-day Minotaur. Wonder what his name is?'

'Signor Collo Taurino,' Elodie said, laughing.

'What does that mean?'

'Mr Bull Neck.'

'Signor Collo Taurino has a message for you Signora Tanner. "*Via il cane da qua dentro!*"' Cordelia screamed in Italian-accented English and English-accented Italian, then said to Elodie, 'I'm ready hon. Lead me in.'

She addressed "Valentina" and thanked her for coming.

'Doctor l'Archambeau, always a pleasure. So glad you left that awful friend of yours outside in the rain. Now, I'm far too important to be hanging around so I'll come straight to the point. I have the painting.'

'I cannot wait to see it.'

'Take a close look Doctor. What you won't see are the tears of the volunteers at the museum from which it was nicked. Now, do you want it or not?'

Cordelia came out of character to say, 'Have you done any research on the sale value of the artist?'

'Yes, and I'm sure Valkyrie will cheat me. I'll agree the purchase then delay the payment so I don't hand money over. Can we rehearse that part?'

'Doctor l'Archambeau, this is a one-of-a-kind painting and if you are not interested I have other clients who are, so make up your mind.'

'Yes, I do want it.'

'Then the deal is done. Now, pay me in diamond-encrusted, solid gold ingots that I will pile up in my jewel house with all my other corrupt income.'

'If that is not where she keeps her fortune I shall be disappointed,' Elodie giggled.

'Of course she'll be a kitten to you. None of the death-to-Cordelia-Tanner attitude she shows me.'

'Should we try it again. I'm concerned I will not be convincing.'

'As long as you switch on your poker face you'll be inscrutable,' Rex assured her.

'This is my first experience of entrapping someone. I feel confident now but I might be nervous tomorrow.'

'Do you want me to be in the room as support?' Cordelia offered.

'Thank you, but it will be better for me to do it alone. If you're there I will laugh and picture you as Signor Collo Taurino.'

'Good point. And talking of which, she's bound to be escorted by the herd. Where will you corral them?'

'I shall chat with Valentina in the Worship bar and ask them to wait by the painting of Io, who was transformed into a cow by Zeus. They will not realise the irony ...'

Elodie reminded the others that concealed cameras and listening devices were to be temporarily installed in the gallery. 'One of the Globo Pol techies will do it first thing tomorrow morning. I'll be there to let her in.'

'This is no half-hearted attempt to seek proof of Valkyrie's guilt is it?' Cordelia declared. 'Impressive!'

Cordelia always awoke early but, anticipating Valentina's visit, she was up earlier than normal. Blanche, who was committed to her sleep, did not wake until Cordelia had finished her ablutions and was ready for a walk. She tickled the dog's nose and jiggled the lead because its tell-tale tinkling was the equivalent of a cockerel heralding the dawn. Blanche shot out of bed and chased her tail in excitement.

'That's how I feel Waggy because today is the day that horrible woman who was nasty to you will implicate herself in wrongdoing.'

Blanche did not understand but she smiled and bounded down the stairs of House of Tanner followed by Cordelia. On the street the growl of Nike's engine announced Elodie's arrival.

'Good morning undercover agent. How are you feeling and did you sleep?' Cordelia asked.

'*Bonjour chérie,* I'm excited and that prevented me sleeping, so I've been up for hours doing yoga and writing letters.'

'Here's the Worship key. I'll take doglina for a meander. Back in an hour and then need to don my close-encounters-of-the-vampire-kind cloak of invincibility. Brekkie at Ant's afterwards?'

'That's just what I need.'

Valentina was due at House of Tanner for a 10am final fitting, after which she was to meet Elodie and sell the painting. If all went to plan both transactions would be resolved by late morning.

Elodie had a laboratory in House of Tanner for her shoe research and was meeting Manon there to be fitted with a lapel brooch inside which a hidden camera would record and relay footage. Manon was staying in the lab to study the real-time activity on a laptop and had invited Cordelia to watch.

Deep breath and smile. It'll be over soon and then you can scowl,

Cordelia thought as Valentina entered the lobby of House of Tanner. '*Buongiorno e benvenuta.* Please follow me. The shoes are magnificent. I will be sorry to see them go.' She doubted Valentina was taking any notice, so she slipped in a 'you thieving cow' at the end of the sentence. They ascended the stairs and entered the Boudoir of Pulchritude where the Long-Tailed Widowbirds were waiting on a black damask cushion.

Valentina showed a flicker of pleasure as Cordelia fitted them to her feet and asked, 'How do they feel?'

'As though they were made for me, which they were.' She tried to smile at her own witticism.

Ouch, don't come the happy face you humourless gorgon, Cordelia said to herself but was considerate enough to give Valentina a mercy laugh. 'Excellent. If you are happy then they are complete. Thank you for your business.' *The pleasure was all … neither of ours.* She took the shoes and laid them in a box lined in violet satin and adorned by feathers in the colours of the Wilson's Bird of Paradise. She placed it in a large purple paper carrier bag, emblazoned with House of Tanner in metallic gold.

'I will accompany you to Worship where Elodie is waiting. Please excuse me a moment, I will send a message to say we are on our way.'

Valkyrie with you in 2 minutes.

Outside on the street Valentina took the carrier bag and said, 'Signora Tanner, the shoes are beautiful.'

'I am pleased. They suit you.' *Be sure to wear them when Lady Justice comes knocking.*

Elodie came to greet them. Cordelia telepathed a quick, *She tried a joke and I wish she hadn't cos I prefer her rigor mortis attitude. Anyway, bon courage, I'll be next to WoManon relishing your Oscar worthy performance. Give me a wave if she's not looking.*

I'm primed, feeling poised and ready for the cameras to start rolling. Elodie replied, then led Valentina into Worship. To ensure a private transaction, the gallery was temporarily closed and Winnie had gone to run errands. Elodie soon exhausted her small talk, so Valentina changed the subject to business and summoned one of the guards, who was holding a briefcase. She opened it, took a pair of latex gloves and put them on, then removed and unwrapped a package.

'Here is the painting you are interested in,' she said holding the watercolour of a Crown Imperial, its vibrant orange clusters of bell-shaped flowers shimmering on the vellum. 'As you will appreciate, it was a long negotiation because the owner was reluctant to sell. But because of my status in the art world they eventually assented and are asking a premium price.' She quoted a figure that was five times the market rate for works by the same artist.

Manon, watching the interaction, was translating the Italian for Cordelia, who tutted and rolled her eyes. 'Elodie predicted she would rip her off, the fleecing git.' Manon gave nothing away, despite being pleased the target had already incriminated herself and Globo Pol had the proof they needed.

'How beautiful. May I hold it?' Elodie carefully handled the painting and admired the work. 'A work to brighten any room.' She smiled at how the artist's representation of the plant's green foliage resembled the tangled snakes of Medusa's hair. In the silence she sensed Valentina was staring in a manner meant to intimidate her.

'Please remind me of the price.' Valentina stated a higher figure than the one she had quoted only minutes earlier, but Elodie replied, 'I will accept that.'

Valentina looked satisfied and said, 'I will give you a 10% discount if you use Bitcoin.'

'I appreciate the offer. However, the payment needs to go via Worship, which does not have a cryptocurrency account.'

'Then you shall receive an invoice. My secretary will be in contact to arrange payment. And now, here is the painting.'

Ordinarily a deal would have been sealed by a handshake but that was not Valentina's way and instead she said, 'Doctor l'Archambeau, you are easy to do business with. Do not forget, I can secure artworks that other brokers find impossible to source. That is why I am the best.'

Elodie, still cautious of saying too much, responded noncommittally, 'You have an excellent reputation.'

They stood up to leave but Elodie could not resist asking Valentina to show her the new shoes. Valentina slipped them on and needed no persuasion to sashay around like a model on a runway, past the guards slumped in armchairs. They were shocked to see their employer acting a giddy manner and revealing a secret side that few people knew. With all eyes focused elsewhere Elodie took the opportunity to send a high five to the nearest wide-angle camera, hoping Cordelia would notice.

Elodie returned to her lab after Valentina had departed and Cordelia cried, 'You were brilliant in every way. Brilliant!'

Manon, circumspect as usual, said, 'What a good job. Now we have the proof Valentina attempted to sell stolen property. Thank you both for everything.'

Elodie placed the painting on the lab bench and said, 'That was easier than I'd assumed and any doubts on whether or not I should be doing it disappeared once she lied about the provenance and increased the price.'

'We saw everything and had a choice of several cameras. The one in your brooch showed Valkyrie's stony glare as you were examining the painting. No wonder she's such a successful dealer, she petrifies people into making a decision,' Cordelia commented.

'I felt it and what you probably did not hear was an impatient sigh and her fingers drumming on the table.'

'Do you want to see the footage?' Manon asked.

Elodie watched intently. 'Oh yes, she is terrifying. I'm so relieved

I do not need to engage with her again. What will happen to the painting?'

Manon explained that it was to be returned to La Maison des Fleurs. The trustees had collaborated with Globo Pol and now security measures were to be initiated and staff would receive extra training on scam awareness.

'Elodie, I need to take your fingerprints to exclude them from the frame examination. Valentina is a professional and was wearing gloves, but we might identify those of the robbery suspect.' Manon picked up a portable scanner and switched on the power.

'Do dogs have fingerprints?' Cordelia asked.

'Yes, and they also have unique nose prints.'

Cordelia was happy to know that Blanche had exclusive identifying marks and a snout like no other canine.

Manon concluded her work and was packing her equipment. 'Things will go quiet between us now. We have some issues to resolve on this case. I will call as soon as I have an update.' The sleuths escorted her to the taxi and she kissed them goodbye, saying, 'I do not expect to have much fun in my profession but working together is something I enjoy very much. I hope it is the same for you.'

They agreed wholeheartedly. As they waved her off Cordelia said to Elodie, 'I hope "issues to resolve" is legal speak for "Valentina will be locked up in the Tower of London."'

'Without a river view. I wish we knew more of how the painting was tracked and if they arrest the perpetrator. Maybe Manon will enlighten us later.' Elodie looked at her watch, 'Our antidote to *quella ladra di una Italiana* will be here soon. Do we have time for a quick lunch? I am ravenous for a Croque Madame le Docteur.'

'Me too. We'll have to scarf it though. What does *quella ladra di una Italiana* mean?'

'Thieving Italian.'

They ate a hasty meal and went back to House of Tanner to await the arrival of a group from Blessed St Jude Primary School. Ever since the exhibition at Worship the TannerBeaus had taken great interest in the pupils, who were always welcome to visit. That day, they had been invited purposely to balance Valentina's corruption with innocence. It worked perfectly and afterwards Cordelia and Elodie were full of joy having spent several hours in the company of 30 delightful eight-year-olds. Cordelia had given them a primer on how handmade footwear is produced and they'd been surprised by how many stages were involved. 'So, now you know how complicated it is who's going to treat their shoes more respectfully and stop scuffing them?' All hands went up. Then they were transfixed by the shoes in the archive and tried to guess which birds they represented, and giggled as the teacher had her feet measured because she was ticklish and unable to stop laughing. Shoeseum was their favourite part of the visit. 'This is everyone's fave – mine too,' Cordelia told them. 'Some of the shoes belonged to people who are significant in history. Here, you will be pleased to know that the woman who owned these introduced ice cream to Europe.' The children cheered as she held up Catherine de Medici's green and yellow brocade Louis heel slip-ons.

Elodie's contribution to the visit was more sedentary and the children sat on the floor listening intently as she explained the symbolism of shoes in fairy tales and myths and how they often represented punishment, as in *The Red Shoes*, or status and power, as in *Puss in Boots*. She told them that the Cinderella fable appeared in numerous cultures and the material composition of the slipper varied. In the earliest recorded version it was made of gold.

One of the children asked if she had a job and they were fascinated to learn how she worked as a surgeon in war zones. She did not discuss details, she never did, even with her friends, but said it was satisfying to know her patients had been helped. Elodie, full of tenderness towards them, realised she could be an inspiration because a girl said, 'When I grow up I want to do what you do.' While a boy asked, 'Can men be doctors too?'

She'd already planned to play her piano accordion and swiftly changed the lyrics to Irving Berlin's 'Anything You Can Do (I Can Do Better)' and sang instead, 'Anything I can do you can do too. You can do anything so make sure you do'.

The children quickly learnt the lines and skipped alongside her, singing loudly as she led them through Shoeseum, accordion strapped to her chest. Rex heard the commotion and popped in to film the scene on his phone. Elodie saw it later and said, 'How adorable, some of them are pretending to play the accordion.'

'Remember at Karaokeverse and my idea for an air orchestra tournament? What fun it would be to stage one for juniors. Their innocent outlook is much more agreeable than cynical adults,' he replied.

Rex was keen on the school visits to Worship and the children's enthusiasm. After the first one he had commented to the others that it was, 'All the pleasure, none of the responsibility. That's how life should be,' a sentiment of which they all approved.

Chapter Seventeen

'What are you up to this afternoon?' Rex asked Cordelia one workday morning.

'Judging by your upbeat tone, I shall answer "whatever you have up your sleeve".'

'Fablings. Bertie has invited us to watch the auditions for the person who will play him in the musical.'

Victory in the Turnaround Trophy had been a coup for Left To Their Own Devices but it had been an even bigger one for Bertie. His participation in the acceptance speech charmed almost everyone who saw it and social media referred to him as a national treasure. He was inundated by invitations to appear on TV talk shows and his sassy campery was exactly what the country needed, so talent agents came calling. He chose the one who promised a spread in a men's glossy fashion magazine and when that materialised it led to bookings as a mature model. The most significant result of his new celebrity was *Bertie And The Beat*, an autobiographical musical to be staged at the London Palladium. Bertie was having a blast and, as executive producer, he could make such decisions as hiring Cordelia to design the shoes for the main characters' costumes.

'Bunking off is one of the benefits of running our own biz. Where are the auditions?' Cordelia asked.

'The scene of Blanche's greatest triumphs.' He meant London's Most Photogenic Dog annual competition, staged in a crumbling old music hall in Shadwell, which Blanche had won an unprecedented three times.

'Love that place. So characterful. It's a gorgeous day so we can walk and do the Charlie D.'

The Charlie D was a favoured route they had devised for a school project on how writers were inspired by London's built environment. They based it on Charles Dickens and included: Smithfield market, mentioned in *David Copperfield*; Bleeding Heart Yard, location of the Plornish family residence in *Little Dorrit*; and The One Tun pub, which doubled as Bill Sikes' local boozer The Three Cripples in *Oliver Twist*.

When they arrived at the venue Bertie was sitting outside sunning himself. 'My sweet peas! Come here and let me plant a mwah mwah on those lovely cheeks of yours.' He kissed them both and said, 'We're having a break. We've met ten young men so far and I have my eyes on a couple for a call back. Larry, he's the producer, instructed them all to ramp up the camp, which they did, but he asked for more. So I said to him, "Am I really that mincey?" He just looked at me. To be honest I'm a bit Bertied out and we still have a few booked in.'

They went inside for a pot of tea. Cordelia hoped Bertie would divulge some anecdotes from his showbiz past. He did not disappoint and revealed details of some naughty goings-on and diva behaviour by well-known stars. They hooted as he told them of the internationally renowned crooner who was too drunk to go on stage, so the theatre substituted him with a tribute act so convincing the audience did not notice.

Neither Cordelia nor Rex had ever watched an audition and thought each of the actors would make a good Bertie. All were pretty, danced well, and had attractive singing voices. Then one man came on stage and Cordelia nudged Rex and whispered, 'Cor, he's a looker. Wonder which team he plays for?'

'Definitely a goalie for Queen's Park Rangers,' Rex replied, eyes focused on the comely young man who moved in an athletic but balletic style and had an intangible magical aura. His name was Billy Angel and he exuded star quality.

'He's the one,' they heard Bertie whisper to the producer who nodded discreetly.

When the auditions were over Bertie asked if any of the actors had impressed them and they both shouted, 'The angelic Billy!'

'Isn't he marvellous,' he replied. 'I'm so thrilled you concur with me and Larry because we've all seen his inner light and that means audiences will too. And he's the quite the mover isn't he. We're going to offer him the role.'

Cordelia and Rex left the theatre and walked through Whitechapel, chatting about the shoes Cordelia was to design for the production. Bertie had agreed to her suggestion that, because the musical had a surreal element, Billy should wear phantasmagorical Footloose creations. 'He'll need real dancing shoes underneath the holograms, to be handmade at House of Tanner. They will fit so perfectly he'll think he's not actually wearing anything on his feet because they will be light, soft, and completely glovely.'

'I'm definitely coming to his shoe fittings,' Rex said as they turned onto Blossom Street. 'What are your thoughts for the Footloosers?'

'Should I tell him he needs to come more frequently than normal for fittings?' Cordelia replied mischievously. 'This is what I have in mind for the virtuals. Shoes are transformational. For a dancer they are an armour, a uniform, and emblematic of their identity. Dancing changed Bertie's life. It liberated him. And what creature is most associated with freedom?'

'Does it begin with b and end with ird,' Rex replied, knowing the answer.

'Some birds perform a dance to attract a lover and, to quote the epigram, dancing is the vertical expression of the horizontal desire.' She had a flashback to her first meeting with Oscar and felt breathless at the thought. 'I'm going big on birds. The designs will start modest to reflect Bertie's early days and gradually become more flamboyant as his career progresses. Actually, male birds are a perfect analogy and I'll begin with the sharp-tailed grouse, cos they gather in groups and, in perfect sync, rapidly tap their feet, like a chorus line. Then we'll move on to the flamingo – they are natural performers, stepping and marching, rhythmically swaying their body. And one of my favourites – the red-capped manakin (although that should be renamed the womanakin). They have fancy footwork, a bit like a moondance as they glide along a branch. Finally, I must have the peacock – it's the law. Billy will come on for the finale in the finest display of feathers the London Palladium has seen since Liberace headlined!'

Wish Manon had some updates. It was a couple of weeks since Valentina had sold the painting to Elodie, and Cordelia was eager to know the conclusion. *What if they can't pin it on her and are still investigating.* She had been reading up on criminal law and discovered trans-national crimes were complicated because of sundry jurisdictions. *I'll send her some "please hurry up, I'm impatient vibes" then they will manifest into a telephone call.*

Miraculously, her cosmic ordering worked and the next day Elodie sent a text message. *Manon has summoned us. How does a visit to Marseilles sound?*

Crikey, I should try manifesting more often. Could it be cos of my chackalacka-ed brain? She-She should give it a go and see if it works for her, Cordelia thought.

A week later Manon was greeting them at Globo Pol HQ. 'I have news.' Rather than the familiar conference room she took them to the basement and a secure operations room where computers and a bank of screens covered one wall.

'This is where we analyse the intelligence you provide. Your success in solving cases needs to be clandestine so our secret weapon – you – is unknown to the criminal world. That means I am unable to invite you on stage to make a formal presentation in front of a large audience, so please accept this to show my gratitude.' She pinned star-shaped metal badges, engraved with the words Special Agent, on Cordelia and Elodie's jackets and stood back. 'Yes, exactly the impression I aimed for.'

The special agents laughed and effusively thanked Manon, who said she'd been inspired by *The Good, The Bad, And The Ugly* film. 'They were in the Wild West of America, and we are in the Wild West of Europe.'

'If you are the Sheriff and we are the Good, who are the Bad and the Ugly?' Elodie asked.

'Daniel Tredd – total minger and majorly B.A.D.' Cordelia interjected.

Manon called them to attention, saying, 'I believe you will be satisfied by what I have to reveal. Make yourselves comfortable, there is a lot to tell.' She switched on a large screen, accessed a computer file and clicked on a video. Hidden cameras had been installed in La Maison Des Fleurs and they recorded someone in dark clothing lifting a frame off a wall, placing it in a bag, then leaving the room. As the perpetrator walked to the gate a camera recorded a clear view of their face. It was Dmitri.

'Oh Dmitri! Naughty, naughty,' Cordelia exclaimed.

'As you know, the painting contained a tracking device, so it was monitored from Gervaliar to Villa Veritas. We did not want to arrest him and alert Valentina, so we waited until she transported the work to London and sold it to Elodie. When that transpired he was taken into custody.'

'How did you know where he was?' Elodie asked.

'A combination of facial recognition software, CCTV, and mobile phone signals.'

Manon revealed that Dmitri was really an Australian citizen called Shane Diggling who, after seeing the film *Anna Karenina*, had so admired the Prince Stepan Oblonksy character that he'd adopted a Russian persona.

'That explains his overcooked accent,' Cordelia said. 'I did wonder. Especially as he used vernacular English and occasionally started his sentences with "Look" which is an Aussie thing to do. And he let slip "mate" a few times.'

Dmitri was not, as he claimed, a wealthy art dealer. He had a modest lifestyle and lived on a tiny yacht called Monte in a marina in Malta.

'How funny,' Elodie said. 'Do you remember he boasted of where he lived and Rex assumed it was Monte Carlo.'

They were gripped by the revelations and even more so as Manon described how he had become involved with Valentina.

'He is a petty larcenist and one day in a Portofino café he took a smartphone from a table without the owner realising. Valentina noticed and sent one of her guards to insist he put it back. If he refused, the guard would, in Dmitri's words, ruin his pretty face. Being a pragmatic sort, he did as commanded and was escorted to meet Valentina, who had tested him to see how efficient he was as a sneak thief because she had a business proposition. She offered him a job and made it apparent he had no choice about accepting it.'

'Poor Dmitri, I'll still call him that, got himself into trouble with the wrong person.'

'Cordelia, you are being sentimental – he was already making a living by stealing, so he is not innocent,' Manon reminded her.

'Oh yes – he's The Bad. But Val's worse. She could star as The Badder in a sequel to *The Good, The Bad, and The Ugly*.'

'Now I can tell you that, because of your work, all the art theft cold cases have been solved. And this is the culprit.' She brought up a photograph of Valentina.

'WHAT! All of them?'

'Yes, even the works she sent back. That was a scam.'

Cordelia and Elodie were flabbergasted.

'I don't understand, why was she interested in that type of art when it has such little monetary value?' Elodie asked.

'She had no interest at the beginning of the collaboration with Dmitri, but he had lied about his art knowledge and when ordered to lift a specific work he took the wrong painting.'

Dmitri admitted under questioning that Valentina's steely anger terrified him and, to fix his mistake, he'd suggested she contact the museum's insurers in case they were offering a reward. Valentina approved of the plan and, after she realised how grateful the museum was for the work's recovery, conceived a scheme whereby Dmitri purposely took items of emotional value to local communities. Then Valentina would return them at flashy public events, as witnessed in Berlesheim.

'Dmitri always gave valid reasons to the museum staff about why he was taking the work. He got a kick out of being brazen and employed the same technique at La Maison des Fleurs.'

'What excuse did he use?' Elodie asked.

'He showed the volunteer a fake letter from *le Ministère de la Culture*, advising them that the painting was to be removed for analysis by an academic.'

'Cor, he was blatant. I suppose that is a characteristic of successful thieving. What will happen to him?' Cordelia asked.

'It is complex because his crimes occurred in several countries. The legal process is so slow, and prosecutors in each jurisdiction will need to decide whether to charge him. Dmitri is not violent and has been released but if Valentina becomes aware he has spoken to us then he is not safe, so Globo Pol has agreed to place him in a witness protection programme.'

'He'll need some films to help him choose a new identity.' Cordelia said. 'Dmitri's quite sweet and he needs to keep out of trouble so he should consider taking inspiration from Forrest Gump.'

She and Elodie sniggered, Manon did not and continued, 'This is a good time for lunch, then afterwards I will continue the update on Valentina. Cordelia, you enjoy eating local delicacies so I recommend a restaurant nearby for the best *bouillabaisse*.'

'Yum. Always up for a fish stew. I am not familiar with Provençal food. What else is typical?'

'If you are partial to anchovies then you must have anchoïade. It is in the same family as tapenade and it also contains capers, olive oil and garlic.'

Cordelia's eyes lit up. 'Yes please, and will you teach me some French terms for various law-breaking related subjects.' Every conversation was a learning opportunity and during lunch she added *le chapardeur* (pilferer) and *le cambrioleur* (burglar) to her lexicon. She was enamoured of the Provençal dishes and the French way of taking a lengthy break – no al desko grazing as in Anglo cultures. She said quietly, 'Manon, I hope you will find more reasons for us to work together so we have excuses to visit. And would you always schedule us for mid-morning and make it a long session so we need to break for lunch?'

'That is deal I am happy to make,' Manon replied, then she murmured, 'We have many missing persons cold cases. This is something to contemplate.' She winked and reverted to her normal pitch. 'And now you are refreshed let us return to the office so we can complete the business of the day.'

Back in the operations room Manon began. 'I will go

chronologically from when Dmitri stole the Herolt-Graff painting. He then travelled immediately to Rome and an agent on surveillance witnessed him enter Villa Veritas holding a briefcase and soon after he exited empty handed.'

'So, what did he do then?' Elodie asked eagerly.

'According to CCTV he spent two days in Rome being a tourist and flirting with women at the Trevi Fountain before flying to Malta. We waited until Valentina was back in Villa Veritas after selling the painting to you then he was arrested on his yacht. At that point we had no idea she was responsible for so many burglaries. It was only once he co-operated that we learnt the extent of her criminality.'

Egotism was Valentina's weak spot and she had become addicted to the glory derived from the Rightful Owner service, so she'd encouraged Dmitri to visit regional museums across Europe to check their security, or lack of, and identify easy to steal works for her to return. Globo Pol needed a motive unconnected to the painting from La Maison des Fleurs as a reason to search Villa Veritas, so Dmitri was instructed to tempt her with the most popular exhibit at a folk museum in the Austrian village of Pamsdorf. The painting portrayed an event for which the municipality was famous. Centuries earlier a lone elephant had mysteriously appeared in the village and became a beloved mascot because it saved a group of children by jumping into the lake and swimming to their rescue after their boat capsized. They were able to clamber on its back and it transported them to safety. This was the type of treasured artefact Valentina sought and she immediately said yes to its theft, which Dmitri executed efficiently.

'A warrant was issued so our agents entered Villa Veritas accompanied by police officers. Soon, Valentina's lawyer arrived and demanded to know the reason for the search. Upon being informed of the connection with museum thefts he disclosed that his client was one of the world's leading art authorities and her professional services included locating missing works so it was likely the police would indeed find stolen property.'

Globo Pol suspected that Valentina would be crafty but had underestimated her slipperiness. One of the agents found the elephant painting and told her they had tracked it from Pamsdorf, so she said, 'That is no surprise. I am well known for working with insurance companies to retrieve missing works and I am often offered goods by the thieves themselves. That is the case with this property.'

Cordelia looked at Manon in alarm, 'Is she going to wriggle out of it?'

'I'm afraid we do need to prepare for that eventuality. Now, there is more to tell and I have something to show you.' She went to a computer and clicked play on a video. The camera moved through all the public rooms in Villa Veritas and then to Valentina's gallery, from where she sold high value works. 'Rubens, Vermeer, Caravaggio …' Elodie reeled off the names of artists she recognised.

'Yes, and take a look here,' Manon replied. 'This is in the art school area.' Footage showed a paint-splashed studio where canvases on easels appeared to be works by cubists Marcel Duchamp and Georges Braque.

'These are all forgeries, just like the works in Valentina's private gallery. The students are in a bone fide class to learn the techniques of assorted art movements and they produce facsimiles of well-known works. She was forensic in her deceit, because students used ancient pigments in colours available when the original artist was alive. They often worked on re-used canvases, which was a common practice in previous centuries, and completed paintings were placed in antique frames. Teacher and students were unaware that Valentina was selling them. Her clients were individuals with newly acquired wealth, wanting to show their good taste by owning art by recognisable names.'

'But what about authentication? Most collectors buying high

profile works demand to see documentation from a recognised professional,' Elodie commented.

'She hired a corrupt attribution expert to issue the necessary false certificates.' Manon opened up a photo file to show them an example.

'The search warrant gave us access to her personal apartment, where we discovered her own collection. It included some of the works appropriated by Dmitri. She appears to be fond of bull paintings.'

Elodie telepathed to Cordelia, *Signora Feticcio di Tori, Madam Bull Fetish*.

Manon, who was unaware the special agents were able to communicate telepathically, smiled as Cordelia waggled her forefingers on her head like horns.

'There is something else you should see.' Manon fast forwarded to large canvases piled in a corner, splattered with rudimentary splodges.

'Which idiot abstract impressionists have they copied?' Cordelia said sarcastically.

'Left To Their Own Devices.'

She and Elodie laughed so much they had to check their mascara had not smudged. Manon was confused. 'I assumed you would be upset to learn she is exploiting your client's name.'

They calmed down and Cordelia answered, 'Yes, but I was laughing because of the shock.'

'And I was laughing at Cordelia's rude comment,' Elodie explained.

Both felt as if they had been hauled in front of the school headmistress to explain a misdemeanour.

'I am compelled to warn you that it will be difficult to prosecute Valentina for all her felonies. We know she commissioned Dmitri to steal the works, but it cannot be proven because we only have his word. As for the issue of handling misappropriated goods, she will claim to be unaware of the provenance, or use the defence that she was negotiating with insurance companies to return the properties.'

Cordelia and Elodie looked disappointed, so Manon informed them that under Italian law it was possible to indict Istituto d'Arte Villa Veritas for forgery, which meant Left To Their Own Devices had the option to initiate proceedings. She smiled and said, 'And in addition, let us not undervalue your personal satisfaction for having solved the cold cases.'

On the train to Paris, Cordelia and Elodie discussed developments and how frustrating it would be if Valentina was not prosecuted for the robberies she had solicited.

'She claims to revere art so how can she cause such strife by stealing it?' Elodie sighed.

'Zero empathy. It will be so unfair if she finds a way to evade the law.'

'I wonder if she sold the piece to Tredd or are other studios churning them out? And what should we do about that pile of LefDevs at Villa Veritas?'

'Let's talk to Rexicles and decide what to do regarding the fakes.'

'Yes, and now let us take a break from that woman and think of our priorities – tomorrow's cultural highlight.' They had tickets for a recital featuring Natalie Rousseau at the Palais Garnier, one of Cordelia's ultimate buildings with its more-is-more-and-then-add-some-more Beaux Arts design.

Later, when they told Rex how Manon had shown them a video of Left To Their Own Devices forgeries, he asked for a description.

'Random watercolours, much better than our daubs. The students were too talented to get the concept that it had to be embarrassingly terrible.'

'It made us laugh so hard, and Manon did not understand our

reaction, so we had to make up an excuse. I sometimes forget she is a serious person and maintains a professional demeanour. She was the same at school,' Elodie explained.

'So, what do we reckon on the Italian copyright law?' Rex asked. 'I will read up on it and then consult Jeffrey and Joffrey and ask for their advice.'

Two days later he was fully briefed.

'We do have an option to press a civil case against Istituto d'Arte Villa Veritas, but do we really want to endure all the legal shenanigans? I feel LefDev was then, and we are now.'

Cordelia shuddered at the notion of being involved any further with Valentina and was about to express her reservations just as Elodie said, 'She is a vindictive character and I believe that if we go ahead we will forever be looking behind us.'

'Ditto She-She. So we are in agreement then, it's arrivederci Valentina Feticcio di Tori.'

'Wonder if any of the oligarchs she flogged the fake Old Masters to will sue,' Rex mused.

'If I consult my motivation-for-owning-art rule book, then no, because it is more important for them to boast of their wealth by showing off an art collection than to acknowledge they were conned,' Elodie explained.

'They might have revenge up their sleeves. Poisoning and defenestration springs to mind. I advise Valkyrie to stay away from windows and never take sweets from strangers,' Rex replied.

'Now we know of the fakes, I am suspicious of the Glenora Richards miniature that she sold me. *Chérie*, will you psy-comm it and check?'

Cordelia nodded and said 'Of course. I'll do it now.'

They all went over to Worship and stood by a tiny painting of daffodils in a vase. Cordelia placed her hand on the frame and concentrated. Two minutes later she turned to Elodie and said, 'The good news is that it was not nicked. The bad news is it's from that infernal woman's forgery factory.'

'*Quelle scélérate!*' Elodie responded with frustration.

'She totally is. Are you upset?'

'Yes, and aggrieved. But more than anything I feel sorry for her. Such dishonesty must surely be bad for her soul.'

'You are lovely. If she'd have done that to me I'd want to wrap the handles of her Hermès handbag around her neck and pull them tight. Which of course I'd never do cos she's too scary and I'm a wimp.'

'We could act it out. That would be a satisfying conclusion,' Rex suggested.

'Good idea. Let's produce an effigy,' Elodie said.

'Come to mine, I have loads of space for taking a swing at it.'

'I was considering swearing therapy rather than physical violence.'

'Can we have a mistress-class in French swearwords please?' Cordelia asked.

'What rating of vulgarity do you want?'

'The gamut from one to ten plus. It's what that cow deserves.'

Despite all Globo Pol's efforts, they were unable to pin any charges on Valentina. Dmitri was deemed to be an unreliable witness and, apart from his accusations, there was nothing to link her with the crimes. As her lawyer had intimated, she had a valid excuse for possessing stolen artworks. Globo Pol agents knew Valentina was guilty and they were peeved about her escaping justice so someone involved in the case – no one knew who – informed Dmitri, by now in a protection programme, that there would be no repercussions for his erstwhile boss. He was exceptionally miffed to hear this news, not least because she was carrying on with her life as normal, while he was forced to live under another assumed name and no longer had the pleasure of being received as a Russian prince. The mysterious Globo Pol revelator also happened to mention that the Istituto d'Arte Villa Veritas sold forgeries for inflated prices, which Art Is Life and Life Is Art would be very interested to learn. Considering how he was scraping by in reduced circumstances this news made him vengeful and a few days later Sandrine's assistant opened an email from a Han Solo who claimed to know that Valentina was up to no good. They provided enough intelligence to warrant Sandrine sending an investigative reporter to Rome. Valentina denied the allegations and threatened to sue, not a wise move. When the reporter tracked down Valentina's former secretary, she found him willing to spill as long as it was off the record. 'What a horrible imperious employer. No one liked her but she paid well and bought loyalty. I can confirm that she operated a production line of counterfeit art and sold it to oligarchs. That is the foundation of her wealth.'

Art Is Life and Life Is Art was cautious about accusing Valentina publicly and chose to start a discussion on social media about what it meant for art in general when unnamed sources made claims of wrongdoing about one of its leading players. That was enough for rumours to start spreading. It was a disaster for Valentina's reputation. She knew her credibility was ruined and, because she had always been standoffish with peers, support was not forthcoming. As there was no chance of status rehabilitation by the art world, Valentina was forced to take early retirement. No one missed her.

Chapter Eighteen

'I have a plan.'

Elodie's words were guaranteed to kindle excitement in Cordelia and Rex.

'Tell us more!'

'When did you last take a holiday that was not merely a couple of days off with some business included?'

'Hmm, let me think.' Cordelia's face switched to ponder mode. 'Quite possibly never. I don't really do holidays. As children we didn't either.'

'Cel took us on culture and architecture city breaks instead. Or we joined her on production design research trips,' Rex explained. 'Our school mates felt sorry for us because we'd never had a seasidey package hol. Not that we wanted one.'

'Little did they know that instead of building sandcastles on a beach in Benidorm we'd be clambering over sand dunes in the Namib desert and visiting real castles,' Cordelia added.

'I clearly recall Drumlanrig in Scotland – Rembrandts and Gainsboroughs inside and the best adventure playground outside,' Rex reminisced.

'Cel once took us to Poland cos she was starting work on a Little Red Riding Hood film. We went exploring in the Białowieża Forest and Rexicles worked out roughly how many trees there were by counting the number in a small area and extrapolating.'

'Are you envious of my nerdicity because you still can't do long division?'

'That is true, but I figure I don't need to know how cos I have my own personal maths genius in you. Anyway She-She, back to your plan. No doubt it will be heroic.'

Elodie's proposal meant taking a three-week break around the date of their shared birthday, which also coincided with the anniversary of her being unofficially adopted by Cordelia and Rex.

'You'll need a passport. Other than that I will reveal nothing.'

The Tanners loved a surprise and were feeling a delicious anticipation. Having experienced her earlier productions they knew it would be a blockbuster.

On the day of departure Elodie hired a taxi to take them to London City Airport where Gladys, the private jet, was waiting. They had packed casual and smart clothing for both warm and cool weather. Consequently, all three required large steamer trunks, which had been sent ahead and loaded on the plane.

Collette the pilot was standing in the cabin to welcome them. '*Bonjour et bienvenue* to you all. We will be leaving imminently and Boniface will look after you well.' Boniface, the flight attendant, was married to Elodie's personal assistant Cédric, who was also on the trip to supervise the logistics.

When the plane was airborne Elodie said, 'We are flying east and by the time we are back in London we will have circumnavigated the globe. I've named our holiday Voyage of The Frenglish, a clumsy title I know, to celebrate the areas of unity between the English and French languages, to explore local food and drink, but most importantly to rejoice in our personal union. We will visit three places where both English and French are spoken and use phrases and partake of activities that are French-derived English terms.' Elodie held up a desk bell. 'I will ding it if a French word is used in English. There are thousands so I won't do it on every occasion.' She gave them a bingo card on which English French phrases were printed. 'This is the first and there will be a few more throughout the sojourn (ding) so listen carefully.'

Rex, who was an inveterate player of bingo, said, 'Even if we do nothing else apart from this I already consider our voyage to be the best time ever.'

'Whoever ticks off the most will earn applause, acclaim, and admiration. Now, I think we deserve an aperitif and amuse-bouche.' Elodie gave the bell five dings and the others checked their cards for those words. Boniface opened a bottle of Bonheur, produced in the year of their birth, placed a dish of gougères on the table and said, 'Bon appétit!' so she dinged it again.

'Do you remember at the Élysée Palace entente cordiale event the British Prime Minister said that almost half of English vocabulary derives from French? I hadn't thought of it before and now I'll never stop,' Cordelia mused.

They started listing places to go and things to do using French loan words. 'We will hire a taxi to chauffeur us, stay in hotels, have breakfast in a café, eat cordon bleu food in restaurants, hopefully will not have to queue for anything, go shopping in a boutique, and take home some souvenirs.' It all sounded too exciting not to know more so Elodie revealed the schedule.

First stop was the Seychelles archipelago in the Indian Ocean, which had been occupied by the French and was a former British colony – hence French and English being two of the nation's three official languages – Seychellois Creole was the third. It was not the tropical climate and pristine sandy beaches that had enthused Elodie, although they were a big draw, but rather the natural landscape of lush vegetation and the diversity of its avian life. Cordelia performed a little dance of delight to learn they were travelling to an islet called Bird Island and might spot Seychelles Paradise Flycatchers and Blue-Cheeked Bee-Eaters.

Two days after arriving they celebrated their birthday on a bar crawl and visited several lakanbiz, informal shed-like premises licensed to sell the traditional hooch – baka made by fermenting sugar cane juice, and kalou, fermented coconut sap. Cordelia, who enjoyed shaking hands to greet people with whom she was not on kissing terms, was pleased to discover that a handshake was almost mandatory, so she went for it with such gusto her arm started to ache. She had memorised a few Seychellois phrases, so she added, '*Koma sava?*' and '*Mon apel* Cordelia' and because the Creole derived from French she found it easy. 'All I need do is pretend I'm speaking bad accented French. Oh hang on, *c'est moi* already!'

After a glass of kalou Elodie stood up and said, 'I'm feeling rather emotional and want to say something.' She gathered herself. 'Becoming a member of your family has been the greatest joy of my life and each day is better than the last.'

This scene had echoes of the night Cordelia and Rex had asked Elodie to become their unofficially adoptive sister and they gazed affectionately at her and felt weepy to hear such heartfelt sentiments. It struck them how deeply they loved her and the three of them had a long hug and agreed that, together, they were the best versions of themselves.

'Here is a gift to represent our familyhood.' Elodie placed three japanned boxes on the table and handed one to Cordelia and one to Rex. Inside each was a decorative silver ring made up of three flattened interlocking triangles.

'Borromean knots – how marvellous!' Rex exclaimed. 'They are a favourite of mathematicians and used as a metaphor for the interdependence of three parts. Either all three are linked, or none are.'

'That is exactly why I chose them for our clique.' She smiled and dinged the desk bell. 'They have a magical property because if one link is removed the other two are no longer connected.'

'What beautiful symbolism,' Cordelia said and hugged Elodie. All three placed their ring on their left little finger and joined them.

'Togetherness.'

'Goodbye Seychelles or should I say *orevwar*?' Cordelia said using the Seychellois farewell and waving from the window as they sat on Gladys waiting for air control to authorise take-off.

'Vanuatu is our next destination. It's a South Pacific archipelago colonised in separate periods by France and Britain. There are three official languages – Bislama, followed by English, then French – plus 138 indigenous tongues,' Elodie explained.

'I loved speaking Seychellois. I hope I'll be as eloquent in Bislama.' Cordelia grabbed her phone to look for a dictionary. 'It's an English based pidgin,' she read. 'Guess what I'm saying. "*Gudmoning. Nem blong mi Cordelia. Mi blong London. Gud mitim yu. Plis, yu wanem danis witim mi? No? Baibai.*'

'Good morning, then something to do with your name and place of birth?' Elodie wondered.

'You asked us for something, not sure what, and were disappointed because we declined, so you bid us farewell?' Rex guessed.

'You two should work for the United Nations as translators. I said it was good to meet you and asked if you wanted to dance. How miserable that you refused.'

'Only because the musical choice was so dull, but I can do something about that,' Elodie said. By then Gladys was at cruising altitude so she asked Boniface to hang the mirrored ball above a spacious area in the back of the plane, dim the lights and play some tunes. 'Time for the discothèque – ding!'

Elodie had chosen a special pursuit for Cordelia in the Seychelles, in Vanuatu she chose something for Rex – sand drawing, listed by UNESCO as a Masterpiece of the Oral and Intangible Heritage of Humanity. They watched as a man crouched on sandy ground and used a finger to trace a continuous line on an imagined grid to form a complicated symmetrical geometric pattern. He executed it without retracing a line or lifting his finger off the sand. Rex was mesmerised and told the others it reminded him of a Eulerian graph in which a line touches each edge one time only and returns to the starting point. Cordelia's eyes glazed over, as they did with most mathematical concepts, but she was captivated by the combination of creativity and practicality and was riveted to learn that the technique had evolved as a method of communication between Vanuatu's myriad language groups.

Voyage of The Frenglish was also a gastronomic tour and they were intrigued to observe how hot stones were used to cook food, and pleased to taste how coconut and banana so often appeared as ingredients. They savoured simboro, laplap, and other traditional dishes sold by street hawkers, leading Cordelia to comment, 'If we weren't such dedicated gourmands,' (she pressed an imaginary desk-bell) 'we'd have to scoff burgers or eat in faceless hotel dining rooms and wouldn't experience the culture via our tastebuds.'

Normally, in addition to the local food, they sought out typical drinks to sample. In Vanuatu they visited nakamals, traditional meeting places of slatted wooden walls and a palm leaf roof, to imbibe kava, a libation made by grinding the root of a native plant and used in ceremonies to communicate with the spirits.

'I'm not keen on the earthy taste, although the hypnotic effect is groovy,' Rex said, as he took another sip of the murky liquid. 'My lips are tingly and my mouth is a bit numb.'

They all felt dreamy and sat, quietly sedated, gormless expressions on their faces, as far as it was possible to be from their customary lively demeanour.

For the final third of their holiday, they landed in the Inuit homeland of Nunavik, northern Québec, in English-French bilingual Canada. Their intention was to witness a light show to end all light shows – the aurora borealis.

'I'm afraid my fluency in Seychellois and Bislama will not be matched by Inuktitut, but I'll probably manage the polite words,' Cordelia commented as she searched for phrases. 'Ulaakut and nakurmiik, good morning and thank you. Oh, and this is a useful one, mamaqtuq means delicious. Might start saying that back home. Is that considered to be cultural appropriation I wonder? Cos it's not, it's cultural appreciation.'

On arrival in the village of Kangalluit they settled into their accommodation, an eco-lodge that was exactly what they'd hoped it would be – a rustic log cabin on a riverbank, with a pine forest backdrop and the cleanest, crispest air they had ever breathed. It was the definition of tranquillity and only the sound of rushing water interrupted the silence. When darkness came they walked along the river to a spot with an unobstructed northward view and waited for nature to commence the performance. She did not disappoint. Solar activity was particularly energetic that night, so the sky displayed undulating waves of green highlighted by vivid streaks of blue, violet, and purple as solar particles interacted with gases in the earth's atmosphere. Cordelia, courtesy of her tetrachromacy, also noticed marigold, garnet, and cinnabar. They were tripping with no need for psychedelics and raised their arms in the air and linked little left fingers. Suddenly their vision was dominated by shimmering scarlet and then an iridescent orange light enveloped them, sending a rush of euphoria through their nervous systems and releasing endorphins that gave them an immense feeling of joy.

For what seemed like hours they stood silently, wearing expressions of rapture. Something profound had occurred and it was only when they were back in London that they found the words to describe it, using adjectives such as spiritual and transcendent. Cordelia thought the light was benevolent, Rex said it made him feel as if he had come home to someone who deeply cared, and Elodie believed it to be a warm and kindly friend.

Cordelia and Elodie, accustomed to hallucinating during their chacruhana experiences, were content to accept the encounter as otherworldly and not interrogate it. However Rex, who had a methodical tendency, developed a hypothesis.

'The aurora borealis is caused by the earth's magnetic poles attracting electrically charged particles from the surface of the sun. They pierce the atmosphere and collide with atoms in the gases, thereby initiating a glow. Our rings are made of silver, the most conductive metal. My theory is that the sun's electrical power was drawn by the silver and due to our fingers being linked that was its way into our bodies.'

'It sounds totally plausible and now I shall add a mystical explanation to your logic,' Cordelia said. 'Astrologically we are sun signs and perhaps the sun knew and chose us especially.'

Elodie, scientific in her medical career but always open to unexplainable phenomena, accepted both hypotheses. 'Our Borromean knot rings already had supernatural power because of the combination of the three of us and it has been enhanced by the sun. Do you feel any different? I am sleeping deeply and for much longer than normal.'

'Good point, I have no jet lag, which is unusual cos ordinarily I'm discombobulated for a few days,' Cordelia replied.

'And I feel spry and full of energy – no hint of weariness,' Rex confirmed.

It was only when Oscar commented in passing on how they had changed since their holiday that they comprehended the impact of the sun bolt. He had invited them to help him redevelop The Weasel's afternoon tea menu. 'It needs game upping and you three are the coaches I need.'

They sat in a private glade in the garden surrounded by a circular pergola of trailing fragrant plants and taste-tested the menu.

'Mmm, what are these cheese straws? I like the texture,' Rex asked.

'I'm trying to reduce waste, so they are made of crusts cut from the sandwiches. And the fruit in the scones – cream first is a hill I'm prepared to lie, not die on – will be soaked in brandy distilled from the plums on the trees over there.'

'Ooh, opera cake, gorge.' Cordelia took a bite of a coffee-flavoured slice. 'Can we call them after opera titles? Wagner for heavier ones and Strauss for the lighter options.'

Elodie took a sip of her Rose Pouchong. 'How delightful, you've used flowers grown here to add to the black tea. This is so refreshing.'

'Your comments are really positive, thanks loves.' Oscar smiled in contentment. 'So, what have you three been taking? You're exuding even more verve than usual – even you Rex.'

'Really? You've noticed a difference? We've been feeling it and didn't realise it was obvious,' he replied.

'Definitely, and I can actually feel how restorative it is. What's the reason?'

They explained how a glittering light had entered their nervous system, giving them a euphoric high. Now they were full of vigour, never felt tired, and all aspects of their lives seemed much easier. Cordelia's designs were escaping from her imagination and onto the paper with even greater frequency. Rex constantly won at cards. And Elodie found surgical planning more straightforward.

'We think it's something connected to the sun,' Cordelia said. Then she paused, 'What if it's radioactive? Should we get a Geiger counter and check?'

'I don't feel as if I've been zapped by anything bad. In fact, I have never felt as positive as I do being with the three of you together. If only it could be bottled!' Oscar said.

The following week Elodie sent a video to Cordelia and Rex. 'I have a plan. I've been considering Oscar's joke on bottling whatever magical factor we were gifted in Nunavik. Let's try an experiment by brewing a beer at The Weasel. We'll wear our rings and link fingers together as we handle the ingredients, then do the same as we pitch the yeast so we transfer our essence. I remember Oscar once explained to me that fermentation was a miracle of nature and whatever was being fermented underwent a process called biological ennoblement, which augments its nutrition. If we make a beer it might soak up our sun-enhanced spirit, which will seep into the liquid and be present when it is consumed.'

The Tanners were excited about this proposal and Cordelia discussed it with Oscar. He enthusiastically consented and, aware that it was esoteric, recommended that he rather than Daisy did the brewing to keep knowledge of The Enlightenment, as they had taken to calling it, in the family.

In terms of preternatural activity brew day was uneventful, even as the yeast was added, so the TannerBeaus wondered if all they had done was make a porter that would be delicious but hardly out-of-the-ordinary. Oscar reassured them, saying it took a while for fermentation to reach its peak and that even now he felt their combined energy and was sure of its presence in the beer.

A fortnight later it was ready for double-blind testing. They asked their associates to drink a bottle each day for a week and make a note of any unexpected changes in their lives. Some were to receive the enlightenment elixir and others a placebo.

When they reported back, the results from the elixir guinea pigs were astounding: Sebastian said he was able to lift heavier weights at the gym; Drag King Wenceslas, who was always gently mocked for singing off-key, told them that the congregants at a Monkey Business Ministries service could not believe how melodically she sang the hymns; and Professor Dorothy McInnes was astonished at being able to translate cuneiform without the need of a reference book.

'How completely amazing,' Cordelia declared as she read the feedback.

'It is extraordinary. However, my scientist's brain recommends doing more trials using alternative styles of beer,' Elodie suggested.

They did as she advised and a golden ale and a barley wine were brewed to test another group.

The results were just as impressive: Bertie, a devotee of Botox, was convinced his skin looked younger; Wilbur was surprised not to have caught Shantina's cold despite them sharing a bed; and Celestine was full of beans because it made her feel so upbeat that she invited the horrible neighbours round for supper and offered them a glass of the beer, which warmed them up sufficiently to be pleasant in their future interactions.

'Un-blooming-believable!' Rex cried.

'Have we created an actual panacea?' Elodie marvelled.

'We need to put our potion into motion,' Cordelia said.

'We certainly do, poet laureate,' Oscar agreed.

Cordelia, Rex, and Elodie did not need to drink the beer to unleash their positive internal power, but they noticed how it affected other people with whom they were in contact. Matty, part of the House of Tanner production team had asked Cordelia to teach him how to waltz in preparation for his wedding reception. During the first lesson he had no rhythm, but in the second, post The Enlightenment, he was so adept she congratulated him, saying all the practice had worked wonders. 'Actually I didn't do any,' Matty admitted, 'Must be your excellent teaching skills.'

Months later Billy Angel was named Best Actor in a Musical at the Olivier Awards, and in his acceptance speech he thanked Cordelia saying that the replacement dance shoes (the first ones she'd made had worn out) had immeasurably improved his performance and he wondered if they were imbued with magic.

Rex was pleased to see the intolerant grumpy owner of the corner shop near his house start to greet everyone cheerily, regardless of their race or sexuality. As for Elodie, she was staggered to observe how swiftly her patients' wounds healed.

Bright Side, as they named the beer, was brewed regularly in small batches for close friends and family who knew it was adaptogenic but were unaware of the active ingredient. Drinking it made all members of the sole brethren feel healthy, full of vitality, and happy. They relished how perky they were and how their lives changed for the better.

After one brew day the TannerBeaus left Oscar to finish the cleaning up – 'Sorry darling, too thirsty to help,' – and were having a drink in The Weasel. Blanche, snoozing by the fireplace, was benefiting from her own version of Bright Side, a non-alcoholic concoction minus hops because they are poisonous to dogs. Her fur was glossier, her teeth whiter, and her tail wagged with even more elation.

Sole Brethren

Elodie carried a bottle of Bonheur rosé and three glasses from the bar and sat down at the table. 'What are we toasting?'

'Our Borromean rings,' Rex said.

'To the three of us, linked for eternity,' she proclaimed.

Cordelia looked lovingly at the other two, kissed their cheeks and raised her glass, 'Long live the Whole-ey Trinity.'

Author's Note

After completing my first novel, *Sole Brethren: If The Shoe Fits,* I missed spending my waking and sleeping hours with the loveable characters I had developed, so I started writing a sequel and this is it.

Sole Brethren: Left To Their Own Devices begins a few months after the first novel ended. What joy it was to be reunited with Cordelia, Rex, Elodie, Oscar, and of course Blanche the adorable spangold. It was so lovely to read the feedback from my first novel and to realise that readers were as keen on them as I am and wished they were their friends in real life (as I do).

Many readers of the first novel sent queries about whether Cordelia's psychic ability exists in real life and the answer is yes, parts of it do, although I gave her a turbocharged combination of several real techniques and made up a name (psychomatricks) to describe it. In this sequel Cordelia finds a practical application for her amazing and unique extrasensory talent.

Other queries about *Sole Brethren: If The Shoe Fits* were whether the historical characters I mention really existed and the answer is that some of them did and some I invented. It's the same in this book, so please Google to find out more about the inestimable Bessie Stringfield, Annie Edson Taylor, Constance Markievicz, Mary Jackson, Dorothy Vaughan, Katherine Johnson, Marie-Sophie Germain, Ada Lovelace, Gladys Ingle, and the female artists, all of whom existed in real life.

Grateful thanks to Alison Shakspeare of Shakspeare Editorial who so expertly copyedited my manuscript and corrected my terrible grammar and turned what I had written into a property that could be published.

In this story I included several French and Italian phrases. Many thanks to Vincent Laurentin and Gabriele Bertucci for ensuring the language and grammar were correct. They also suggested some insulting terms in French and Italian for a particular character, which will be useful in my own life (I collect swear words!).

To G.P. Willy who advised on the scientific content and prevented me from embarrassing myself with incorrect information – a very big phew and thanks.

Thank you to all my lovely family and friends who were so enthusiastic about *Sole Brethren: If The Shoe Fits* and spurred me on for this sequel. And to all the readers I do not know but who purchased and left positive reviews for the first novel– it is very much appreciated – thank you! I hope you will enjoy this one too.

B.A. Summer (pen name of Jane Peyton), Brighton, UK.

Also By B.A. Summer

Sole Brethren: If The Shoe Fits

"Step into a glittering universe that you'll never want to leave. Buckle up your Louboutin's and hang on for an unforgettable ride with a cast of characters as preternaturally gifted as they are charming. Summer has whipped up an irresistible treat."

- Gail Willumsen, three-time Emmy-winning writer and film maker

One of Shelf Media's 100 Notable Independently Published Books 2023.

Mixing magic, footwear and all things fabulous, this is the story of Cordelia Tanner and her glittering life with charming twin brother Rex, and enigmatic best friend Dr Elodie l'Archambeau, which is threatened by the unintended consequences of an invention that she thought was a very good idea at the time – a 3D wearable holographic shoe technology called Footloose.

Fortunately for Cordelia she can periodically escape all the shenanigans because of an extrasensory ability she calls psychomatricks, which allows her magically to enter historic realms for adventures galore.

Meanwhile, back in the real world, will her nemesis, the dastardly Richard Nailer, succeed in destroying her or will Cordelia triumph?

Paperback from Elfado Island Ltd (signed copies), book retailers, and Amazon. ISBN: 978-1-7396102-2-7

E-Book from Draft 2 Digital, and Amazon. ISBN: 978-1-7396102-3-4

Author Details

B.A. Summer is the pen name of Jane Peyton. Jane loves novels with magical elements and loveable colourful characters, which is why she conceived the Sole Brethren series.

Jane started her working life in fashion PR, with shoe clients including Salvatore Ferragamo, and after careers in TV production and journalism she founded the School of Booze alcoholic drinks consultancy and is accredited in wine, spirits, beer, and cider knowledge. Writing as Jane Peyton she has published non-fiction books about architecture, design, and alcohol, including several titles in the British Library's 'The Philosophy of …' series.

She lives in Brighton, UK. and strolls along the seafront every day for inspiration on storylines and to smile at all the dogs out for their morning walk.

More information about author B.A. Summer on Amazon Author Central, and Elfado Island website.

Please sign up to Elfado Island mailing list for occasional updates. https://elfadoisland.com

Printed in Great Britain
by Amazon